EVERYTHING
UNDER
THE MOON

EVERYTHING UNDER THE MOON

A NOVEL

JEFF JOHNSON

SOFT SKULL PRESS
BERKELEY

Library of Congress Cataloging-in-Publication Data

Names: Johnson, Jeff, 1969- author.
Title: Everything under the moon : a novel / Jeff Johnson.
Description: Berkeley : Soft Skull Press, an imprint of Counterpoint Press,
   [2016]
Identifiers: LCCN 2016020237 | ISBN 9781593766481 (paperback)
Subjects: LCSH: Werewolves—Fiction. | Portland (Or.)—Fiction. | Law
   enforcement—Technological innovations—Fiction. | BISAC: FICTION /
   Literary. | GSAFD: Horror fiction.
Classification: LCC PS3610.O3554 E94 2016 | DDC 813/.6--dc23
LC record available at https://lccn.loc.gov/2016020237

Cover design by Michael Fusco Straub
Interior design by Megan Jones Design

SOFT SKULL PRESS
An imprint of Counterpoint
2560 Ninth Street, Suite 318
Berkeley, CA 94710
www.softskull.com

Printed in the United States of America
Distributed by Publishers Group West

10 9 8 7 6 5 4 3 2 1

For tomorrow night

PART

ONE

The Hiding Moon

CHAPTER

ONE

THE EXPERIMENT WASN'T working.

I stared at my funhouse reflection in the bathroom mirror. It was different than a bad hair day. The mirror was smeared and speckled with any number of things, and some inept dildo had keyed "Rupe" across the surface in square, uneven ghetto script. The white scratches hummed with the tiny vibrations from the throbbing jukebox on the other side of the door. Somehow around that time of the month, I invariably found myself snorkeling a dive bar made temporarily popular by the red zero on its hipster horoscope, and I didn't even know the name of this one. Odds were Rupe didn't, either.

Some kind of clear slime was coming off my scalp, and while it concerned me, it did give my hair an extra-special sheen. I leaned in closer and examined my new teeth. I could smell my breath on the mirror, a mixture of rain and pine needles and the discount whiskey I'd been pounding all night. Rust and mustard and darkly molding cake mix roiled up from the dry sink drain in dense little curlicues. The sweaty humanity outside, empowered by the perfect shittyness of everything, were ultimately afraid of the sink, so their experiment wasn't a complete success, either. Experiment. Experiment.

The Experiment wasn't working.

I'd only have a minute before some downward-spiraling cretin came crashing through the door, and then I'd lose my last marble. I knew it. Grooming is a sacred thing, even in a nameless public bathroom with my face pointing back at me. I listened through the swell of grind and the screams and the laughter for a heartbeat. Bass hurricane wreck, tittering I'm sexy, oh man I might puke, fuck I forgot . . . Sound soup. Larynx stew. Babble sauce. A social slurpee with a coke chaser.

I'd selected an orange jacket for the evening, an oversized thing that fashionably blended mystic Okie duck hunter and deadbomb urban junkie. It had big pockets, which I needed, and I thought it went well with my black jeans and my black tee shirt, the shiny black rain boots. I wanted to project a vague warning signal that complemented my aura of steely shoplifter and possible dime-bag dipshit, but still look good enough to get laid.

I took a pair of shortened tin snips out of one of my pockets and opened my mouth again. Always the left incisor. I bared it and neatly snipped off the end. The sharp piece of enamel skittered around in the sink and went down the sighing drain hole. I studied the results. Passable. Then I held out my left hand. I'd noticed it while I was drinking. Left pinky nail, way too fucking long. Made me look like a Mandarin coke dealer from a Swiss B movie. It was too thick for toenail clippers, so I snipped it back and it bounced into the assorted crap on the floor. There was no point in picking it up. I didn't feel like carrying around one of my new fingernails all night long, and I didn't want to get any of whatever was down there on my fingers, either.

Fast. I put the snips away and took out my new shaving razor, turned on the water. It was a cold rusty trickle and there was no soap, but it didn't really matter. I had the new hair slime to work with, so I wetted my face and ran my hand through my hair, then rubbed the new stubble with it and got to scraping. I was just about halfway through when the door opened on the raging landscape of jabbering drunks and the mule staggered in.

He was bigger than me. With my boots on I'm almost a six-footer, so he only had a few inches, but I ran on the lean side and he was definitely fat. Bald, too, and he smelled as bad as everything else in the place. Flabby skinhead, out on a full moon trolling for pussy and fueled by cheap beer and what could only be French fries.

He went straight to the reeking urinal trough and unzipped, let fly a manly arc of yellow. He glanced over at me midway through.

"The fuck you doing?" he asked. Slurred, but pro. Mean, but also genuinely curious.

I tapped the safety razor on the edge of the sink. A clump of hair came free. I examined my face and got to carving on the other cheek.

"Impressive," I said. He just kept staring. His horse bladder maintained a steady output. He was close to a pitcher.

"What?" A tiny crease, high on the bridge of his flat nose, right where it shook hands with the rest of his face.

"Your question." *Don't pick a fight.* "You must have a big-ass brain in that bald thing on your neck. Scooter."

"What?" A second tiny furrow appeared between his beady brown eyes. He didn't really have much of a neck, I noticed, and it looked like his eyebrows were gone. Got carried away maintaining his dome, which was shining with meat oil.

"I'm shaving, fuckin' retard." *Maybe too late.* I turned fully to him. "How's my hair look?"

He stared and finally shook his head. I turned back to Rupe and heard him zip up. I watched in the crusty surface reflection as he passed behind me. Not even a bump. I rubbed my face down, pocketed my razor, wiped my face with the top of my shirt, and studied my reflection. No nicks. Slime worked like an expensive Euro super lube. Interesting.

I'd already taken fifteen Xanax, a Thorazine, and I'd added two roofies to the mix, just to see what happened. The roofies were behind the hair-gel look, and the odd glossiness in the vision of my right eye, which rimmed everything in the dark with Spanish-orchid pink. Another new addition. I took two more and dry-swallowed them. They smelled weird, brown, and greasy and as alien as the roaches in the wall behind me.

Done. I put my sunglasses back on.

The explosion of light and sound and smell when I opened the door slapped me like an electrified shockwave of hot mud, but I swanned right into it. That was the Thorazine. The place was packed with overheating bodies, even though it was sleeting outside. Maximum capacity for a place that size was around sixty, but the washed-out beardo doorman had crammed in a dozen few more. I'd noticed him selling coke earlier. He certainly smelled like it. A train smell, wintry and surgical, with a touch of tragedy. How many people had died to get it into the noses of the people flirting and scowling in this shithole was anyone's guess.

No one had taken my barstool. Five bucks had secured it for five minutes. I settled back in place and picked up my drink. The bartender was sort of good-looking, slightly sweaty, with too much makeup and not enough shirt. Flouncy dyed-brown hair, hoop earrings, chipped emerald fingernails, and an iPhone bulge on her round but heading-south ass. I could smell her molars when she flashed her low-pro, all-mouth smile.

"Another?" Skeptical. I'd lost count at sixteen.

"Yep," I wheezed after I downed number whatever. I slid the glass over.

"Glad I'm not your liver," she said, dumping instead of pouring. It was close to cutoff time, she was saying, which was fine because it was almost time for me to go.

"I'm glad, too. It's always so dark in there. You'd be miserable." Conversationally, she was crappy for someone behind the stick. Giving a power drinker health advice from the other side of the bar was financially irresponsible and borderline provocative. Rookie. I'd give her one more year before burnout or the place around her caved in, whichever came first.

"The hell you talkin' about?" She looked perplexed and slightly disgusted, like I'd just given her a sticky debit card.

"You ever want to swallow one of those little LED lights? I saw them at the Dollar Store." I tossed another five on the bar. It was loud, but she heard me. She actually smiled a little out of reflex, but then what I'd asked her registered and the smile pancaked and her eyes went all the way off.

"Why the hell would I do that?"

"Because it's . . . never mind." I waved her away.

She snapped up the fiver and spun back into action, our short conversation already forgotten. I turned on my stool and studied the crowd, nursing my drink. It would be my last one in that place for as long as the bartender worked there, I knew, because I was planning to leave soon and do the kind of thing that made ever coming back potentially tricky.

Hot, flushed faces, laughter both fake and real, whispers, some sexy royal cheesy, some pleading, some straight-up gossip. Lots of nerves. Dudes over at the pool table sermonizing about cars, way in the back some woman crying as she told her friend about something involving a bus stop. Scattered everywhere, work, music trivia, bragging, bad news, fancy illness. I glanced at the woman on the stool to my left. She had her back to me and was talking to the guy right next to her. The guy I'd been stalking for the last three and a half weeks.

Miss Soon-To-Be-Miserable's name was Linda. The dead man was Vince Percy, and he was a weird one. Big, handsome, and charming as a motherfucker. Loaded, too. I could smell money on him, literally. Vinnie could easily have any woman he wanted, but it made him feel entitled to just take it because he considered pussy his right, like free air. The psychology of the situation was totally irrelevant this late in the game. I didn't really give much of a shit about his motivations in life. I'm not a rapist, but I do kill people. All the time, unfortunately, hence the complicated bar situation. Vinnie had been hunting in my neck of the woods. Trespassing. I tuned back in.

"—place in Cabo last weekend and, girl, I got so fried on these—"

"Cabo?" Miss Misery interrupted. God. I could just picture her glancing over his shoulder, out the big safety-glass windows at the midnight street and imagining hot sand under her bare feet, a beat-up, swollen cooter, daiquiris . . . adventure, romance

. . . sombreros. Maybe even a maid. I could feel her moist, flowery crotch radiation on the side of my face.

Vinnie laughed. A politician's laugh. I sucked back a drop of saliva. I smelled his hands go up, a waft of perfume and lotion with a tiny bit of pre-sex perspiration.

"I'm not rich," Vinnie said. He was smiling. I could smell his big white horse teeth, his ten-dollar breath mints. "It was my aunt's place. I sort of inherited it and then I thought, what the hell? The market sucks. Maybe I'll hold on to it for a while until things turn around. Been five years now."

"I'd fuckin' love to go to Cabo," Miss Misery gushed. She was teetering somewhere between way buzzed and obnoxious in the drunk department. Vinnie would strike soon. His heart rate was going up. I could hear it beginning to thrum in his chest. His armpits smelled like shampoo. His hair was high-end hotel gel and his scalp was moistening.

"It's loud in here," he said, leaning closer to her. "There's a way nicer place down the street. Tapas. Feel like a late snack?"

"We're out of here." Miss Misery's heart rate spiked as well. All three of us were hunting now, and it was so damn adorable. For the moment, anyway.

They got up together. When Miss Misery knelt to pick up her purse, I had my back to them. I scanned the crowd one last time and got up, moved to the door in their wake as they wove through the bodies. As I passed their stools I reached out and brushed the lip of Vinnie's glass, lightly, just for the fun of it.

The blast of cold air hardened the skin on my face and blew some of the stink out of my coat. I watched the two of them stroll north arm in arm, laughing, heads down against the weather. Vinnie was very well dressed, as always. I particularly liked his coat, a big black wool thing with an elegant collar. I let them fade into Thorazine pink tracery in the gloom as I lit up a smoke, cupping fire against the wind. Indoor smoking was against the law everywhere. As I exhaled I turned my face up to the rain. The sign above me read "The Hell Factory" in tangerine plastic and halogen. I snorted and closed my eyes. The sleet felt alive, beads of it skipping down my face like freezing termites. I took my sunglasses off and there they were, one block down, right in front of the alley I'd visited earlier. I'd picked the lock on the dumpster and the big trash truck was due just after 5:00 AM. I watched as Vinnie pulled Miss Misery in and then I broke into a light jog, just one more idiot trying to figure out why he never had an umbrella. Even over and under the patter of slushy rain and wet street I could hear them. Vinnie must have really liked her, because he wasn't wasting any time.

"—the fuck away!" she insisted. Mint. Fear smell. Street. Wires. Clouds. A train behind me. Cloth tearing. Breath. Sucking heart valve. Vinnie sounded so sincere.

"As soon as I'm finished," he sort of hissed, but there was something new in his voice. For some reason it reminded me of talk radio.

I rounded the corner at a good clip, slid a little, and stopped for an instant to admire how perfectly I'd imagined the tableau. He had her against the brick wall about ten feet in, one hand on her face, the other one in her hair. She looked like she was about to fight. *Too late.* Too big. Too empty inside.

Vinnie never even saw me, not even once. I plowed right into his side in a smooth dive, the top of my forehead hitting him in the neck, my hands locking his wrists. His neck broke on impact and we went tumbling. I rose over Vinnie's spazzing corpse and turned to Miss Misery, who was just standing there, her mouth open in a wide, red-rimmed oval.

"Run, dummy," I snarled.

Frozen like a deer in the headlights. Then she turned and hit the gas as fast as she could in high heels. I estimated that I had less than three minutes before the sirens, a sound I truly love. I knelt next to Vince and looked him over. For a monster, he was doing a remarkably crappy job. He was already dead.

I went through his pockets, fast. Keys, wallet, cell phone, breath mints, three condoms, a roll of twenties an inch thick, and a bag of coke. I pocketed it all and then stripped his coat off. It smelled wet and expensive, and even though it was too big, it fit well enough with my coat on underneath it. I buttoned it up and adjusted the collar, shot the cuffs, then dragged Vinnie down to the dumpster.

No one had locked it up. I tossed the lid open and took a few bags out, then heaved Vinnie in and dropped the bags on top of him, locked the whole thing. In the distance I could hear the first siren, about fifteen blocks away. I listened for three heartbeats, eyes closed and face to the sky, as the sirens dopplered closer. Time to walk. At the edge of the alley, just before the sidewalk, Miss Misery's purse was lying in a puddle, a forlorn little fake-leather clutch bag. I scoped it up as I passed and tucked it under my arm. The sleet was beginning to thicken into a wet rain. I reached into my new coat pocket and took out my new keys, pressed the car fob. A Lexus down the street chirped.

Time to go see what Vinnie had in the fridge.

TWO

T HE FIRST THING I did was take a slow breath through
my nostrils. No one else lived there. No pets. Someone,
a black man, had been around in the last three days.
His scent was faint, almost masked by dense Vinnie perfume,
carpet, furniture polish, and a thousand other things. I walked
slowly through the place, looking at every item in turn. Vinnie
had expensive taste, but no cohesive style, a twin reflection of
his income. The somewhat common condition was sometimes
remedied by a designer, who always left a telltale of fakery, but
Vinnie had skipped the fixer and shopped from what appeared
to be a random assortment of busy rich bachelor catalogues. I'd
predicted as much.

Rifling someone's house is always sort of fun. Especially
when they're in a dumpster. Or at the bottom of the river, or
burning somewhere, or in the trunk of a car at the bottom of a
lake and no one would be interrupting the otherwise relaxing
process. Walking up to the place I'd felt fairly confident. I was

driving his car and I was wearing his coat. The neighborhood was upper-middle-class new, with spruce-lined streets and clever yard stones. It was a Friday, and it was a little after 1:00 AM. No one else was awake and the only lights in all the houses were porch lamps. I'd even imitated Vinnie's swagger as I went up to the front door and let myself in. None of his lights were on, either, but I didn't really need them, so I left the switches alone.

The living room had a matching black leather sofa and twin chair set, with a low glass and chrome coffee table and a big flat-screen on the wall. Past that was the dining room, with a large table for eight and a fruit basket in the center. The fruit was artificial, but it didn't have any dust on it. Empty modernist sideboard.

Beyond that was the kitchen. It didn't look promising. The flecked Mexican marble counters were spotless. There was a knife rack that still smelled like the plastic factory wrap it had come in, a row of copper-bottom pots that had never seen a stovetop, a decorative spice rack with unopened jars, and not much else.

"Shit." I opened the refrigerator door and discovered why everything was so fingerprint free. Vinnie had been a strictly takeout and microwave man.

Korean pork salad, still good. A bowl of Bing cherries. Half a pizza, vegetarian down to the broccoli, a deli portion of potato salad, some exotic cheese, half a bottle of expensive white wine, and some fancy mustard to go with the Reuben on the top shelf. I took the Reuben and the wine out and closed the refrigerator door. The Reuben was good, but the wine was unfortunately a Chardonnay, which even at its most impressive is usually flabby and oversweet. While I was eating and drinking I continued my search of the dark house, eventually drifting into the imposing master bedroom.

Some action had taken place, but not recently. The bed was huge, perfectly made with snappy edges. There was a dresser with no framed pictures or knickknacks, and another flat-screen. I set the wine bottle on the dresser and opened the top center drawer, where people usually kept things like watches and rings and change, precious photos of dead cats, and mommy artifacts. My eyebrows went up.

A Rolex. A thick gold necklace. Another roll of money, smaller than the one I had taken off him earlier. I finished the Reuben, wiped my hands on my pants, took it all, and put it in the inside pocket of my orange coat. There was nothing else, just clothes. Nothing under the bed, either. I went to the walk-in closet and closed the door behind me. It was pitch black, without even sketchy pink edges, so I turned on the light.

Rows and rows of shoes. Maybe fifty suits. A tie rack. A bunch of hats. Matching luggage. A file cabinet. I sniffed. No money. I took one of the shoes and held it up to my foot. A perfect fit. That was good, so I took the biggest suitcase out and tossed in my five favorite pairs, then tidied up the collection so that it would look like nothing was missing when the official body hunters came snooping around at the end of the month. Then I opened the file cabinet.

Mortgage crap. Car insurance, the car title, bills, and receipts. At the back was something written in Spanish. I took it out and read it.

"I'll be damned," I said to myself. He really did have a place in Cabo. On impulse I tossed it in with the shoes and the car title. There was no telling what my fence could do with it.

Money smells like a tropical sewer mixed with really old milk. Most people can't smell it unless they hold a stack of twenties under their nose, but I was sure it was a factor in the trending preference of digital currency. A wave of it hit me when I opened the door to the master bathroom. It's odd, really, how so many people hide money in their bathrooms. I tracked it right to the underside of the sink, about six grand in hundreds, duct-taped to the back of the basin. I stripped it out and looked at it. Not even gift-wrapped, just naked, smelly paper. I stuffed it deep inside my coat next to the tin snips and then raided the medicine cabinet.

Vinnie had a huge constellation of pills, some of them pretty valuable and some of them really tedious to find. The amphetamines were spendy, and there were mood stabilizers and weird drugs I'd have to look up later. There were roofies and Valium, both useful, plus sturdy representatives of the rest of the drug kingdom. I put the stuff I wanted personally in the pockets of my orange coat, dumped the rest in with the shoes, and then stood there in the middle of the bedroom, thinking.

I'd pretty well looted the place, but there was something more. I could feel it. Vinnie had secrets. All baby monsters had secrets. I sniffed more, and then I dropped down and began directly scenting the carpet. I went through the entire house like that again, really going over it for almost an hour, but in the end there was nothing. I went back to the refrigerator and got the Korean pork salad out and slowly chewed through it. I thought the pistachios were a nice touch, and that's when it hit me, just as the horizon was beginning to turn blue.

There were no books. No art on the perfectly painted walls. The fake fruit on the polished dining room table. Vinnie's secret was with him in the dumpster, inside his cold head. He was bland. Stale. Painfully so. He'd been an actor in his own life. It had probably been at the heart of his behavioral issues. He hadn't had a personality in the classical sense, and the knowledge of something so awful had taken the place of it. A self Möbius of craptaculation. Fucking dummy. Taking all his shit was a small fee for hitting his do-over button for him.

When I was done I tidied up and went back into the master bedroom and took down the smaller flat-screen. It just fit into the suitcase. It was 5:00 AM by then and people would be waking up soon, even though it was Saturday. It was time to leave.

Outside, the sleet had turned to no-stick snow, so before I went out the door I returned to the closet and got a hat, which fit just like the shoes. It was good cover in case there were any early birds. Suitcase in hand, I went out into the predawn cold, head down. I locked the door behind me in case I wanted to come back in the next few days, and I certainly didn't want anyone else robbing the place if I did.

The streets were quiet and empty. I started the Lexus and slowly pulled away, in no hurry. When I hit the first stoplight I opened the glove box. Standard stuff. Miss Misery's purse was on the passenger-side floor, so while I waited on the light I picked it up and looked through it. Sixty-eight dollars, two credit cards, and an ATM card. Driver's license. Linda Morgan. 311 N. Coulier, apartment number eleven. I took the money out as a finder's fee. I'd toss the rest in a mailbox later.

The dawn, when it finally came, was bleak and gray. I drifted through the dark byways of an industrial zone and listened to the radio for a while, finally parked in front of a gutted phone booth by the train tracks. The actual phone and the dial box were long gone and layers of graffiti covered the entire thing.

Street art, undoing the vague bad taste in my brain that had smeared me at the dead guy's place. Looking at it, I felt a sudden wave of wonder. I'd found the telephone booth artifact over a year ago and watched as the layers changed. It was only a matter of time before someone tore it out, probably right around when Starbucks moved into the neighborhood. So one more ounce of Vinnie's world would spread into the fabric of things. That blandness was how he was having his babies, and no one seemed to notice, and wondering about anything like that at all made me wonder if I was finally becoming a pussy. I shook my head and changed gears.

I was still hungry, but nothing good would be open for a few more hours and I needed to get rid of the car and all the crap in it first anyway. My fence, Lemont, was three blocks north, but I didn't want to bother him at six-thirty on a dreary Saturday morning, even though it was impossible to tell what hours he kept. Lemont was a seriously smart kid and we had a good working relationship, down to some humor and the kind of completely marginal camaraderie only available to marginalia, but I was careful not to test it. Like most bright young criminals, Lemont was slightly unstable. I considered picking up some coffee to wash out the mints I'd eaten to cover up the bourbon I drank to mitigate the indescribable taste of the hiding moon, but instead I popped a few more Xanax and snuggled into the big new coat and pulled the new hat down. With the heater on and some nameless sonata purring quietly in tandem with the random hiss of passing delivery trucks, I was relaxing nicely when Vinnie's cell phone rang. I slowly took it out of my pocket and looked at it. Max. DC area code. I answered it and cleared my throat by way of greeting, purely out of boredom.

"You dumb prick," the Max guy said.

I made a hungover chirp and sneezed. The growing light was making the phone booth take on a pleasing lurid quality as muted reds and values of gray emerged from the stomach of the thing. One new piece of graffiti kept catching my eye, a particularly unpleasant phrase that threw the rest of it off. "Pause-n-Leeze," with a little skull under it in the same blurry white. It made me wonder if the dead guy in the dumpster had an understudy.

"I just got a call from the ballroom," this Max guy went on. "If this shit isn't in somebody's inbox by noon then both our asses are officially fired. And that's noon your time, so get the fuck up, put on that smile, and get down there and start scanning. Now." Then he hung up.

Max was the kind of name I always associated with the worst sort of Bill Blass suit. I put the phone away and took out mine, punched in Lemont's number from memory. I never programmed a cell phone. It was too dangerous, plus I didn't know how. Lemont answered on the first ring.

"Yo homie," he said brightly. Lemont called everyone homie. Occasionally baby. "Waz up?" There was a birdlike quality in the way he spoke. A double-dipped-in-lunacy candy warbler. Chipper. Crackling.

"You awake?"

"Baby, Lemont don't sleep." He also referred to himself in the third person. "Roll on up, back gate be open in four minutes. We even got coffee."

Four minutes later, the back gate to a junk-cluttered four-car parking lot in front of Lemont's soot-streaked tin warehouse rolled back. I pulled in and a black guy in a leather trench coat ground the gate shut behind me. The warehouse doors opened and Lemont gestured for me to pull the car forward out of the rain. He was all smiles, even more than usual.

The inside of the warehouse was relatively dark, but my eyes adjusted in a beat and I could instantly see why Lemont was so effervescent. There were at least twenty-five flat-screen TVs leaning up against the far wall, along with three deep racks of fur coats. I sighed. The flat-screens were all bigger than the now completely worthless one I had in the suitcase. Lemont was already sitting at his cluttered desk wearing one of the coats. It looked real, huge on his skinny frame. His bare chest was showing just at the top, even though when I got out it was cold enough in the warehouse to see my breath.

The gate man, Larry or Barry, closed the warehouse doors and watched me, polite, with his hands out and clear of his body. In the one year plus I'd been doing business with Lemont, the gate man had never said a word. He was African-dark, so it was possible he didn't even speak English. I gave him a quick nod and he nodded back. Lemont spun around a few times in his office chair.

"Yo baby, what you think of this coat?" He held his arms out. Lemont was from Detroit, originally. He and a handful of his old kindergarten chums could probably take over a small South American country in less than a week, which pretty much made Portland a cakewalk for him. He'd been fired in a hotter kiln.

"I think it's a woman's coat," I replied. He cackled gleefully, white and gold molars.

"Maybe so, maybe so. But damn, thing so fuckin' warm Lemont don't even need no pants."

"Way to go, dude."

Lemont gestured at the chair across from him and I crashed down into it. "Coffee?" He held his cup up. "It's like, from far the fuck away . . . Ethiopia, maybe."

"Black. And there's a suitcase in the car."

Lemont snapped his fingers and I heard the Lexus open and close behind me. The gate guy brought it over and gently set it down beside me, then wandered off to examine the road outside through one of the many peepholes. Lemont handed me the cup and the warmth instantly flowed into my hands. He eyed the case.

"Whatcha bring Lemont this lovin'-ass mornin'?"

I set the coffee down on his desk and put the case on its side, clicked it open and spun it so he could see. He leaned over and looked in. The flat-screen was on top.

"I know, I know," I said. Lemont shook his head.

"Yesterday this might have been worth somethin'. Today? Hold on to it for a week, then we see."

"You can just have it. I already have one. I never watch."

Lemont shrugged. "So be it. Lemont put this in the bathroom at home."

I winced ever so slightly, but he didn't notice. I dug the Rolex and the gold chain out of my pocket and handed them over. He weighed them both in his hand.

"Now these is good. Aw yeah, baby. Two Gs."

"Three."

"Two and some change."

"Three and the screen." The Rolex had a diamond centerpiece.

Lemont shrugged. "We can swing that." He looked back in. "Shoes?"

"Those are mine, but there's all kinds of pills in there. Most of them I have no idea about."

Lemont rubbed his hands together and took out the first five bottles, spun twenty degrees to his computer. "We look 'em up. Lemont don't need no Rolex of laxatives."

"And that car."

Lemont nodded, already typing. I got up and lit a cigarette, wandered back over to the Lexus and took out Linda's little clutch purse, put it in the inside pocket of my orange coat, which was seriously close to overload.

"What about that coat?" he called over his shoulder.

I frowned. "C'mon man. It's fuckin' cold out there. It's cold in here! Plus, I dunno. I like it."

"It's too big, it ain't your style, it got mud all up the back and it make you look like a hobo in a stole coat. Need a shave, homie mountain. Lemont get it dry-cleaned and add it to the collection. Another fifty."

"This is like a seven-hundred-dollar coat."

"Maybe, but dry cleanin' be expensive as hell these days."

"Jesus." I took the coat off and tossed it on the hood of the car, stuffed my hands into the bulging pockets of my own coat, and wandered around looking at crap while he dug around the Internet to figure out the pill situation.

"We got migraine shit. Useful, but not too useful. Lemont take 'em off your hands. Speed's good. Some epilepsy shit. Take that, too. The rest for ulcers. Looks like your boy," he read off a bottle, "Vincent Percy, he had him some stomach problems. Or the butt pipe. That usually be the stress or the cocaine. Shit be worthless."

"Toss it, but burn the names off."

"Course. How hot is that car?"

I shrugged. "No real heat for a day or two. Maybe a week. Then it's gonna be on fire."

Lemont didn't bother to look up from his computer. He was totaling sums by then.

"Know me some Mesicans have that shit in pieces all over the West Coast by tonight." He opened a drawer and took out a cash box, began counting out bills. When he was done he put them in an envelope. To count it in front of him would have been insulting this far into our arrangement, so I stuffed it into the only pocket it would fit into. He smiled up at me.

"Next week?"

I nodded.

"All right then." He turned back to his computer. "Store around the corner is open. You look like some freaky-ass punk construction dude, but they be hippies anyway. Neighborhood goin' to shit."

"It's happening everywhere. I blame TV actually, so I don't know what to tell you. I'll head over to your local and get some supplies, take a cab back to my car. Sometimes, Lemont, some-times I wonder if there's such a thing as a lifestyle pension. I mean, this gig doesn't really have a retirement plan built into it. What's our gold watch look like?"

"Box fo' 'dem shoes?" How clever.

✳

THE GROCERY STORE was newer and relatively swank, and indeed staffed by sleepy hipster boys and yawning hippie chicks. I put the big box of shoes by the register and got a smile, pulled a cart out of the rack and started shopping. Red wine, some sheep cheese I'd never heard of, corn tortillas, lard, four filet mignons, an onion, some jalapeños, a lime and some cilantro, and the three biggest heirloom tomatoes they had, grapefruit-sized bulbous purple things that looked and smelled promising. When they rang me up I had a little trouble digging one of Vinnie's rolls out, which thankfully went unnoticed. Then I went outside and called a cab with my box and my bag. My pants felt wet, which was sort of deflating considering how much shit I still had to go through just to get home. The snow had reverted back to sleet and the wind had kicked up, so it felt like it was getting colder.

The ride home after a night on the town could easily bum me out, so I tried to fixate on the shoes, which had been unexpected after all. Cab number one took me all the way into North Portland, but the part with the tacky, floundering artsy streak. I walked a few blocks under awnings as cafés opened and bed-head sweater-nerd proto yuppies fired up their Macs inside, ghostly through the already steamy windows. A few blocks down, a different cab service took me all the way across town again to within striking distance of my car, which was parked in front of an anonymous apartment sprawl fifteen blocks south of The Hell Factory, right at the edge of my current hunting grounds. I hoofed it through slush from there and by the time I finally got into my white Camry I was thoroughly soaked and cold.

My house was a small white Victorian set among other small white Victorians four miles north, with a few fruit trees out front for show; a forever-stunted lazy pear Bonsai, a hearty Bing cherry, and a Ladysmith apple, the latter two favorites for many on my street. The house would need a paint job in the next year or two. The neighborhood was middle class and family oriented, and everyone on the block was on friendly terms, which was soothing considering my nature and line of work. Comfortable. I carried all my stuff up the steps and let myself in.

The living room was lined with bookshelves, very different from Vince Percy's post-trust-fund mannequin box. It smelled like books and fireplace and a complex history of fine cooking. I dropped the box by the door, put the grocery bag on top of it, and went straight to the fireplace. I tossed in a few logs and some kindling and lit it up, then picked up my groceries and went into my kitchen, passing through the dining room. The table and chairs were beautifully kept Amish and there was a Norway china hutch with china in it. Original paintings, mostly turn-of-the-century Russian landscapes, all stolen but tasteful, their provenance only part of their charm. The books, even the cookbooks, were all first editions, many of them signed and all of them with an interesting story of how I had gotten them.

I set the bag down on the kitchen counter and got to work. I rubbed the steaks with salt and quickly seared them in butter, then added a clove of garlic and water to the pan, set it to simmer for later shredding. I fired up the old gas stove, wrapped the tortillas in foil, and tossed them in the oven at a low temperature and left the rest. The fire was just getting going, so I went to the dining room table and began emptying my pockets, neatly lining everything up. It was an impressive amount of crap, even for me.

Tin snips, some piano wire, two rolls of bills, an envelope full of bills, a naked stack of bills, five bottles of pills, a short, hooked knife, the rest of Vinnie's mints, Miss Misery's loose bills, some pliers, a lock-pick set, a roll of duct tape, a safety razor, a straight razor, two packs of smokes, two lighters, two cell phones, a trash bag, and a purse. I looked at it all, laid out with perfect precision, and I smiled with all of my teeth. Most of it was going into the safe in the basement, but first things first.

I went into the ground-floor bathroom and turned on the shower in the old claw-foot bathtub, and while the water heated I stripped my soaking clothes off. When steam was rolling over the top of the shower curtain I stepped in and let the hot water pound on me. I washed the chemical slime out of my hair and shaved one more time, lathering the transparent alien film of other people off of my entire body, and then got out, flipped the curtain up, and ran the bath. While it was filling, I put my robe on and padded back out into the kitchen.

The beef would be ready to fork apart in about thirty minutes. I chopped up half the onion and a few jalapeños and the cilantro and one fat tomato and made a type of salsa, squeezing lime over the top and tossing in the rind. Then I went and sat in front of the fire, which was crackling away. I was a little tired. Hungry. I thought about Vinnie's personality-free house again, and for the first time in a few weeks, I looked at the paintings and the books. It felt good, but maybe it was the drugs talking. Maybe it was all some kind of insulation. Maybe the gathering wimp in me had developed wallpaper for a cage. Maybe dead, empty Vinnie's place had left a residue on me after all.

Just when I'd levered myself into the hot water and settled back with a glass of red wine, Vinnie's phone rang again. I let it go and sank lower into the water, blew a few bubbles. The phone rang five times and went to voice mail and then a minute later it rang again. And again. And again. Whatever the dead man in the dumpster had done for a living was either damned important or he had missed an appointment to massage his mother's feet, but whatever the case, after a while the ringing began to get irritating, so I got out and toweled off, put my robe back on, and walked steaming to my new collection of stuff and turned his phone off, then tossed it in the kitchen trash. In the first twenty-four hours, a phone could be a nifty passport into the financial planning of a fresh ghost. After that it would be bad news to have around, and I was too hungry to perform a half-baked forensic root canal on it anyway.

After I shredded the beef, I put everything on two big platters and carried it out to the dining room table with a bottle of hot sauce in my bathrobe pocket. It was everything I'd hoped it would be. After taco number ten, my mouth was on fire and I slowed down a little. Idly, I reached out as I chewed and flipped opened Linda Misery's purse. It was troubling that she'd seen my face, even if it was just a trauma-blurred glimpse in a rainy alley after dark. It was true that Lenny or Vinnie or whatever his name was had some seriously nasty things in mind at the time of his death, but I'd killed him right in front of her. She might not have known that I'd broken his neck and put him in a dumpster. Maybe she didn't even remember his name. It was already slipping away from me now that the whole thing was over. But a witness was a witness.

I had her address. At least the last one she had given the DMV. Her credit cards. I wiped my hands and took out the thin sheaf of business cards. There were four of them. A real estate place. Dentist. Car repair. Bingo. Her card. Linda Morgan, Salt Street Development, Personnel, and an address, phone number, and email. The card was tasteful, even understated, without any gloss. I sniffed it. It didn't smell like her, but then she hadn't been a powerful stinker. It was almost like she had never touched it.

I shrugged and picked up another taco. Going to her apartment would be potentially grisly if she recognized me, and other people's targets weren't my cup of tea. Monday I'd put on a suit and pay her a visit at work just to sniff-probe, take a temperature on how freaked out she was. It was something to do while I waited for something to do while I waited for something to do.

That turned out to be one of the worst mistakes of my very long life.

THREE

S ALT STREET DEVELOPMENT turned out to be a big four-story brick building by the train station, a few blocks away from the old hardware store where I got my blowtorch ephemera. The area had changed over the last few years. Gone were the days of gutters full of blood and bum puke and spent syringes, replaced with the occasional "slim" condom and the odd Starbucks cup. The cars were nicer. Everything was clean. Soon it would be so clean that they'd have to tear down all the turn-of-the-century brick and mortar and bring in the architects from California or Canada to ensure the total ruination of the district's charm, but that pinnacle of progress was still a few years from fertilization.

I'd showered and shaved and put on one of my better suits, a black Armani. I'd gone with a collarless black V-neck, mostly because collars don't appeal to me, and over all that a perfectly tailored knee-length white leather jacket. I'd liked the look of my hair the other day, so I rubbed in some gel until the tornado

mop on my head was a fashionably shiny messy. I had no choice
on the mess angle. My hair did something thick and wild all by
itself, but in the last few years I'd been immensely pleased that
the look had come around again. The beatniks may have made
a big dent in the poetry department of the downtown library,
but they made a distressingly cyclical impression when it came
to hairstyles. To round out the ensemble, I brought along a slim
leather briefcase with a specially rigged but mostly blank computer, and my Really Cool Pen.

It had taken Lemont about ten minutes to crank out a web-
site that looked good, and he'd even tossed in a small stack of
business cards that were actually quite impressive. All it had cost
me was some of the coke I'd lifted off of Vince or whatever his
name had been, so I was glad I'd held it in reserve. Free is forever
the best price, and the barter haggle was liberating in some old-
fashioned way.

Salt Street's foyer was quite different than what the aged brick
exterior suggested, almost as if all the anonymous brick was hiding something, or if the cancer of gentrification had metastasized
inside exclusively, sparing the skin of the place for the bitter end.
Everything was brightly lit, full of glass and metal and mirrors.
It reminded me of some kind of advanced tech operation, or
possibly the far-flung secret outpost of a Taiwanese firm special-
izing in next-generation dentures and Soylent Green. A receptionist looked up from her terminal, a termite hexagon of bur-
nished copper. Half Japanese, half maybe Norwegian, with dead
Apache eyes. Her smile was a phony professional crack in her
ageless face and it came nowhere close to the piercing eyes. The
floor-to-ceiling mirrors to either side of me had the greasy sheen

of one-ways. Twin elevators were just behind her to either side. I tapped smartly across the blond marble floor and gave her my most convincing smile, one far different than the molar-to-molar I had pointed at the collection on my dining room table.

"Welcome to Salt Street Development," she said, her voice flat and perfectly unmodulated. She cocked her head, very robot. "Do you have an appointment?"

I decided to pour on everything I had in the way of charm. It usually worked. I leaned casually up against the metal bug nest, smiling, blatantly admiring her beauty. The artificial rictus crack never wavered. Hmm. I took my card out and handed it to her, my smile fixed as well.

"Gelson Verber," I said with a touch of purr. "I have an appointment with someone in HR."

She accepted the card and flicked it with her glassy eyes.

"Human Resources has a sizable staff, Mr. Verber. Whom exactly are you meeting with?"

I shrugged amiably, projecting slumming rich guy just back from a ski trip. "You tell me. Something to do with a joint water reclamation deal in the Pearl. That little park with the fountains. Normally I would have sent one of my people, but I'd heard so much about your building. It should be in your fancy computer somewhere." I looked around. There were no chairs. "Can I just stand here and look at you while you figure out your end?" My smile broadened. It was getting painful.

She pressed a button under her terminal and there was a muffled pneumatic hiss to my left and a flash of blue over her face as her computer did something new. I glanced over. A portion of the forty-foot-long one-way mirror slipped back.

"The waiting room is through there, Mr. Verber. Someone will be with you shortly." She looked down and began typing. Still smiling. Splendid facial muscles.

"I absolutely have to get one of those," I said, putting marvel into the statement. It was an appalling waste of capital and red-zone paranoid creepy at the same time. I picked up my briefcase and went through.

The waiting room was huge and airy, with several widely spaced round tables and a self-serve espresso stand. There were three coffee dispensers with a silver tray of white porcelain cups and assorted coffee-related condiments next to it. Scones. Recessed halogen lighting. A flat-screen was spooling off a summary of the week's ticker tape at record speed below a muted commentator's analysis of something that was almost certainly grave.

The room was also empty of anyone but me.

I helped myself to some black coffee. Expensive. Everything reeked of investment. I sat down at a table and took out the blank laptop and my Very Cool Pen. I put the pen next to the computer and initiated the single application on the laptop, projecting relaxed and distracted. I didn't need the computer for anything but taking pictures. Which it immediately began doing. I angled it around a little as I got comfortable. I was being watched. I could feel it.

Five minutes passed before a door opened behind me. She had a null scent, scrubbed away and replaced with something cast off and three people distant, but the pattern of her footfalls, the rhythm of her heart: Linda Misery in the flesh, draped in someone else. She came around and settled lightly across from me, all made up and tricked out in a maroon power suit, a thick file tucked under her arm. She looked completely changed. Smart, confident, even proud. And slightly disdainful.

"Mr. Verber," she said smoothly. She put the file on the table in between us. "We have a gift for you."

I smiled pleasantly. "Wonderful, Miss . . ."

"Linda, please. Call me Linda." She nodded at the file. I spun it around and opened it. The very first picture was a photo of my house, taken almost a year ago. I knew because of the car in the driveway. I'd wrecked it early last winter. When I looked up she was holding her little black clutch purse. It had been on my dining room table when I left an hour earlier. "And I'll take that sixty-eight dollars back whenever it's convenient for you. Our employer will see you now."

FOUR

I SHOULD HAVE KILLED her right then. Just crushed her throat. Anyone who could break into my house that fast, even knew where I lived in the first place, well . . . I was already toast. Plus, I'd probably be making my exit under steady gunfire if I did, and I really liked everything about the outfit I was wearing. People heal, especially me. Clothes never do.

"Lead the way," I said, my smile unchanged. I pocketed my Pen and slipped the laptop into my case while she watched, then I nodded at her. Sardonic came back, just under the surface.

Miss Misery picked up my file and led me to the door she had come through. It went straight into an elevator. She ran a swipe card through the slot and pressed four. We waited in silence. I yawned. *Ding.*

The fourth floor was one huge office, but not as big as the building's footprint. Something was behind the west wall, roughly the size of a small house. There was one desk and two chairs. A man sat at the desk with his back to us, looking out the window. I followed Miss Misery over to the desk, where she set the file down and then stood at something like parade rest. The man spoke without turning away from the gray morning.

"Have a seat, Mr. . . . . Verber. We have a lot to talk about."

I smelled it then. He smelled like me, but different. More like two of me, or even three. Rain and dust and lavender, but in his case mingled with something old, like paper from a forgotten attic, or the things at the bottom of a dry well. Not bad, just musky in a very certain way, a living and vibrant scent that came from a healthy passage through a century or so. I sat in one of the chairs, put my briefcase down.

"Germany. 1944. You were Lieutenant Daniel Reed at the time. Daylight of the One-Oh-Six Special Demolitions. Bit off the real Gelson Verber's testicles and then disappeared into the forest for three months. Found naked and starving in the middle of winter. Honorable discharge. You were the only survivor in your entire platoon." He clicked his tongue and turned a page. "You killed quite a few Germans. Real zest for it."

The plane had crashed and only sixteen of us had made it out of the wreckage alive. I had Chuck Desoto's foot in my hand and I was running before I realized the rest of him wasn't attached to it. The first bullet hit me in the thigh and wadded up in the meat. Jimmy's head blew off next to me and a piece of his skull went right through my cheek. I'd dropped the foot and gone to all fours for a jump. The gunner was solo, just mowing us down. Someone had managed to take out the guy next to him as we made for the tree line. Verber could never have known that I could jump that high or that far. I made it into his hole from fifteen meters, going right over his line of fire. It tore the boots off my feet. When I landed in a crouch in front of him my leg gave out, so I bit his package off. It was quiet for a moment because everyone was dead. Then I heard shouts in the distance. Germany. I disappeared and had one of my blackouts, the longest one I'd ever had. Three months of it.

"Who are you?" I asked, very casual. He slowly spun in his chair. Pale, pale blue eyes, hair almost white, an Armani as black as mine. Shoulders as wide as wings, thin as a rail, long fingers steepled under his chin. I look somewhere around thirty. He looked like porcelain.

"Christophe." A smile. Very toothy. "Coffee?"

I shook my head, smiling back. "Had some, thanks. What were you people doing in my house?"

He shrugged. "Well bourbon? Pills?"

I looked up at Miss Misery. "You bitch."

She remained at attention, but I caught the smirk.

Christophe leaned forward and picked up my file, began thumbing through it. "Herbert Franklin. Not very original. Right after the war. Then you're Brian Clark. Suitably innocuous. Except for today. Today your name comes from a man you ate part of." He snapped the file closed. "So who were you before the war?"

"This is all bullshit." I didn't really even know. "You people are fucking crazy. Is this a reality show?"

Christophe laughed.

"1892. Orphanage in St. Louis called Mama Heads. The groundskeeper, Laurence, taught you how to read. He also chained you in the basement every full moon. You killed him when you turned thirteen and you were never seen again in that squalid little corner of nowhere."

Laurence. I hadn't thought about him in a long, long time. He'd been okay in a way, except he'd tried to beat what he called "the Devil" out of me. Those years had blurred over time, like copies of copies of copies of an already old cassette tape.

"Exactly what do you want?" I asked evenly. Christophe gave me a measured stare.

"Do you even know what you are, Mr. . . . Let's stick with Verber. I like that. Points for style." .

I stared back. I could feel my face going white as the blood pooled around my organs and oxygenated my muscles, leaving my skin. Christophe sniffed like a dog, scenting me.

"You're a half-breed, just like me, except my line is more pure. My mother was a werewolf. Your grandfather was one, too. Raped your grandmother. Then your father in turn raped your mother, carrying on the family tradition. So that makes you, what . . . one-eighth rapist dog?"

I was over the desk faster than most people can blink, but it wasn't fast enough. Not by a long shot. Christophe didn't even leave his chair, just tossed me over his head like a toy. I smashed into the window and was about to spring up and bring it on, but he was there, instantly, one shoe on my neck. He smiled down at me like I was a moron.

"Moron," he confirmed. "I know what you're thinking. You see, Verber, I'm stronger than you. Faster. Younger and older, both. And I'm rich. Essentially better in every conceivable way." I couldn't breathe. Black spirals danced at the edges of my vision. His foot felt like an iron tractor strut.

"Now, I'm going to release you so that you don't die today, but if you try any more shenanigans," he wagged a finger at me, "it will test my limited humanity."

Christophe let his foot off and I gasped for air. He sat back down at his desk and began shuffling calmly through my past.

"I'll give you this file for now, Mr. Verber. All I ask is that you hear me out when you're finished reading it. You can take as long as you like. No telling how effective dear slaughtered Laurence's tutorials were."

I got up and inspected myself. Thank God he hadn't torn my coat or wrinkled my pants. Then the whole day would have been truly ruined. I walked around his desk and sat down across from him again, panting. I looked up at Miss Misery, who was staring straight forward, that faint smirk still in place.

"What the hell do you want?" I croaked. I calmly smoothed back my hair. He didn't bother looking up.

"I'm offering you a job, Verber. Wolves run in packs, not that you seem to have noticed. Details to follow. Linda, please show Verber to the door." He put the file on my side of the desk and spun back to the window. I'd been dismissed.

"This way, Verber," Miss Misery said brightly.

I put my file into the briefcase, then followed her to the elevator. As soon as the doors were closed I turned to her and smiled.

"Is it okay if I give you my personal cell phone number?" I asked.

"We already have it." Primly. Satisfied to point that out to me.

"You don't." I took out one of my cards and my Very Cool Pen. It was a Montblanc, but with a modified nib. I wrote out a series of numbers on the back and handed it to her. When she reached out to take it I stabbed her through the back of the hand. The razor-sharp titanium went through her flesh like butter. I held it there. She let out a muffled gasp and almost went down to her knees. Almost. A toughie. The sulfur in her eyes was red and possessed of spirit. Her tiny black heart had earned the corporate seal of approval.

"All that shit he said may be true, but it applies to you, too, sweetheart." I pulled her closer. "So it's *Mr. Verber* from now on. Got it?" My face was too tired to smile again so I didn't. She stared, burning.

"Good." I slid the nib out and wiped it on her shoulder. She immediately applied direct pressure and faced forward again. There were several drops of blood on the floor, but not a gory pool of it. I've been stabbed through the hand dozens of times. A stubbed toe hurts worse. She was pale, but the fear sweat wasn't really there. Building security, I guessed. We both faced forward again.

"That was a pretty clever trap," I admired. I watched Linda's blurry reflection shrug.

"Your profile suggested you'd go for it."

"My profile." Puzzling. My game was slipping. *Ding.*

The doors opened on the lobby. I sauntered to the main exit without pausing for a final pass at the receptionist. Miss Misery remained where she was, holding her hand.

"Mr. Verber," she called after me. I turned. "You still owe me sixty-eight dollars."

I had to smile, as painful as it was. "Dinner it is."

The elevator doors closed on her with our eyes still locked.

CHAPTER

FIVE

T HE FIRST THING I did when I got home was go
straight to the wine rack and take down the '58. I'd stolen it more than twenty years ago from a crooked little
man who taught at PNCA and freelanced as a forgeries broker
for several former students. I uncorked it, and rather than let it
breathe I drained about a quarter of it and smacked my lips. I
needed it to rinse down the bitter aftertaste of the four Xanax I'd
crunched up on the drive. I was sort of rattled after getting my
ass kicked, especially since it had never happened before. Then
I stripped naked and went down to the basement to deal with
my safe.

My basement was an orderly place. Canned goods, some of
which I'd put up myself, tools that I used for various crimes but
could pass as standard homeowner stuff, a disguise weakling
weight bench, a heavy bag, and my washer and dryer. There was
a wet vac with the tools in case of a flood. I used it every week
or so, right after I visited Lemont.

The entire process was time consuming and dirty, but it had to be done. In the end I wasted a few hours, got truly filthy, and swore a lot, and I did it all naked. And it was cold. Fun. First, I had to remove a four-hundred-pound slab of concrete without cracking it or tearing off one of my fingernails. That demanded a crowbar, sweat, and a near-constant dialogue with myself that would have made the crazy Pentecostal idiots at Mama Heads commit suicide. Below the slab was the safe. That was the really grubby part. I knelt into the wet hole and dialed in the combination and opened it. Empty. The safe weighed just under a thousand pounds, too heavy for me to lift unless it was a total all-out crisis, as in it was sitting on my chest. I had a makeshift winch from a tow truck built into my sissy workout setup, so I hooked the inside lip of the empty armored box and then hit the green spool button and waited the twenty minutes it took to lever the fucking thing out of the ground. As soon as it cleared the floor by a quarter inch I gently pivoted it to one side and set it down beside the hole. Then I looked down at the mud. The real safe was two inches below it. Cursing more and with inspired invention, I wheeled over the muddy wet vac and turned it on, then waited as it slorped out about ten pounds of runny brown sludge, spattering me as it did so. When it was finally clear I got down on my stomach and wiped up the rest with a rag until the surface was grit free. Then I dialed in the combination. It opened with a soft, smelly *plunk*.

Two and a half million reeking dollars, with enough room to spare for maybe half a mil more, as long as they were hundreds. On top of it all was a note on pink stationery. I pulled it out and read it in the dim light. Something with small, icy feet danced up my back and capered across my scalp.

Dear Mr. Verber,

If I wanted your money, it wouldn't be here.

-C

He had the handwriting of a nun.

I put the note on top of the dryer and then reversed the process. By the time I was done the basement was spotless once again, with the exception of the filthy naked thing that was me. I walked slowly up the stairs with the note in my hand and turned out the light.

After wiping my feet on the bath mat I had thoughtfully laid down, I padded naked into the kitchen and washed my hands, then took down a wineglass. It had taken me five hours to figure out that:

A) I hadn't been ripped off yet, and—

B) Christophe's sense of humor was eerily similar
to my own, and—

C) Someone had been watching me very closely,
right at that moment, and—

D) My house was bugged.

Whatever the case, there had been plenty of time for the wine to breathe. I drained the glass in three big sips and padded into the bathroom. While the shower heated up, I studied my muddy reflection in the mirror.

Determining how long I'd been under surveillance was key to determining exactly how raw the situation was. There was good stuff buried in my neighbor's backyard, for instance. Three years ago, Barry and Kim had gone to Cleveland for two weeks and I'd house-sat for them. In between watering the plants and feeding the goldfish, I'd buried a sniper rifle, body armor, fifty grand, and some grade-A fake IDs in their backyard. The grass was perfect by the time they returned. So were the rose bushes. I'd even pruned their trees. There was a fake passport in their mattress, and four grenades in the attic. A first-edition of Ivor Gurney. A small vacuum-sealed bag of pearls in the plumbing. I had to shake my head.

I had a restored 1977 Lincoln Town Car in storage out by the airport under yet another name, a beautiful thing I'd been forced to steal from the woman who ran me over with it. Someone at the garage presumably started it every month. There was forty grand in the spare tire in the trunk and various kinds of hand weaponry magnetized to the undercarriage. The ID set for that was buried a few houses down.

I stepped into the steaming shower and watched mud swirl down the drain. I had more than a decade's worth of stuff stashed all over the place, really. Enough to cut and run twice over. There was nothing in my office of any value, but the dentist next door had let me volunteer to supervise the installation of some new sinks while he was on vacation in Belize, provided that he did the same for me the next time I was out of town, which turned out to be never. I'd hidden a Sig with a silencer and twenty grand in the wall behind them with an incredible antique necklace I found in a burglar's stash. Verber, jeweler, dental assistant, killer.

When the water ran clean I stepped out and dried off. There was grit in my mouth, so I wiped the mirror down before brushing my teeth, and that's when I noticed it. A heel-shaped bruise high on my left rib cage. It would be gone in a day, but still,

Christophe had been so fast that he'd kicked me and I hadn't even seen it. I stared at it for a minute and then brushed my teeth again. Christophe's own file was getting more and more interesting.

As I put my suit back on I realized that there was only one logical thing to do. The first rule of spying, it seemed to me, was that if someone was spying on you, it was in your best interest to spy on them in return. I took out my wallet and dug up Miss Misery's phone number, dialed it from my regular cell. She answered on the first ring.

"My hand smarts, Mr. Verber," she said. Her tone was professionally bored.

"I'm eating at Jake's tonight at six," I said smoothly. "I owe you that sixty and change. You can stab me afterward if you like."

"Are you . . . You can't be serious."

"Offer's on the table. So is my hand. Maybe I'll see you there." I hung up.

Six gave me about an hour to kill, so I finished the wine and checked all the locks on the doors and windows. I plucked one of my hairs at every stop and used a little saliva to adhere them to where things opened and closed. Low craft, but sometimes it worked. I was tempted to drive around the corner and sneak back in and wait, see if anyone came in, but that would have been potentially unsatisfying, counterproductive, and possibly boring all at the same time. With a few minutes left, I thumbed through my file for the first time and immediately wished I hadn't. It was totally damning, documenting almost every strange thing I had done for a long time, all the way back to my ancestral tree, which had attached to it another hundred pages of what were presumably the horrors of my father's side of the family.

Someone, perhaps many people, had taken a long time to compile it. Half of it I'd forgotten and didn't need to remember. But there were blank spots, and that was the only comfort. A few of the blank spots were usable. It was interesting in some ways to learn exactly where I had left a trail so faint that even Christophe, with the resources he evidently had, couldn't pick up the scent. I closed it without reading very much once I'd established that single hard fact. It was hard to guess why.

Just before I left, I took a quick look around my place in case any of the bugs were wildly obvious, like screw marks around wall sockets and books that were out of place, but I didn't find anything until I took out the trash. The usual smells came out, coffee grounds and onion skins, but the other bags in the trash can had been opened. There wasn't much, because I recycle, but it was hard to miss since I knew what they would take.

Vinnie's cell phone was gone.

✳

I PULLED UP at Jake's at ten till six and got valet parking to minimize the amount of sleet that might screw up my hair, then ducked inside. It was Monday, so the bar was only three-quarters full. I ordered an expensive scotch from the bartender, stipulating only "expensive" with an apologetic grin of feigned ignorance, and after I paid I went through the bar to the main restaurant.

Jake's was an old place, even venerable. The staff was uniformly immaculate, the lights were low, and everything was brass and dark wood and white linen. I checked the oyster specials on the ancient chalkboard as I passed and approached the maître d' station just inside the restaurant side's front door. A beautiful woman with blond hair and bright green eyes looked up at me and smiled. I smiled back.

"Got a table for two available, nowish?"

She consulted the reservation sheet, a thing still done on paper, then looked back up. "Table or booth?"

"Booth, please."

"Name, so we can direct the other half of your party?" Her pupils flashed. She was wearing contacts. She'd smoked weed that morning and used eye drops. Her clothes smelled like a half a dozen different fabric softeners and detergents, so she lived in an apartment. Her natural color was light brown. Her car had newer leather seats.

"Verber. Gelson Verber."

She jotted it down and led me to a booth with a view of the street on one side. I took the side with the view. She placed the menus on the table.

"Can I get you started on something?"

"Oysters," I replied. "Sort of big ones, even dozen, whatever you recommend. And a bottle of the Château Margaux."

"Very good. I'll let your waiter know." Another smile. I watched her ass as she walked away. Fit, on a limited-personal-trainer level. She knew it and tossed a final sparkle back at me. I sighed and took my jacket off and folded it on the space next to me. I was staring at the softly guttering candle on the table in a meditative trance when Linda settled lightly across from me. She was wearing a low-cut black Prada evening gown and pearls and her hair was up. Just a hint of makeup and a French perfume I remembered from a long, long time ago, Petit Lac de Nénuphar Blanc. I was sure it was in my file.

"Why the long face, soldier boy." It wasn't a question. I shrugged.

"I have to get my fireplace cleaned. Almost time to get a Christmas tree, so I'm mentally going over my ornament scheme. Do I get the glowing reindeer for the yard this year? Plus, I ordered these books from the Rare Book Exchange and they still haven't come. Amazon. You begin to see."

She had a small bandage on her hand. A precise cut is a very special thing. The waiter arrived with oysters and the wine. He poured for us and we sampled and nodded. He departed quietly and Linda leaned in.

"Our second date and you flirt with the hostess. After stabbing me."

"She was flirting with me," I protested. "And it was more of an incision. I bet it doesn't even hurt."

"It stings. And I saw you staring at her ass. Just like you were staring at mine the other night."

"Wrong. I was sniffing your ass, which is different. In fact I'm doing it right now. And I was only admiring how her dress complements her eyes."

She picked up an oyster. "So you're an artist. A painter."

I picked up an oyster, too. "A longtime collector."

We sucked them down in tandem, eyes locked. She broke contact first.

"So Christophe," I began.

"Will not enter into this conversation. Don't even try to pump me for information. That's my job."

"Fair enough. What were you going to do if I didn't show the other night? With the rapist guy?"

"Shoot him in the stomach." She shrugged. "There was a sniper on the roof across the street anyway, but I sort of wanted to do it myself."

I nodded and picked up a second oyster. So did she.

"Stomach shot. Painful."

"Yeah." We sucked in tandem again. I was measuring her perfectly and it was working. She was relaxing a little. "He deserved it. Did you find anything interesting in his house?"

I shook my head. "Not really. Some cash. Small-time drug stash. A Korean pork salad. Oh! But this!" I held up one foot for her to inspect. A brilliantly buffed Italian leather with a pointed toe. "We had the same shoe size." I shrugged. "I also stole one of his flat-screens, but it turned out to be worthless."

"Aw baby," she crooned. "And they're so heavy, too."

"Yeah. Bummer. Mostly I discovered that he was a pretty bland guy with migraines and ulcers."

"Problems from head to colon. Foot powder?"

"Didn't look. Sorry."

She snapped her fingers. "Damn. "

The waiter took her snap as a call to attention and silently appeared. I took notice of him for the first time and my nostrils flared for a heartbeat. He'd been drinking rum in the kitchen, which is where the bleach smell came from, and he hadn't washed his hands after he went to the restroom. He had diabetes, sugary around the scalp and armpits, the trace urine on his fingers and on the tops of his orthopedic shoes.

"Lobster," Linda said, twinkling at me. "All the trimmings. Vinaigrette."

"I'll take two lobsters and two filet mignons with everything. Rare. Vinaigrette. And an order of those big prawns. And can you bring us another bottle of this with dinner? I'll have a martini in the meantime."

"Make that two," Linda said. "Extra olives for both of us."

Date number two. Three lobsters. And it wasn't even a date. I leaned back.

"So what's your story?" I asked. "Garden-variety dummy or what?"

"No story." She picked up another oyster.

"Then how come you work for a . . . you know, a Christophe?"

Her giggle was purely for the stage and she put her hand over her mouth until she swallowed, then took another sip of wine and wiped her lips. "Why would I eat dinner with a creature like you?"

"I'm handsome. Charming. Witty." I picked up an oyster of my own.

"Also a serial killer, a thief, a drunk, and a pillhead."

"You shouldn't address all of a man's bad points at dinner. Especially after you ordered the lobster."

That got a chuckle out of her, but she said nothing.

"I could list yours, of course, but I won't."

"And why is that?" Her eyes glittered, but she was still smiling. I yawned and looked out at the street. The same white sedan had gone by three times. A little too slowly. They had finally found a parking place with a bird's-eye view of me. Two men, dark suits.

"Manners."

"Manners," she repeated. She picked up another oyster and so did I. "What did you think about your file?"

"Didn't really look at it." I tossed my oyster shell back. She paused with hers halfway to her mouth.

"What? Why?"

I made a vague tossing gesture. "Who cares, really."

"Do you mean that no one really cares if you read it, or that you don't care what's inside?"

I took a sip of wine. "Both, I guess. But mostly I mean that I don't care what's inside. Other people can think whatever they want."

"Why?" She seemed genuinely mystified. "Don't you want to know your birth name? Your mother's name? Your father's? Where you were born? Where your genes come from? Which line? That kind of thing?"

I sighed. "Not really. It's not like it's going to do me any good tomorrow. Or the next day."

Miss Misery stared up at the ceiling for a moment, then trained her eyes on me again. Her expression was grim. "You're not a very cooperative thing, are you?"

It was my turn to look grim. "I've been alive for a long time, lady. You read my file. I'm not going to change my ways just for you. Keep your hand in mind."

There was a shimmering on the window. It would be undetectable to the human eye, but I picked it up as something just beyond purple.

"Your friends out there don't trust you. They're bouncing a laser off the window to pick up the vibrations of our conversation."

"White sedan?"

I nodded. She shook her head in disgust.

We sat in silence until the dinner came. By then the place was even louder. The best surveillance laser could probably still follow us, but it was irritating even if it couldn't. The purple strobed on and off as they adjusted it, plus other cars kept cutting through it. I flipped out my backup phone and dialed 911, listened to the spiel until I got a live person. Linda was already scooping flesh out of her tail, watching me curiously.

"Yeah, this is Cameron Marshal. I'm at Jake's downtown. My wife and I are trying to eat dinner and there's this white sedan across the street. Two guys throwing beer cans at prostitutes and screaming about snakes and Jesus. Did the restaurant call? It's disturbing us."

Pause. Linda looked delighted.

"Oh wait, one of them just flashed a badge. Shit, assault in progress. I'm going over." I hung up and winked at her. "There we go."

Whoever was in the sedan must have had a live police scanner, because thirty seconds later when I looked up from lobster number two they were gone. Even over the clink and chatter of polite diners, I could hear the thrilling howl of sirens in the distance. I carved into one of my steaks with relish.

"You going to eat any of your salad?" she asked. I shook my head.

"Probably not. Go ahead."

She took one of my salad bowls and started munching away. Eventually she gestured with her fork. The second bottle of wine arrived and the waiter cleared the oyster debris, interrupting what she was about to say.

"You know, I was thinking for our next date," she began. I arched an eyebrow, mouth too full to talk. "I was thinking we could visit this wonderful geneticist Christophe wants you to see. I'll even buy you ice cream afterward."

I swallowed and poured us more wine. She expertly swirled her glass. So did I. I even held it up to the light to study it.

"I already did that. I'm surprised you guys didn't catch it."

"And?"

I shrugged. "Had to kill him."

"So that'd be . . . a no?" She ate more of my salad. Linda ate with real appetite, like a woman who worked out more than twice a week. I shrugged, chewing meditatively.

"Unless you need the guy dead. But I charge for that. And he still doesn't get to peek at my molecules."

She nodded and turned her attention to the shrimp.

"So what happened with this geneticist?" She seemed genuinely curious, enough so to pose the question with her eyes down.

"Not over dinner. It was sort of sticky. There was even arson involved, which really isn't my thing."

"Oooh. Now I really want to know. Sticky followed by sloppy arson. What'd you do afterward?"

"I think I went to the movies. That was during my quaalude phase. It's a shame they're so hard to find anymore."

She arched an eyebrow mischievously. "They grow on trees in France."

I almost choked. "Figures," I managed.

"Microlabs in the Basque Country. Want some?"

"Nah. They're fun, but they don't work."

She picked up a second prawn. She was finally slowing down. "Work for what? Sounds like you have some kind of drug program going on."

"I do," I confessed, surprising myself. "I call it The Experiment."

"You're kidding."

I plucked up a prawn. In the booth behind us a couple were quietly discussing their tenth wedding anniversary. She was on the nasty side. He was playing along, but it wasn't in his pulse. I could even hear the boredom in his short replies. Probably having an affair, or he'd reached the wilted-man years a decade early. He didn't smell particularly old. The waiter wafted by. Still hadn't washed his hands. The hostess glanced over at us. I had her scent by then. Chanel Number Five, high-end mousse, a hint of rust, all over a subtle base of her natural burnt cinnamon. She also had herpes, freshly dried up, that still smelled like ketchup. Across from me, Linda smelled like seafood and fabric softener. I wondered if Christophe has warned her about my sense of smell. She'd showered with a baking soda scrub before she came, erasing herself.

"Yeah. The Experiment. I use a lot of drugs, especially around the full moon. Always looking for the right combination."

"To . . ."

"Damp it down, or at least blur it up. You should see some of the shit I get up to right around moon time. The rest of the month is bad enough, but it's just like the tides. And the full moon is high tide with fucked-up waves. Unpredictable, stormy weather. I usually give myself something to do to focus the hunt. Otherwise I'm driven to improvise, and that's led to several epic disasters. They have new stuff on the market every month, but no single pill will ever work all by itself. So I experiment."

"I remember. You were loaded to the gills on a river of bourbon on top of it."

I chewed meditatively. "Yeah. I'd added roofies to the cocktail. Four or five of them. Not that it did Vinnie much good. I didn't even have it together enough to talk to him. There was banking information, shit he might have hidden. Total mess."

"So the net results of experimental roofie consumption were?" More genuine curiosity. She was a hard worker. She enjoyed her job.

"I manufactured my own hair jelly."

She laughed. So did I.

"It looked cool." I couldn't help myself.

"Not cool enough to get you laid that night. We were watching."

That didn't surprise me. "All night? That must have been boring."

She nibbled at her prawn. "Not really. Picking the lock on the dumpster. Setting up the kill. You had your act together. Doing all of that seemed to calm you down. Then the shaving in the bathroom. We sent one of our people in to see what you were doing. The bald guy. Then your insane conversation with that poor little bartender? Swallowing little flashlights from the dollar store? When I heard the playback I laughed so hard I . . . That was fantastic. Downhill with the diving head butt to the neck, true. But then you spoke to me, even if it was mostly snarl. The funeral by trash. The calming burglary. We took Vincent Percy out of the dumpster after the cops left to cover your tracks. Just in case."

I feigned offense. "What the hell for?"

"You never can be too careful these days. Especially when it comes to the new guy. We ran him through a grinder and fed him to the river in itty-bitty pieces."

I nodded approvingly. At the table next to us, two well-dressed gay men were talking about shower curtains. They had strong heartbeats in strong frames, fit and relaxed. Dial soap. Espresso. Just beyond them another couple were discussing their kids. Benny was doing great in math. They seemed to be concerned that their daughter wasn't being encouraged enough. Two booths behind us four businessmen had brought their water cooler gossip to dinner. Someone named Janelle was getting a divorce and all four of them were queuing up. Golf on Sunday. The new BMW got a bad review. Sports droning. Competitive cloud of aftershaves and stifled flatulence and vermouth. It was embarrassing.

"So back to The Experiment? Anything working?" She was a little bit cautious now. I tried to focus.

"Who's asking? The lady who set me up, got my ass kicked, and then got shanked in the elevator for her trouble? Or the lady who thoughtfully scrubbed her scent down to Bounce and ate my salad."

"The setup ass-kicking shank lady, but salad lady wants to know, too."

I sighed. "The Experiment, then. I haven't been looking for a cure. The dead and burned genetics guy assured me that there wasn't one. That guy really tried to fuck with me, too, just so you know. Greedy little bastard. Anyway, it's a mitigation-type thing. I've been at it for about fifty years now. Sometimes I hit on a cocktail that works for a few months, but then something happens. My system adapts. A gland reboots. So I start all over again. Fuckin' tedious."

"We are aware of your attempts at self-medication," she said slowly. "Christophe called it quaint. Pharmacology is a hobby of his as well. His approach is more . . . advanced. He has access to things you won't hear about for another ten years, if ever. It's one of the things on the table."

"Fuck that guy," I said lightly. She chuckled and wiped her mouth.

"Don't let him hear you say that. He has a temper underneath all that chemical calm." She studied a prawn tail.

"He kicked me somehow. I didn't even notice until I got home."

"But that splendid white coat was fine, wasn't it? Undamaged?"

I didn't reply.

"He never messes up the clothes. Says it's sloppy. Christophe is exceptionally tidy. His pharmaceutical control program works. Even around the full moon."

More data for the file. I was learning more than she could imagine. She admired him, for one thing. That could be useful.

"So how do you like Portland?" It was time to put some cards on the table and hit my stack of chips. Linda shrugged.

"Two years of rain? Fine. Better than some godforsaken desert or the East Coast."

Bingo. Backup ride, rifle, dentist stash, all safe. I almost breathed a sigh of relief, but I kept my breezy poker face in place.

"The rain grows on you. I spent a winter in Nebraska." I shook my head. "What in the world was I thinking?" I looked back down at my steak.

"I dunno," she replied. "What were you thinking?"

I took the last bite and chewed. *Stalking deer through the snow. Quiet. Quiet. Still. Killing with a knife. The little log cabin with the big tin bathtub. The old potbellied stove. Coffeepot with a blue ceramic handle. That damn bag of potatoes. It had been forty miles to the gas station/convenience store. Running naked through the frozen woods. The spear I made. The two whiskey-bent hunters who broke in. The bodies on the roof.*

"I guess I was trying to get away from it all. It was right after the war. Wasn't as bad as I make it sound when I get to talking about it. The people were nice and I did some hunting. Venison mostly. Ice fishing. Used to play cards with the old guy who worked at the general, name was Theo Watts, vet from the

Great War. We ate pickled herring, drank moonshine. That kind of thing."

"Sounds lovely. Why'd you enlist?"

"Now there's a story for your psych profile. The guy who taught me how to read at the orphanage? Laurence? My first big kill? Christophe was talking about him." Gelson Verber: Missouri Axe Bandit.

She nodded. "I read your entire file. Go on."

"Well, in the end I didn't like him so much. Part of it was the reading thing. And the beatings. He smelled a certain way, like apple brandy, the cheap kind that used to cost a nickel. Anger sweat on his hands and his back. Mr. Bee's Powder For Men and lemon hair tonic. Fertilizer. Corn pollen. Anyway, he was German." I trailed off. Linda waited for me to continue. Clearly being German wasn't enough information, so after a sip of wine I continued. "When I heard we were going over there to kill a bunch of them, well, I thought it was a wonderful idea. It was almost as if I could kill Laurence over and over again. Plus, I really like Jewish food. All that fat. Just can't get enough of it. So I went. Had a great time up until the end."

"What happened?"

I toyed with my glass. "Difficult to say. Christophe was right about one thing, though. I do have a pack instinct, and it really came out with the soldiers I was fighting with. Teddy Caldwell. Crazy Minnesota Todd. Dan, the two tall guys from California. This one little guy with a crooked finger. They were good kids. When they all died, I just sort of lost my shit. Went feral, like the night with the neck snap in the alley. Killed a whole bunch more Germans, but I didn't use my gun. I don't think I could have figured out how."

"Hmm." It was a grim sound accompanied by a grim expression. "How many?"

"I wasn't in the frame of mind to count. And I wasn't for weeks. Months."

Gelson Verber: Unrepentant Blackout Killing Machine, Stealer Of Names. Buddy To The Dead.

She nodded. We sat in silence. I though about ordering another steak, but that kind of thing made me stand out.

"Christophe's drug cocktails," she suggested again. I made a dismissive gesture. Water cooler guys had moved on to time-share swapping. The horn yuppies were diving for deep pervert, snorkeling around the kinds of things that made me feel prudish and ancient. The hostess was watching us. Me.

"It's that alpha thing, isn't it?" Linda cocked her head, studying me. I met her eyes. Shower curtain discussion had moved on to bath mats.

"Of course it is."

Now I had even more data. Score: Verber, Nebraska Butcher Of Dickheads, up seven; Miss Misery, up mostly not that much. And the wine was loosening her up. At a little under three thousand a bottle, it was worth it.

"He's faster than you," she said softly. "Stronger. Smarter. He has more wolf in him. He has more money. More power. Knowledge. He knows things about your history. My history. Everyone's."

I shrugged. "I have more guile. Certainly more charm. My hair is better. I'm whimsical. And I bet I know more about music than he does. I'm definitely a more devoted reader. Plus, I have fantastic taste in wine."

She snorted. "You definitely have matching egos."

I had to laugh. "I'm sure we do."

"You can't take him, Mr. Verber. If he wanted you dead, it would have happened yesterday." She said it softly. I nodded.

"I know, honey. I know."

"And you're not worried."

"Nah. Christophe's okay. I'm just not a joiner. He'll get it."

Abruptly she sat back and crossed her arms. Her heart rate had gone up. Potty-talk couple was whispering now. She finally had his complete attention. I could smell his stiffy. Operation Homo Bath Mat looked promising. Those guys were really up on things.

"He won't take no for an answer."

I shrugged with my face. We stared at each other.

"How was your dinner," I asked quietly.

"I ordered the lobster just to piss you off."

"I one-upped you with the wine to show you that it didn't work."

"How was yours?"

"Still hungry."

Then she laughed and the tension broke. It was her first genuine laugh of the evening, maybe brought on by my deadpan delivery. She was too cold inside for it to transform her in a miraculous way, but it made her measurably less disgusting. I leaned forward.

"Let's pony up and blow," I suggested. "Go get some dessert. I know a great place right down the street, just a few blocks from here."

Linda leaned forward, too. "What'd you have in mind?"

"Sushi," I breathed. "It's what I always have for dessert."

"We don't have an umbrella," she purred back.

"Mmn. There's a rack by the door. We'll steal one that matches our outfits."

We stared at each other. Her skin was slightly flushed.

"You're even stranger than your psych profile suggests, Mr. Verber." She gave me a sleepy half-smile.

"Psychology is a French science at best."

The space between us was positively intimate. We were playing each other and we both knew it, but at least we were finally enjoying it. I was, anyway.

"I think I'll pass," she whispered.

"I knew you would," I whispered back. "I'm a pig. A walrus."

"It's not that," she murmured, our faces even closer. "It's the whole homicidal-kleptomaniac-who-stabbed-me thing."

"You better not have naughty dreams about me," I chided. She winked.

"Not a chance."

And with that she got up and slowly walked out without a backward glance. I motioned at the waiter and made the fingers-rubbing-together money sign. He didn't even bat an eyelash when I paid in cash. The lobster and the wine came out of the stash I'd taken from behind Vinnie's toilet, and as such was a thematically appropriate salute to his prospects in the afterlife.

I put on my jacket and straightened the sleeves. Maybe one more drink at the bar, I thought. As I passed the hostess station, I slowed. The green-eyed woman looked up and blinked. The slow kind of blink.

"How were the oysters?" she asked. I licked my lips. The slow kind of lick.

"Delicious. Thanks for the recommendation. Smoothed over the whole business dinner thing."

"That looked like a date to me," she said. Again with the blink.

"Ah." I leaned on the antique counter and looked at her hands. No ring. "I think I'm going to get a drink at the bar. What time do you get off, Miss . . ."

"Katie. In about fifteen."

"Do you like sushi? There's this fabulous place right down the street . . ."

I'm immune to herpes.

SIX

A T EXACTLY 8:00 AM there was a knock at the door. I was asleep naked in the upstairs bedroom, Katie the hostess next to me on her stomach, snoring. She'd kicked the blanket off of one long leg, so I covered her up and put my robe on, went down the clothing-strewn stairs to the door and pulled the curtain on the little door window aside. A bullet didn't come through, but it was almost that bad. Linda was standing there with a truly icy expression, flanked by two big guys in dark suits. It was gray and raining outside, but the two men were wearing sunglasses. I opened the door.

"You fucked the hostess," Miss Misery spat.

"Like three or four times," I said in hushed tones. "She turned out to be kinda demanding. It must be going around."

"Christophe would like to see—"

"Keep it down," I hissed. I tossed my thumb at the stairs behind me. "She's still sleeping. Lemme gracefully kick her out first, okay?"

Linda crossed her arms.

"C'mon in and make us some coffee."

She reluctantly crossed the threshold and brushed past me. The two men made to follow. I held my hand up.

"You two fuckers wait in the car." I slammed the door on them. But not too loud. From the kitchen I heard the sound of Linda banging around. I picked up Katie's coat and her skirt and wandered into the doorway.

"For God's sake, the coffee and the filters are in the cabinet above the coffee machine."

"I've never known a bachelor with this much cooking crap," she said, flagrantly disgusted.

"It's all stolen, if that helps."

She glared at me and then glanced at Katie's skirt. I put it behind my back.

"I told the fat dudes to go wait in the car. I didn't hear them go down the stairs. They're still standing there. When you're finished making coffee, go tell them to do what I said or I'm going to drag them in here and beat the fuck out of them. And call a cab. Tell them twenty minutes. I think Katie might have a wicked hangover, so this could go south fast. And pour her some coffee. The go cups are next to the filters. Let's give her the Mickey Mouse one, much as I hate to part with it."

Linda narrowed her eyes.

I gathered clothes as I went up the stairs. When I finally got to the top my arms were loaded. We'd made it to the top close to naked. I dropped them in a pile and sat down on the edge of the bed. When she didn't stir I reached under the blanket and rubbed the nearest butt cheek. She moaned.

"Sweetheart," I whispered. "Wakey wakey."

She moaned again, a little louder this time.

"We overslept. I have to be at work in half an hour."

Her eyes flickered open. "Holy shit. How much did we drink?"

"I can't remember, so just enough, I guess."

"Water," she mumbled. "Coffee."

"Coffee's coming. My maid is making it right now. Water is on the bed stand."

She sat up and picked up the pint glass, drained it, then ran a hand through her hair.

"Upstairs shower is right there," I said, pointing at the bathroom door. "Clothes are all over the place, but mostly in that pile. Cab is in twenty. Coffee's almost done." I tousled her hair. "I wish I had time to make you breakfast." She gave me a sleepy smile.

"You're fantastic, Gelsie. I'll be out in a jiff." She got up and limped naked into the bathroom. A moment later I heard the shower running. I went to the window and peeked out. The sky was slate gray, so I selected a silicon-colored suit to match it. I'd picked it up a few months ago the day before an estate sale and worn it the next day when I went back to shop for anything I might have missed. Underwear and gray socks, shiny gray patent-leather shoes, and then I was back downstairs, in and out of the shower and dressed in about six minutes. After fucking with my hair and shaving and brushing my teeth, I was ready to face Linda again. I emerged from the steaming bathroom and adjusted a moist forelock.

"I heard all that," she said. Her morning face was a tight, mean thing. "Your maid?" She handed me a cup of coffee and as soon as she did I could tell she instantly regretted it. I grinned.

"You'll do in a pinch." I sipped. "So what's the story, mornin' glory?"

She shook her head, cheek muscles flexing as she bit her own teeth. "Fucking pathetic. I've only seen pictures of this place. Now that I'm here, I still can't believe they were real."

"You weren't part of the B-and-E team that cracked my safe?" I gave her a skeptical look.

"Not my department. Clear that bimbo out and let's get rolling. She can wait for her cab on the porch."

"No fuckin' way! It's cold out there and her hair is probably wet. And I'm not so sure I'm going anywhere in the first place."

"You are," she said firmly. "Christophe wants to see you. Now."

Upstairs I heard the shower turn off. Katie was humming softly. The rustle of clothes. The house had a very subtle under sniff of pussy and ass, too subtle for Linda to detect, which was a shame, considering. I looked past Linda and saw she had filled the Mickey Mouse cup and put the lid on. She saw me looking and scowled. I went around her and picked it up, then came back and whispered in her ear.

"Hang back. No need to frighten her with your death mask."

Linda spun on her heel and walked to the little breakfast nook at the back of the kitchen, she sat down and stared out at my weedy lawn, willing my grass to die. I could hear Katie coming down the stairs, so I greeted her at the bottom with the Mickey cup. She took it and smiled warmly.

"Thank you," she said shyly. "Last night was . . . I mean, I never . . . It's just . . ." She stamped one high heel. "Damn." She took a dainty sip. I brushed her earlobe with my index finger. I'd told Miss Misery where we would be dining, and Katie had been her most logical potential bribe to dig around in my pants, but people make poor liars in the throes of passion, and there had been nothing there more than a lonely woman looking for a little joy.

"You're a special flower, Katie."

"When can I . . . can we, I mean . . ." She shook her wet hair.

"I'll see you as soon as I can. I know where to find you."

She smiled, now playing the shy dummy. "I left my number on your bathroom mirror. Red lipstick."

I smiled in earnest. "I'll have my maid write it down."

"Promise?" She squirmed a little.

"Swear it on my heart, babe."

Outside, the cab beeped. I kissed her lightly and she gave me a shy wave and limped out. I watched her go. Linda appeared beside. I could feel the negative juju.

"The limp of shame," she observed.

"Touch of stagger as well."

She snorted. "How was the sushi?"

"Katie liked it well enough. For such a tiny thing she can really pack it in." I turned and looked down at her. "So exactly what the fuck is on today's increasingly hypothetical menu?"

Linda sipped her coffee. "I wish I knew."

✳

THE RIDE WAS a hulking black SUV with tinted windows. One of the beefy guys was in front, the other one in back. Linda opened the back door and tossed her head at the backseat meat.

"Get up front. Now." There was steel in her voice. The guy got out and walked around. I bristled at him and Linda gave me a gentle nudge, so I climbed in and she got in after me. I could smell them. Both took steroids and testosterone and they both had gas. The driver had dentures he soaked in bleach at night. Black beans and boiled eggs oozed out of their pores. A thousand other scents mingled in with those overpowering ones, and their trail for the last twenty-four hours hit me so hard and with so much detail that I almost gagged. A trip to the gun range. Cleaning the guns. Hot long-string polymers from a cluster of computers. The oriental woman at the Salt Street front desk. A hotel, the trace scents of more than a hundred other people from the common washing machines. They were chewing some overly minty gum in time with each other.

"These fuckers are disgusting," I announced. I turned to Linda. "We're taking my car. I just can't stand it."

"Meet you there, gentlemen," Linda said sourly. The passenger turned, craning his wide neck, and drew a breath to say something. I slapped him on the top of his baldish head, hard. His heart rate spiked.

"And stay the fuck out of my house."

I got out and stormed over to my car. Linda clicked along behind me. We got in and I started the engine, waited for the SUV to pull away before I backed out and followed them. She waited for a few blocks before she started talking. I rolled my eyes, but she wasn't looking.

"We're starting the day off on the wrong foot. Why did you think those guys had been in your house?"

"Smell of denture glue. That blue crap. It even smells blue, if you can believe it. Like spearmint algae mixed with antibiotics."

"Huh. What do I smell like?"

"I already told you. Exactly what your boss wants you to smell like. Nothing." I turned to her. "You lead a charmed life, woman. You smell like a thing that never even got born. Congrats."

She frowned at me. "Did you take your medicine? This is a bad time to stop your Experiment."

I shook my head. "Didn't take anything this morning. S'why I'm all pissy."

She blew out a long breath. "Are you sure that's a good idea? Today, I mean? Can't you just act like an asshole tomorrow?"

Even my laugh was off.

"I'm serious, Mr. . . . What should I call you? We did have dinner, and I just made you coffee."

"Gelson. Or Verber. Gelson Verber. Who gives a shit."

"Well, I'm serious, Gelson. Christophe is extremely dangerous. If you go in there with this kind of attitude, you'll be coming out in half a dozen trash bags."

I shot her a mean look. "You say that with such conviction. Almost like you're proud of something involving trash bags. You've added up to zero twice in the same conversation."

She gave me an exasperated hiss and rubbed her forehead, stared out at the gray that matched my suit.

"Tell the rich man to keep his fingers away from my mouth. I'm hungry. I had to skip breakfast thanks to this idiot operation."

"Jesus," she said, mostly to herself.

There was no sign of the beefy guys when we entered the lobby. Just the weirdo insect lady at the front desk/podium, wearing the same Formula 409 face. Linda swiped her card on one of the elevator slots and we waited. My mood had not improved.

"Yo, lady cake," I called. The receptionist turned. "Quit calling me in the middle of the night. No means no."

Her expression broke for an instant with a flash of panic. That was followed by an equal microsecond of fury, and then it was back to the CGI perfect corporate model. *Ding.* Linda pulled me into the elevator. The receptionist turned quickly away as the doors closed.

"Take your medicine. Now."

"No."

"Gelson!"

"Only if you let me make dinner for you." I had to spy on her after the meeting.

"Fuck you." She paused. "Okay then. Do it!"

I took a small tin out of my pocket and fished out six Xanax, chewed and swallowed. The results were almost immediate, though they wouldn't last long. I needed a drink to really make them sink in.

"I'll need a whiskey or something to make these things get any traction, so find me a drink before I get myself killed." I turned to face her. "I told you he kicked me, didn't I?"

"In the ribs. I remember. There's a fully stocked bar in his office."

"Hmm." That was the first good news I'd had all morning. "How do you feel about roasted pork medallions in a red wine walnut—" *Ding.*

Christophe was seated at his desk again, this time facing forward, looking at a computer. He was dressed in a perfectly tailored black suit that looked somehow Japanese. He didn't look up, but his fine nostrils flared.

"Mr. Verber. Please have a seat. Linda, where are you going?"

Linda cleared her throat. I could hear the nerves in her voice. "Mr. Verber has requested a drink, sir."

"Good," he said with sharp enthusiasm, eyes still down. "One for me, too, please. Scotch. Neat."

I slumped down in the chair across from him. He remained engrossed in his computer until Linda set our drinks down, coasters and all, very well trained. I instantly picked mine up and drained it, handed the empty back to her and flashed a finger for one more. Christophe ignored his. When he finally looked up, I was struck again at how pale his eyes were. He just stared at me, like I would be hypnotized or something. It was the long stare of wolves, the kind that could never be penetrated; fixed, unwavering, and unreadable. I made the opening move.

"What." It was a statement.

He smiled tightly, flashing it on and off, light to ancient stone. "I understand you haven't read your file."

I looked at my empty glass. "It's my life. I already know what's in it."

Suddenly Christophe was standing. He was so fast. He casually walked around the desk and sat on the edge, the very definition of grace, every movement fluid, absently powerful.

"That was not the point, Mr. Verber. The point was to teach you how exposed you are. If I can find all of that, then so can someone else. I could sell you to the highest bidder, in fact." It didn't sound like he was bragging. He sounded almost indifferent.

"Let's cut to the chase. Exactly what do you want out of me." I met his eyes, my poker face firmly in place. Linda silently set my refill down and backed away. I picked it up and drained it without breaking eye contact.

"Work," he replied, as if it was just that simple. He picked up a thin file from his desk. "Here. Look at this. Linda." He snapped his fingers. "Another drink for Mr. Verber."

I opened the file. The first page was a high-quality photo of a man in a trench coat, obviously wealthy, balding, midstride and walking fast. It was raining and so gray the picture looked black and white at first. I flipped to the next page and began reading.

James Thomasini was a first-generation hacker who had gone into communications, and after two decades had wound up several gory rungs above normal rich. Worth a little over a billion (actual worth unknown, so read—more) and expanding every second of every day. His security was miles beyond professionally tight, his political leverage was grotesquely huge, and he was evidently an asshole of a peculiar variety in many ways. Two dead wives, both of natural causes, which was clearly unnatural, and four children, one of who was in a mental institution and another in upscale private juvie for blowing up police cars. Those were the boys. His girls were still at home and there were no photos or biographical summaries of them at all, just names, which was a tad more than wrong. I wondered what a man that wealthy was doing walking in the rain alone, without an escort, or even a slave like Linda to hold his umbrella and lie down in puddles for him. The answer was in section five, paragraph two.

Thomasini had remarried and was on his way to meet one of his mistresses, a nineteen-year-old transvestite name Comoni Bee Bay. He never took his escort with him. He wasn't afraid his new wife would find out. She was property. He was afraid one of his other mistresses would. I finished reading and flipped to the last page. Photos and addresses of all five mistresses. All were young transvestites. Very convincing ones, too. I snapped the file closed and picked up my drink, then looked at Christophe, who had been watching me for the entire minute it took me to confirm my theories about the creepy side effects of being obnoxiously greedy.

"And?" I sipped. His face darkened.

"I want that fucker in my office, hog-tied, within one week. And no one better be able to trace it back to me." The same fury I struggled with geysered in him. I could see the veins in his face. His heart was a perfect bowling ball of otherworldly perfection, suddenly smacking my face with waves of heat.

"Why?" I asked casually.

"Because he Pissed. Me. Off!" The last word was part inchoate roar, and so loud the windows vibrated. I could feel it in my sternum.

"What's in it for me?" I tried to remain utterly still. The bruise on my chest hurt.

It was like he threw a switch. The fury vanished, instantly. Christophe smiled. His teeth were extremely white.

"Why, money of course." He picked up his drink. "Say half a mill in crispy new hundreds? Enough to top off that safe of yours?"

I opened the file again and took out all the photos. "I'll take these. You can keep the guts. What's he smell like?"

Christophe went back around the desk to his chair and sat. He spun very slowly with his eyes closed, daydreaming. "He smells like fresh jizz. Silicon lubricant. Used motor oil and yeasty pool-cue powder. Plastic. Cashews. Argentine horse leather and cheap rubber and yellow mustard seeds, all of it under an expensive amber and lilac cologne and a lotion made in France he uses for his dry hands and feet. Floral, like a daffodil's pollen after the fog has burned off."

"Got it."

His eyes clicked open like camera shutters. "Now was that so hard?" He spun one last time and stopped, pointed out the window with his scotch glass, his back to me again. "Welcome to the pack, Mr. Verber. It's good to belong somewhere, eh?"

I finished my drink and left.

CHAPTER

SEVEN

IT WAS JUST after 7:00 PM and dark, dark, motherfucking wonderfully dark outside. The freezing rain had a clean smell that mingled favorably with the aroma of the peppers I was roasting on my tiny one-man hibachi operation under the also tiny awning over my back door. The hibachi was custom made, a gift from a Japanese historian to his princess daughter. I'd taken it when I robbed her of the knockoff processor chips she was peddling for coke money after they turned into a dangerous minor empire that overlapped with mine. I was just finishing up searing the pork tenderloin medallions in the kitchen when my cell phone rang. I looked at it, then clicked "Talk" and "Speaker" with one pinkie.

"We still on?" I asked.

"Am I on speaker phone?" It didn't sound like she was driving.

"Yeah. I'm cooking. There's butter all over my hands."

"Cooking."

"I told you I was going to. I'm even wearing an apron. If that helps you envision why you're on speaker."

"I already get it." There was an odd echo. "I'm on your front porch."

I tapped the end button. Damn, she was good. No sound, no smell. I wondered if she was getting paid as much as me, and I sincerely doubted it. In a world where people breathe complex, unnamed poisons fourteen hours a day to give their kid something to eat that they had to steal out of a supervisor's trash can, I was betting she was in the cotton-candyland middle class, with the illusion of a 401(k) and maybe a half-baked dental plan. I'm no Luddite, but then again no one else is, either.

I washed my hands and padded to the front door as I dried them on my apron, then peeked out to make sure she wasn't holding a gun or sporting an escort. She was alone and wet. When I opened the door, she took one look at me and burst out laughing.

"You look ridiculous!"

I snarled and growled, a little too low for her to hear. "I already spit in the food." I leaned out and glanced up and down the street. She'd either come alone or her meat posse was hanging way back. "C'mon then."

Linda had her hair up again. There was a trace of tired around her eyes. I took her coat and hung it on the coat stand, fluffing it first for the folds and droplets and whatnot. That's when I busted her very first genuine scent, faint, like it was days out in the weather, a mixture of potato chip and pencil lead. A gun. There had been a gun in her coat at some point. It had been fired, too. The scent was mingled with woman smell in an ingrained, permanent way.

"Shoes," I said, pointing at her feet.

She slipped out of them and put them next to mine, a delicate little dance. No socks, long toes, no polish. She immediately went to the fireplace and the dance continued. Her back was to me, so I knelt and sniffed her shoes. Nothing.

"Fuckin' cold out there," I observed.

"Did you read your file?" she countered. She squatted and put her hands out to the fire. The bandage on the one I'd stabbed was already smaller.

"Pressed for time."

I went back into the kitchen and looked down at myself. I was still wearing the gray slacks and the crease was still sharp, but I'd changed shirts to a gray designer V-neck tee. Barefoot. White bib apron. It had to be the apron.

I turned down the heat on the pork medallions and checked the scent on the fingerling potatoes and julienned Braeburn apples I'd been roasting in goose fat and rosemary. Almost done. Linda appeared in the arched entryway to the kitchen.

"Something about you and all these knives . . . Maybe I'll just look at your books." And snoop around for anything new.

"The real library is just past the bathroom. The ones out front are my show books."

She stood there studying me for an uncomfortable period of time.

"Wine and a glass on the dining room table," I prompted. I finished wiping down the stove and set the cutting board in the sink. I left the knife on the counter rather than pick it up, just to avoid any more commentary about them. She didn't smell nervous and her heart rate was an athletic normal, but all that could change if I started wandering around with anything long and sharp. I tossed a dishtowel over it instead.

She drifted off. I watched her back as she poured herself a glass of the Repasso and went on to inspect the paintings in the dining room. After a moment I took my smokes off the counter and went quietly out the back door to check on the peppers. I'd invited her for many reasons, so I'd let her have some privacy to screw around so we could get through my agenda undisturbed.

"Gelson, this thing you have with food. Christophe is the same in some ways, but he never talks about it."

"You're asking about my 'thing with food'? You're kidding, right?"

"No." She smiled a little.

"You're a microwave fan, right? Eat out three times a week?"

"Maybe." Condescending. She couldn't help it.

"I can tell. Transparency is a terrible quality in anyone, Linda. You might be tempted to think that cooking has something to do with humanization. Wrong, of course, but if you even thought about it at all, I guess it means you're trying. But that's not it. Old friend of mine, he used to quote this guy Oscar he kicked around with back in the day. 'Food nourishes the body, but good food nourishes the soul.' Stuck with me I guess."

"Tell me about the paintings. I'm curious."

"There's a story behind every one of them," I said. I picked up my wineglass. "Which one?"

"This. It's lovely." She was standing behind a watercolor on wood of two lilies floating on a pond. The petals were ghostly, all of it cast in shadow or maybe dusk.

"1981. It was painted by a guy named Peter Wickwire. Signed on the back. Too bad about that guy."

"Too bad?"

"Yeah. There used to be this gallery, Chamaya. Guy who ran the place had a habit of holding the work of every artist who had a showing. If the artist left the unsold pieces with him, they would appear in his quarterly catalogue. Anyway, when he died his wife wound up with everything. Horrible little woman immediately started selling it all off in secret. I had to kill her for entirely different reasons, but I wound up with that painting. Wickwire had been so disturbed by the entire episode that he didn't want it back." I gestured. "Same with that oil of the bicycles, actually. Different artist from the Chamaya."

I left her with the paintings and carried my wine outside. The sky had decided to shift to sleet mixed with fat drops, and it was coming down hard and flat. My back patio awning was about the size of an economy car hood, so when I squatted in front of the little hibachi on my heels like a Cambodian monk and breathed in the scent of roasting peppers and wintry storm, I could reach out and cup my hand and fill it with water. I did.

Natural beauty is lost on almost everyone, especially and most tragically on its most ardent admirers, who can't ever get past the instant-by-instant shock value of it. Cities are things to prepare to enter. The wild world is a place to prepare to return. There is very little that is natural left in people when they stray from the cities. Day hiking in Gore-Tex with a bag of trail mix and a cell phone in a fanny pack and a bottle of iced chai tea clipped to your belt isn't actually natural, it's tourism, or worse, voyeurism. Bare feet still touch the ground sometimes, and there is a growing, almost desperately evolving knowledge in people of why that is so important. Maybe it's a reaction to the hard greed of the Thomasinis of the world, who are more a manifestation of physics than biology. I held my hand out and let the rain

run over the back of it. I cupped it there for a long minute and
then drank when it was full.

To feel, to run naked, to chase something through starlit
ferns, to watch flowing water and see patterns, to luxuriate in a
wind that was like a thousand wings brushing you with motion,
to listen to the nonsense music of rain on leaves, to savor the
round blindness of stones . . . I didn't diminish the wands of
grass in my backyard by mowing it. If I hadn't had a dinner
guest, I might have stripped naked and rolled in it right then. I'd
be doing something close enough in a few hours, so I didn't feel
all that bad.

"Penny for your thoughts," Linda said softly from behind
me, standing in the open doorway. I'd heard the creak of the
floor and smelled the approaching wine.

"Overpaying," I cautioned. "It's the American way, I know,
but try not to be too crass with the help here."

A car about a block up the street to the north, tires through
puddles as it passes. Donny, the kid next door, playing some kind
of game on his computer, but quietly so his parents won't hear
and thus believe he was finishing his homework. I might bust
him on it later. I was his occasional English tutor, which I did
so I could keep track of the objects I had hidden in their home.
The occasional ping of the cooling engine of the sedan Linda had
driven. A rabbit rustling around the edge of the withering hippie
garden next to the house behind mine. The rabbit smelled old.

"Whatcha got there?" She stepped out, inches from the rain.
I was a little surprised that her skinny feet could take the concrete's bitter cold.

"Fire with peppers on top." I turned them with my fingers
and took a drag off my smoke.

"Are you . . ." She was pensive for some reason. "Are you okay?"

Then I did look up. I had nothing to say to that. Maybe she hadn't been paying attention for the last few days. She took a sip of wine and continued.

"It's just weird to see you crouched over a fire in the rain. We know you can afford a bigger back porch." She sat down in the open doorway. I shrugged and pushed the peppers around.

"I like it as it is." I held my hand out and played with the rain again. There was a shift in the random patter and I knew she was doing the same thing.

"I was looking at your books. Science, philosophy, the classics, but no mythology except for a generalized world history collection. You even have Chinese poetry, which is gay, by the way, but nothing about wolves."

I was silent again. She went on.

"You have a plan to deal with Thomasini?"

Down to business already. "Yeah. After dinner I'll tell you. Peppers are done. Will you grab me that glass bowl on the counter?"

She got up lightly and returned a moment later. When she passed it over my shoulder, I felt a faint smear of her body heat, her breath on my neck. I dropped the peppers in the bowl and stood, gave her a wan smile.

"Just about there." I followed her back into the kitchen.

"Just about starved. Christophe had me on the move today. I even had to pick up his dry cleaning."

I put the bowl in the sink and turned on the cold water to soak the blackened skins off, then put on my oven mitts. More ridiculous by the second. The mitts had roosters on them.

"I keep wondering about your job," I said. I opened the oven and smelled. Done. "Creepy rape sting in an alley. Getting stabbed in an elevator. Eating dinner twice with a . . . well, me. What am I missing here?" I took out the potatoes and the pork and set them on the counter, kneed the oven door closed.

"I like my job," she replied. "How many people can say they do what I do?" She cocked her hip and leaned against the counter, watching me.

"Not many people above ground." I took the lids off of everything. "You're in way over your head. There's a reason guys like me spend a lot of time alone." I took a sauté pan down and heated it up. There was a small antique Chinese bowl of crushed walnuts waiting on the counter next to the stove.

"Christophe seems to have a social life. So do you, in your own way." She watched as I took two white porcelain plates out of the cupboard and set them on the counter, then started peeling and seeding the peppers to take the bite out of them. Smooth, deft moves. One by one I dropped them in the blender.

"I can't imagine. Does his social calendar involve these trannies? Is that why he's so pissed?"

This time it was her turn to remain silent. I dumped the walnuts into the hot pan and toasted nut filled the air. We were both quiet for the minute it took them to become crunchy and leave a thin veneer of walnut oil on the pan. Then I dumped them back into the bowl.

"Where did you learn how to cook?"

I shrugged. "You pick things up."

I plated the steaming fingerlings and apple and the pork medallions. The medallions were so tender they were falling apart. The steam was intoxicating.

"I can't even make a grilled cheese," she confessed.

I poured the wine-infused pork juice into the blender with the peppers, added sea salt, and hit "Go" for the thirty seconds it took to make it smooth. Then I put a few pats of butter into the hot pan and poured in the sauce. It flared and bubbled and reduced quickly.

"I used to be like that," I said. "I was fifteen. The year I spent in Wyoming. It was elk that started me down the culinary highway. Raw elk is okay, but there are options." I glanced over and winked at her. That's when I noticed the big folder on the counter. "Is that in my file?"

"Find out for yourself." She didn't wink back.

The sauce had thickened. I poured it over the medallions and sprinkled the walnuts over it. The dining room was already set for two, so I picked up the plates and gestured with my head, followed her out.

There were no knives on the table. Just cloth napkins and wineglasses. I silently opened the second bottle, a Bordeaux, and poured. She settled lightly into the chair across from me, dropped her napkin in her lap, and inhaled the steam rising from the plate in front of her with her eyes closed. I set her glass down in front of her and she came out of her trance and raised it.

"To this," she saluted.

We clinked glasses.

As I ate, I could feel her eyes on me. After a minute she took a deep breath.

"Delicious. At least you have a fallback career if you decide to give up crime."

"Maybe." I was eating slowly. She took a not-so-dainty bite and nodded. I like watching people eat. It's always revealing in some way. Linda was consistently . . . enthusiastic, in a slightly overmature way. She'd assumed her plate as territory, like a convict or an orphan. Police officers did it, too. It was an unconscious thing for the extreme poles in certain social power dynamics.

"Christophe eats with this kind of laser focus. He has a strict rule. No talking while he's eating, and keep at least three feet away from him."

"Charming," I said. "Maybe he needs to try my version of pill therapy."

"Maybe." She sipped her wine. "So what happens if you go off your drug and alcohol program completely?"

I looked off into space, savoring dinner, patient just to be irritating. Eventually I decided the truth couldn't hurt.

"Not much, to be honest, unless the moon is full. Then I'm out of my comfort zone."

She arched an eyebrow. "Your comfort zone?" Sarcastic.

"Sure. All mammals have one, even borderline reptiles like you."

"Interesting. Is this house part of your comfort zone?"

She was fishing for her boss, adding to my file. I shrugged.

"Not really. To be honest, I'm homesick for a place I've never even been." I don't know why I said it.

"How so?" she asked, feigning casual.

"Too hard to explain." I tried to focus on dinner. When I was done the real interrogation would begin, I knew, so I tried not to focus too hard.

"Give it a shot," she prompted. I was down to one medallion and one fingerling. The walnuts had been a nice touch, as crunchy as little bird bones.

"Well, it's like this. People, and I mean people like you, can find contentment sometimes, although it always surprises me how little importance you place on the concept. Money and career, and the illusion of safety, instead of a sense of place or whatever. I'm just not wired that way. Sometimes I wish I were, but the wishing itself disgusts some other part of me. That in turn makes me angry, which naturally leads to mistakes. Plus, it makes me feel bipolar."

"Sounds like you have quiet a roller coaster in there," she said, tapping her temple with one manicured finger. Feeding her a partially fabricated weakness felt like a good way to blunt what was about to come next, but I was a little put off by how convincing I'd sounded.

"It's a regular funhouse."

I ate my last two bites and drained my wine, refilled the glass, and topped hers off as well. We'd finished eating within seconds of each other. She'd been waiting for me, holding back.

"So let's talk about your plan." It wasn't a request.

I took my wine over to the bearskin in front of the fireplace and she followed. We settled down and I absently stroked the fur, staring into the fire. The pelt had a few holes in it, but the knives had been thin and extremely long, so they were small and the fur was so thick that they were hard to find. I'd have to get a new one in the next decade or so, provided I lived through the week. I kept my eyes on the fire. Miss Misery kept her eyes on me.

"Well," I began slowly, "I think I'm going to start with lady-boy number three. Izelle Tatum. He/she's by far the hottest, so I'll scout her place and everything around it. He spends more time with her than any of the others. And did you notice the jewelry in her photo? I looked at it under a magnifying glass, and while it's impossible to be sure, it looks real to me. And big. Plus, her neighborhood is both the nicest and the most cluttered with people, and I'm reasonably familiar with it. Cafés, restaurants, my favorite grocery store . . . I'm guessing this one is Thomasini's favorite, the one he's the most worried about. The others are backup or variety, I don't know. So I'll deep-scout her place and then I'll run her down. In a nice way, of course. Then lie my way into her life, buddy up. Find her day planner or something like that. Firm everything up from there."

"Hmm. I need more on that last part. Firm up from there is just a little too vague."

I sipped my wine and tried to dumb it down for her, to answer in a way she might have some chance of understanding. It wasn't going to be easy. I sipped again. Her attentive eyes glowed gold in the firelight as they wandered over my face and calculated my demeanor. I finally cleared my throat, shooting for the wise and meditative reflections of a professor of abduction.

"Sometimes, the best plan at this early stage is no plan at all." I paused and looked above her head. "See, people, and once again I mean people like you, they make elaborate plans too far in advance. They scheme. Then they put these crappy half-baked things into play and, oh, well, about 80 percent of the time there's a great big fucking wrinkle. You know that. Everyone does, and yet . . . Then you not only have to make a new plan up on the fly, but you have the additional burden of having to actually disassemble your own original plan as you go. The new plan has to both work and at the same time erase all the evidence of the premature one. That's the difference between an accident and a disaster that leaves a trail that everyone you just irritated can follow without a flashlight. So it always seems to me like the best way to get through a situation like this is to get as many facts as you can and then design something flawless. It takes time. Research. Patience. You can't make these kinds of things up as you go along. I know my file might suggest that I sometimes operate otherwise, but this is a unique situation. Let's do it right, and doing it right means that I'll need to rely on you, as a sounding board and for material support." My boldest lies of the decade. I was totally on a roll.

Linda Misery snorted derisively. "Is that why you picked the lock on the dumpster in advance on rape night? Advanced planning?"

"Sort of. If it hadn't worked, I could have dragged him to his car and trunked him. Or lit him on fire right there in the alley after I yanked the teeth and bit off his fingerprints. Or dragged him up on the roof, maybe even chucked him down a manhole. Could have even put him in someone else's trunk. Dead in an alley means options unlimited. But that was one guy. And he wasn't rich. And there was no Christophe."

"Nothing at all about your plan to rob and kill Vincent Percy worked out, did it?" She wasn't being sarcastic. Just bitchy and factual.

"I dunno. I was going to be sort of bored this week. Half a mil for abducting a rich pervert . . . worse things have happened, I guess."

She sipped her wine, her eyes never leaving my face. I continued.

"Life is like that," I said, returning to my strategy dodge. "Everything travels through the instant, the now. I try to focus on the quality of the moment. It's a lifestyle choice more than any kind of philosophy."

That last part made her laugh.

"Maybe you should write a self-help book," she said, gesturing with her glass. "The smooth-sailing ramblings of a ten-year-old serial killer who refused to grow up."

"Kind of book I would definitely buy," I admitted. "But I think I have another fifty years to go before I turn ten. I'll find you in whatever welfare asylum you wind up in and give you a copy, if I get around to it."

"Sounds sort of bitter. Realistic." The sarcasm had returned. She gave me a tiny smile. I gave her a thoughtful one back before I replied.

"You're probably having a bad effect on me."

She smirked. "Not too bad, I hope."

I pretended to ponder the statement. The fire was getting low so I put another log on, a smaller one, since I was going out later.

"You ever meet any more like you?" she asked casually, leaning back on one elbow. "I mean other than Christophe." More fishing, a little too obvious. This time I told the truth a second time, since I'd been lying all night and she might actually know the answer.

"Twice," I replied. "First time was just outside of Penn Station. 1938. It was really cold that winter. Wind sucked everything out of my cigarette when I stepped outside. I remember I had these boots. Leather, with this rabbit fur on the inside. Wool coats were big at the time. And hats. Everyone had a hat. I'd just had a plate of sausages and boiled potatoes at some place down the street, I forget the name, but the sign was red with cursive writing, something foreign. Maybe they were Polish. Anyway, he was right there, waiting for me in that hard freeze. I killed him."

"Why?" Maybe the story ended a little too abruptly for her taste, and maybe it was in my file and she was testing me, but she was suddenly at maximum perk. It was in her heartbeat, though outwardly she was still relaxed.

"He attacked me," I said shortly.

"Huh." Her heart rate was continuing to ratchet up. I ignored it. "Did you ever learn anything about him?"

"Nope. No wallet or papers and I was in a hurry. I think the train station was his hunting ground. I was trespassing." I shrugged.

"Too bad," she said, almost to herself. "What about the other time?"

"Now that was truly weird, even for me." I absently stroked the fur. "It was at this book fair. Denver." I pointed up at my Dickens set. "I was after those beauties. Anyway, I picked them up, and when I was paying I could smell the dealer. He scented me, too. There was a stare down, but it wasn't like that first time, or with Christophe. Neither of us was hunting, for one thing. Denver wasn't territory for either of us. And we had something in common."

"Books." Linda was too curious to hide it. "So what happened?"

"That was in '77. Coke, disco, big hair. We palled around for a while. He'd had a wife who had died of leukemia. No kids, no family. He was lonely, I guess. His name was John Jack Bridger. That was his real name, actually. He wasn't like me in that respect."

"You must have been lonely, too." Her voice was softer. "All those years alone. No family. Moving from place to place every time the full moon made you do something bad enough to run."

I made a dismissive gesture and stared into the fire, remembering.

"So what happened?"

I was quiet for a long time. When she finally interrupted my stroll down memory lane, I don't know how much time had passed.

"Gelson?"

"He . . . killed himself." I cleared my throat and sipped wine. "We were fishing. Two miles off the coast of Costa Rica. John had been depressed for weeks, and I thought it might cheer him up. We were living in Baltimore in those days, back before the big burnout and John Waters. Bridger had a house right down the street from mine. Brownstone. Fun couple of years. Rum and crappy weed. Ludes. God. Ludes and a river of hairy pussy. Anyway, I cast my line and looked back, gonna toss him a beer. He was on the edge of the boat with the anchor tied around his neck, '38 in his mouth. He gave me this sad smile with his eyes, brained himself, and went right into the drink. Sharks were everywhere in less than thirty seconds."

"What the fuck?" Linda sat up, but something in her voice told me that she already knew. I'd been right, but she wanted more. Maybe she just wanted to hear it out loud, to watch me tell it.

"It was his wife's birthday. They'd been married for over forty years. She died at ninety-six. In the end they'd moved around a lot. Everyone thought he was her grandson." I shook my head. There was more, so much more, but that was all I felt like sharing. We were quiet for several minutes.

"I'm sorry," she said finally. Another lie. It was in her heartbeat again.

"Me too."

Silence again. John had helped me take down the bear we were sitting on. His knife had made the holes mine didn't. The two of us, bounding naked through the woods at night in the Alaskan moonlight with long skinny knives. John knew where all the tendons were, so he'd taken the legs. I'd hugged the huge head. The liver was steaming when we ate it, the ripe glow of the full moon in silver crescents on the red snow. Almost like daylight on the moon itself.

John had been born in New York City, in June, 1901, under the Corn Moon. There were so many things to learn from him, but he hadn't been the talkative type, not really. When he died, there were so many questions left unanswered. Why, for instance, would he never talk about his time in China? And once he had told me that wolves weren't the only creatures to make the jump into the human genome over the last two hundred thousand years. What he knew about that haunted him so deeply that even that one mention of it had brought on a long bout of superstitious silence.

I closed my mind to the memory and watched the fire until Linda finished her wine and rose.

"Tomorrow?" she asked. I rose, too.

"I'll check in early. Need some sleep. It's gonna be a long-ass day."

She slipped into her shoes. I yawned and held her coat out.

"Thanks for dinner," she said, playing sincere.

"Don't flatter yourself," I replied with a sleepy smile. "I was going to make it anyway."

She gave me a curious look and then walked out and away with no good-night, down the steps and out into the rain. I watched for a moment and then closed the door and locked it. Miss Misery got in her sedan and drove off, snapping into her cell phone as she did. It was all too easy to guess who she'd called to feed the head full of lies I'd been telling her.

It was going to be a long night. I turned the lights out, stripped naked, and went into the bathroom. The four Xanax out of the medicine cabinet went down bitter, so I padded out into the dining room and washed them down with the rest of the wine, bottle to lips. Then I took a deep breath and slowly let it out, stilling parts of myself and waking others.

Seconds later I was out the back door and into the freezing rain, running naked through the dark. I bounded the ten-foot chain link fence into the yard behind mine without even touching it and landed in a tight crouch. My heart was singing a song of its own, the opening chorus of a hunt that Christophe and Miss Misery were definitely not expecting.

EIGHT

Mr. and Mrs. Demming lived three houses down on the street behind mine. Clide Demming was a retired civil service engineer and Margret Marie Demming was a not-so-retired homemaker. He was getting progressively more senile and smelled like mothballs, talcum powder, cherry jelly, and the coming cancer. She was slow and arthritic and scented primarily of crappy coffee and peanut butter, with a little pee and wheat mold mixed in to spice things up. I landed in their cluttered backyard and remained in a silent crouch for a moment, listening, sniffing.

They were asleep. Even their ancient cat Bishop was asleep, which wasn't surprising. I moved in a low, slow prowl to the narrow wedge of mud behind the forgotten toolshed at the corner of the yard and started digging with my hands. It only took about thirty seconds to unearth my box. After I wiped my hands in the grass I opened it.

Socks, underwear, tee shirt, an orange and white Nike jogging suit, complete to the sporty shoes, a white watch cap with a tiny bill, a wallet with three grand and a fake driver's license, a short, curved gutting knife, a customized Glock with a spare clip, and a lonesome car key. All triple-wrapped in plastic. I'd even had the foresight to include a towel.

Fashion wise it was all five and a half years out of date, but the careful packaging and the packets of silica had kept it all clean and dry, and when I ripped open the plastic it still smelled a little like detergent and fabric softener. I put the plastic back in the box and buried it, then rinsed off under a leak in the shed's rain gutter, toweled quickly, and dressed at speed before the rain soaked me again. Then I was off. I dropped the towel in the Demmings' trash can as I passed.

Once I was on the street I moved at a fast jogger's clip to the nearest health food store, about fifteen minutes away. I made it in less than ten without breaking a sweat, just before they closed and just a little wet. Planning was everything. I was still amazed Miss Misery had believed a word of my lame irrationalizations suggesting otherwise. The miraculous load of zeros I'd spun for her was little more than a delightful piece of improvisation, and the irony of the moment would forever be wasted on everyone but me, which was tragic.

The bright lights of the store almost blinded me. Like all modern health food stores, New Reasons was ingredient-intensive and had ineffective cleaning products, expensive trash bags and lightbulbs, worthless recycled paper towels, and everything was marked up 400 percent. Plus, the help was reliably too stoned, uniformly snarky, and dependably unhelpful.

"We close in fifteen minutes," the lone checker droned, sneering faintly at my edge-of-retro workout clothes. She was almost as tall as me and rail thin, with wicked BO, a crusty nose ring, and a limp and greasy zigzag rebellion of a haircut only her half-blind vegan roommate could have been responsible for. I smiled pleasantly. She gave me back zombie.

I plucked up a hand basket and conducted a fast stroll. Nothing from produce. Nothing from vitamins. I got a bottle of water and a big Belgian beer, all-natural toothpaste that could never work, and a stick of floral deodorant with chamomile, the most expensive they had. Then it was back to the checker. She was picking at her nose ring, looking out at the vacant parking lot. When I set my basket down she didn't even bother to give me the sneer again, just started scanning.

"Twenty-two fourteen." She said it like she was grudgingly doing me a favor. I took one of the hundred-dollar bills out of my wallet and handed it over. She swiped it with a bill check pen and it came up real, but she held it up to the light anyway, and once she was satisfied she gave me a sour look.

"Where's your bag." Not a question, just a bored confirmation of easily predicted ineptitude on my part. Flunking at checkout time. It appeared to be the story of her life.

"I don't need one."

She gave me my change, sort of scattering it onto the counter. I picked it up and then grabbed the water and the beer and started for the doors.

"Dude," she called, her voice as flat as her hair, "your other crap."

I turned back. "It's for you. Merry Christmas, bitch hole."

She froze, astonished, her eyes miraculously wide. A pound of organic weed had just fallen out of her brain. Sudden spike in BO, and abruptly I could smell her feet. Foreign cheese rind and tangy fried buffalo wings.

"You can get foot powder at Rite Aid." I left her gaping at me and went to the pay phones at the laundromat around the corner to call a cab. The change machine at Wash and Spin didn't take fifties or hundreds, and the bonus beer kept me company for the ten minutes it took for my ride to show up. Careful planning in action.

The cab driver was a middle-age chubby guy with a scraggly beard. There was a copy of George V. Higgins's *The Friends of Eddie Coyle* and a big coffee on the seat divider next to him. He was anticipating a slow night and was just beginning his shift, which was good. I'd be forgotten either by fare number five or chapter three, whichever came first.

"Pioneer Square," I said. I kept my vibe sleepy and distracted.

"Downtown it is."

We rode without talking, listening instead to his dub mix, which wasn't my thing, but not altogether grating. When we got to the bright lights I had him drop me off at Macy's and tipped him average. He cranked up the music as soon as I was out of the car. I'd achieved forgotten passenger status.

Macy's was closed, but it wasn't my target. There were several small shops in a tight run of streets between the bigger buildings a few blocks up, so I put my head down and went through the night-shift panhandlers with their facial tattoos and dogs, just dangerous but spirited kids, by and large, and made it to my actual destination with about forty minutes to spare. It was a vintage clothing place I'd walked past several times over the past few years, run by the quiet little post-hipster guy who was sitting behind the register looking over a men's magazine. I gave him my best smile as I walked in and he smiled pleasantly back. The place was cluttered and warm and tasteful, with the classical station bubbling quietly in the background.

"Evening," he said by way of greeting. He adjusted the lapels of his deep burgundy wool blazer and reflexively smoothed his hair. Behind his antique silver-framed glasses were the eyes of a romantic in the wrong country and the wrong decade both. He smelled like old newspaper, an ironing board, pecan trees, and his girlfriend. "What can I do for you? Feel free to browse."

"I have a small crisis on my hands," I said. "A woman I've been courting for over a year just called me and wants to grab a late dinner. She sounded . . . sad. I have a great deal of money and no time to go home and change. She's at a bar right around the corner, but it's the kind of place I can't really go into in my gym clothes. Can you fix me up?" I held up my wallet and smiled imploringly.

His smile broadened. He adjusted his glasses and put down his reading. "An actual damsel in distress? And on a rainy night? This is too good. You do like vintage . . ."

"I do indeed."

He stood, an exuberant journeyman tailor of Prague, circa 1921. "Let's get to work."

Twenty minutes later, I walked out wearing a gray wool suit from a place I'd never heard of in England, a red tie with gold patterning, a white silk shirt, argyle socks, and buffed but broken-in root beer wingtips, and all of it under a thick black wool coat with a red checkered scarf, topped by a black bowler hat. He'd tossed in the cane and a handkerchief for free after I'd tipped him a hundred dollars, and he'd been delighted with my gift of the soon-to-be retro tracksuit and shoes.

There was a 7-Eleven right up the street from his place. I tapped in smartly and purchased three cell phones, each with unlimited hours. That and a pack of cigarettes and a lighter and I was adequately prepared for phase two.

Back down at Pioneer Square, I boarded the Max train for Beaverton and got off somewhere halfway there, where I picked up a cheap umbrella at yet another convenience store and then smoked out front until the cab I called using phone number one arrived. I waited in the shadows on the side of the place, listening and scenting. If I'd been followed, they were world class. Christophe's people had certainly successfully tracked me from time to time for months at that point, but never when I was acutely conscious of it. After five minutes, I was certain that I was alone.

Cab number two took me into the NW industrial area. I had the driver drop me off in front of a lonely residential strip, and once again tipped average after a silent ride where I projected amiable but preoccupied. After the cab was out of sight, I opened my umbrella and casually tapped along the twenty blocks to my final destination, occasionally ducking through alleys and sprinting over a row of rooftops, until I arrived at the twenty-four-hour-access car storage depot called Billy Wagner's.

Wagner's was where you put your vintage ride if you had no room left in your garage. It was for rich collectors, but it had year-round continuous access, security, and they kept the cars in good shape. Billy Wagner also had a climate-controlled wine and cigar storage building on the same street, ostensibly for the same customers. Expensive. I walked up to the enclosed booth and took my license out and handed it to the security guard, a big black man with tired eyes and gray in his tight Afro. The press of his uniform spelled ex-cop gone private-sector nobody. He read my ID and worked the computer with the same telling echo of authority that was hanging around in his clothes.

"Mr. Fowler. Been six years since your last visit."

"I've been in Europe. How's my baby?"

He chuckled. "Runs like a top. Says here we did an oil change and a brake inspection six months ago. Not that it really needed it, but it's policy. Belts and hoses two years ago. Gas change at the same time as the oil. She's ready to drive to New York. Started every month for an hour just to keep her heart in good shape. Take her out?"

"Oh yes," I replied. "I've missed that ride. I have a conference in Seattle the day after tomorrow and I'll be damned if I'm going to rent a Prius at the airport. Not when I have the Lincoln just waiting. It'll be like sitting inside of an old friend. Without the mess."

His laugh was a genuine one that slewed into uncertain along with his expression as that sunk in. "I'll have Jose bring her down. Uh, coffee?"

"Thanks. Okay if I smoke?"

Ten minutes later, I was behind the wheel of a perfectly tuned, polished, and purring Presidential Black 1977 Lincoln Town Car. I drove a few blocks into a dark patch between streetlights and pulled in behind a warehouse that looked like it had been abandoned for twenty years or so, cut the engine. Then I lit another cigarette and got out, and after I scented and listened carefully for a full minute I went back to the trunk and opened it.

The trunk was huge, easily big enough for the two spare tires and the locked box. The key to the box had been taped under the ashtray. I opened it and surveyed the contents.

Tailored black jeans, expensive alligator cowboy boots, thick black socks, a Western-style long-sleeve shirt, another gun, another knife, a lock-pick set, and a cowboy hat. Underneath all that in a separate bag was a black Nehru suit and black loafers. I slapped the tire with the money stashed inside and the sound came back full, with no ring. Still stuffed with bills. Satisfied, I took the Nehru and the loafers out and quickly changed. I had no idea what I'd been thinking when I'd packed the cowboy getup. Probably deep cover resulting from whatever peculiar variety of paranoia I'd been experiencing at the time. I left the spare tire full of money alone.

After I'd carefully packed away my new suit and coat and shoes, I drove around aimlessly. It was getting close to the darkest hours before sunrise and the streets were empty. I went to ground in short-term parking at the airport and sat in the outdoor smoking area, just one more well-dressed traveler waiting for whatever the people around me were waiting for. Eventually I lit a final smoke and dialed Lemont.

"Dis better not be you again, Momma." It was what he always said when he didn't recognize the number.

"It's me," I replied. "New phone. I dropped the other one in the toilet on accident. It's in a jar of rice drying out."

"Shit, homie," he replied, amused. "That really work?"

"I hope so, but if it doesn't I guess I don't really care."

"Huh. So what can Lemont do for ya?" He sounded perfectly lively, primed for hooliganism, like it was getting close to his lunchtime. It was a little past 4:00 AM.

"I need Gelson Verber firmed up big time. Super solid, two credit cards, bank account, the works."

"Hmm." In the background I could hear him typing. "That is not the cheapest thing in the world, homie."

"Money isn't really a concern. Just quality."

"Whuhell!" A gush of enthusiasm. "Lemont always like the way you roll, baby. Sixty-five grand even get you a dope dopay credit history. But Lemont also need a small favor."

Sixty-five grand was suspiciously high. PayPal had established the roll on a solid fake ID at five grand. So the favor was supposed to be a bargaining chip.

My eyes narrowed. "What kind of favor?"

"We talk when we make the exchange. Deal?"

"Maybe. What's the nature of the favor? Can you tell me that? I don't like speculating. It makes me speculative."

"Take out some trash. It's just one little piece. Lemont ain't the only boy in the game, see. It, ah, well, there be a weensy, teensy-ass problem."

"We'll talk," I said, a sinking feeling in my abdomen. "Just make it fast."

"Take me about three days. Cash on delivery."

"Deal."

"What state Mr. Verber from?"

I thought. "How about Michigan. Detroit. Your hometown. That make it faster?"

He crooned with delight. "Keepin' the money in the family! Lemont knock off five Gs just for that, and one day, too. Makin' the job easy an' shit."

"I'll call you in two days."

"Lemont be waitin'."

After I hung up I realized that it would be hours before any-thing opened, so I picked up the Lincoln and got on the freeway headed north. Salt Street Development staff wouldn't be rolling in for hours, so that gave me plenty of time to look for an all-night diner and eat a few steaks, then do some shopping. Izelle Tatum could wait until evening. If everything worked out, I'd be buying the fetching transvestite dinner. I opened the glove box and took out the pint of whiskey I'd stashed inside, took a few hard pulls, then turned on the radio. Early-morning jazz, no Casio. Just horns, brushes, and the sacred Hammond.

I was actually enjoying myself.

PART

TWO

The Hunting Moon

NINE

HUNTING PEOPLE IS a little different than hunting animals, especially in a city. Then the only possible analogy is the seriously tired and ultimately besmirched wolf in sheep's clothing, but even that can't really hold water. People aren't really animals anymore. John Bridger had first pointed it out to me once when we were in Houston, stalking some cash-heavy pimp through what was then called the World's Biggest Mall. The notion rang as true then as it would next year. They congregated in artificial bubbles constructed within other artificial bubbles, and some kind of gravity was at work, drawing them in closer and closer to whatever the center was, and the closer they got, the more similar they became, until even the brutal pimp we were tracking looked and smelled just like everyone else. But modernity was graciously and consistently secretive enough to design back doors and blind alleys in everything, right down to the brand new. If it kept up, and it almost certainly would, then there would always be a place for

things like me to hide. And a place for things like me to hide
stuff, drag things around out of plain view, that kind of thing.
Everyone was hardwired to behave and stay away from the hidden hallways around them, ones they themselves had blindly created out of some ancient and inescapable instinct in both their
social structures and their material architectures. Technology
had changed nothing in that respect. Push a person and sometimes the pedigree pops up, because humans were frighteningly
dangerous creatures long before they were anything else, and it's
still in there. And sometimes, if it gets really raw, they detour
through their trap doors. It's called crime. Company is always
nice, rare as it is.

I'd given Miss Misery a misleading version of my technique
that had the merit of sounding convincing. If she'd believed any
of it, that was her fault. And her mother's. The truth was that
while I liked everything planned out to the T, I hadn't been
kidding about maintaining a certain fluidity that allowed me
to instantly abandon the most carefully laid plans. Dragging
something through a back door or down a blind alley was
exactly what it sounded like. Part of a plan. Getting that crap
back out required what I often thought of as an emergency flex-
ibility. Poor impulse control was a factor both good and bad at
that point.

When it came to hunting the people of the day, there were
brief moments of thrilling activity punctuated by much longer
moments of absolutely crippling boredom. I endured a particularly lame period of watery stoicism lying on the roof of a building half a block away from Salt Development, watching the front
door through a pair of kid binoculars I'd scored at Walmart for
three bucks. I was supremely spiritless, so much so that I almost

used one of the phones to call the herpes woman from Jake's whose name I had already forgotten. But I'd forgotten the number, too, which led to a solid two hours of paranoid contemplation on the formless nature of my memory.

The only place in the city open at 7:00 AM that sold high-end sports gear was an uber-yuppie kayak place catering to the upscale cubicle set, a lean and eager mob elbowing each other to pick up supplies for their maniac winter sporting needs before they had to report to their cages. The store had been full of muscular men and women in suits, quickly gathering tools, squinting as their colognes and perfumes fought for supremacy. I'd picked up a Gore-Tex outfit, matte black spooky, tight rubber rock-climbing shoes with gripping soles, gloves, and an Aussie-style rain hat. The clerk had been too busy ringing people up to do more than give me a brief nod and my change. An hour later and some quick climbing, and I was top of a four-story roof in the rain, watching. Waiting. And waiting. And then waiting. And then considering my memory, and what The Experiment might be doing to it. Which led me once again to worrying about how long Salt had been spying on me.

But by then I was sure they had no idea where I was. My cell was at home, so they couldn't use it to track me. Ditto with my car. Same with anything they'd put in my clothes. I might have swallowed a technobug, but I doubted it. There were taste buds in my esophagus. If there was even a chance I was still inside sleeping, there was no way they were going to let themselves in and snoop around, because that would have been a fatal mistake and they knew it. There had been no weapons more advanced than kitchen knives, some piano wire, and a curved gutter in the place on their first sweep, but in their minds I'd had plenty of time to move in enough heavy equipment to blow a herd of elephants back into a temporal cloud of grass seeds and tiny baby trees.

At five minutes to eight my target, the insectoid front desk secretary, pulled into the parking garage just across the street. She was driving a white Nissan. When she emerged, she crossed the street in a quick Asian dancer's mince that had a touch of childhood ballerina in it. Her umbrella was black with yellow polka dots. Probably higher on the food chain than I'd thought. She entered the building and I immediately wished I'd brought a snack. I dug four Xanax out of my pocket and rinsed them down with water from the puddle next to me. My mood took another step down. I spent the next several hours watching people going in and out, memorizing cars and faces, walks and body types.

By the time she emerged at five in the afternoon I was bored enough to howl, but I didn't. I was down the side of the building in seconds. My car was three blocks away and had collected three parking tickets, but it was worth it. I was two blocks down and watching with the heater on full while changing back into the Nehru when the Nissan emerged and turned right. I put on some shades and followed.

The Insect Lady, her important title distinction in place, took a right on Burnside and headed up into the hills, where the upper-middle class congregated in quaint new mini-mansions made to look old. She made one stop, at a grocery store where they sold everything from ten-dollar corn dogs to caviar, and came out with one small bag. From there I followed her to a pretty nice two-story gingerbread with a carefully tended yard and no other cars in the drive. She went in quickly to get out of the rain and the lights inside came on.

I cracked my window and listened. Within about five minutes there came the sound of the refrigerator door opening, followed by the pop of a wine bottle. Minutes after that, the sizzle of food, meat, it sounded like. If I got closer I'd be able to tell what, but there would be plenty of time for that later, and it didn't matter anyway. A few minutes after that, porn. I smiled and drove away.

Insect Lady was a lonesome half-drunk porno fiend. Perfect.

✳

PARKING A BOAT like the Lincoln in NW Portland was a bitch, so I went for one of the rental lots about ten blocks out from my target. It was a little after six and dark, rain still hammering the streets. I moved from awning to awning, my head hidden under my umbrella, lost in a sea of umbrellas, invisible by herd proxy.

Humans have a lot in common with herd animals. Even in the rain, carrying dangerous eye pokers, they tended to clump together. The social gravity factor at work again. I stayed at the rear fringe of one such group and finally ducked into a dark little bar across the street from Izelle Ladyboy's apartment.

After putting my umbrella in the stand, I scanned and scented the place. Two hipster secretaries who smelled like Xerox machines and wet paper, a chubby drinker at the bar who smelled like he worked in the produce section of the grocery store down the street, then surface bleach, spilled beer, Windex, and finally food. I sat down at a table in the back that had a view of Izelle's apartment building and flagged the lone waitress down. I wanted a drink, a dozen of them, but I also hadn't eaten in almost twenty hours.

"Sucks out there," she said sweetly. She was around five-three and pretty, with long dark hair, slightly chunky legs and a bigger side ass, tight jeans, and a high-waisted sweater that was just snug enough to show off her generous and genuine tits. Her teeth were a little crooked, but very white. She had a kid at home and smelled like baby powder. "It's still happy hour. Menu or just a drink?"

"I'll start with a double vodka, best you have, and what is that teriyaki beef smell my mouth is watering about?"

"Teriyaki beef." She cocked her hip. Some pleasant jiggle was in it. "Jimmy does it just right. Little garlic, some kind of spice mix, I don't even know. I'll bring you the menu."

"Don't bother. Just bring me three of those and the hooch."

She was good at smiling. "On the way."

I settled back and pretended to be deep in thought, eyes on the door across the street, fist under chin in the classic thinker's pose. A minute later, the waitress dropped my drink off and I gave her a quick nod, then went back to watching, outwardly reviewing imaginary charts and a pressurized day at a fictional office. I had more than a century of practice at public fakery, so I could pull it off without much effort. Whenever I did, I was occasionally reminded of something else John Bridger had told me. Half the trouble he'd gotten into in his life had come from trying to be peaceful. The other half had come from trying to blend in. It was funny at the time. Years later, when the world was quiet and right for introspection, I found that like many of his observations, it made me uneasy.

Fifteen minutes later the food came, three steaming plates of it. Spicy, irregular chunks of tenderloin, flecked with red chili and smothered in a deep brown soy and plum reduction. I chewed through it, still outwardly lost in thought. A few more people had come in by then. Two garishly dressed women who smelled like they worked in a clothing store and a guy with baggy pants and cool boots, who joined the drunk produce guy. They immediately started talking about French cinema, a conversation with long legs between them. Alain Delon. *Un Flic*. The debate over the slap. Cool Boots weighed in on the PC side, while Produce stuck with the party line of get over it. Fifteen minutes later and just after my plates had been cleared and I'd finished my second double vodka, Izelle Tatum emerged, decked out in a glorious gold thigh-length ski coat with a white fur collar, high heels, and a fuzzy white cap. Gorgeous. The ladyboy unfurled a peacock umbrella and strutted south, ass cocked out, in no hurry and as slow as high heels could slow down.

I hit up the waitress and dropped a hundred-dollar bill on her tray. It landed right over the top of a mixed no no with no umbrella.

"That cover everything?" Time for the James Bond eyes.

"More than. Hang back and I'll get you some change."

"Fuck it," I said. "Tip the cook out. I just got buzzed by the office. Gotta run." I smiled, like I was pausing considerately in a frantic world just for her. "I like this place. People watching, the big windows. Good for some high-speed decompression, which sounds totally lame, I know. Anyway, I'll be back." And I'd be welcome. A big tip was the fastest way to buy real estate. One chair with a view, bought and paid for.

"Thanks," she said brightly. "Next time the first round is on me."

I grabbed my umbrella and unfurled it as I went through the door. I used it to shield my face, and a minute later I was stalking

Izelle, glommed onto the back of another anonymous mini-herd, watching ladyboy's long legs. I ducked into Miro Sushi about a minute after she did and shook off my umbrella at the door. It went into the stand right next to hers.

Izelle was seated at a little two-top, staring with too many miles in her big dark eyes out at the rain-swept street, people watching and decompressing for real. A waitress approached and set a menu before her and bowed. They spoke softly and the waitress bowed again. Izelle looked back out.

The place looked expensive and it smelled good. They had opened minutes before and it was empty other than the staff and Izelle and me. Chefs buzzed behind the open line and sleek kimonos put a final touch on the floral arrangements. I crossed to Izelle's table and sat down across from her. She turned to me and smiled curiously. I smiled back.

"This seat taken?" I asked. I leaned back casually, hungry around the eyes, sardonic around the mouth, enigmatic with the forehead. Her eyes narrowed a little, but ladyboy was clearly amused.

"Maybe." Her voice was husky but high, the voice of a jazz singer. The voice of estrogen injections. Big eyelids blinked once, languidly, over big eyes. "Who's asking?" She had the crisp diction of the perfect foreign diplomatic spy. Accent wise, a faint trace of New York with a sprinkling of Chicago, all buried under standard Midwest. The ladyboy smelled like a flower garden in late summer with a hint of oranges from some high and distant greenhouse. Burnt cinnamon. Sesame seeds. Copper. Wood glue. And very faintly, blood. I cocked my head.

"Don't be alarmed. My name is Kevin. I work for Mr. Thomasini."

If she was alarmed, she didn't show it. She just stared at me for a long moment, waiting for me to continue. The waitress set her drink down and placed a menu in front of me while Izelle and I watched each other. I broke eye contact and looked up into the carefully blank face of the Asian woman.

"Double vodka please. *Arigato*."

She nodded and bowed, vanished. Izelle raised an eyebrow when I looked back.

"One of those days?" Again, the soft purr. I nodded.

"Fuckin' always."

It was Izelle's turn to nod. "To what do I owe the pleasure, Kevin?"

I rubbed my face and pretended to gather my thoughts.

"I can see why he likes you so much." I found that I meant it, which made saying it easier.

The languid blink. "Thank you."

I leaned forward a little. "I've been with Tommy for about ten years. What I have here is—"

"Tommy?" Izelle interrupted. "Is that what you call him? Tommy?"

"Well, yeah. Long story. What do you call him?"

"Butterhole." Izelle smirked. I winced.

"I'll just go ahead and forget that," I said, laughing a little, putting some nervous into it. Izelle laughed, too, a ringing silver bell thing that came from deep inside. Her skin was that odd shade of coffee that defied ancestral analysis. Maybe part Cuban and part Vietnamese, possibly part dark Irish and part Filipino with a few drops of Ethiopian. I couldn't tell.

"I won't tattle if you don't."

I zipped my lips. "What's good here?"

Izelle waved a long, skinny hand. "Everything." Ladyboy's nails were perfect, long and red and buffed to perfection. "I think I'm going for the tuna belly and some miso. Miso is so good on a night like this."

"So is vodka." I picked up my menu. "Here we are. Spicy tuna roll. Tuna sashimi. And . . . ooh! Lookie here. They have those seaweed cup deals with the raw quail egg."

"Hungry, Kevin?" Izelle sounded amused. "Lot of food for a skinny man."

I shrugged. "I have a bad workout habit. Mix that with the metabolism of a fruit bat and I eat so much that by the end of the day my face hurts. Especially lately. Smiling has become a part of my job, if you can believe it. I just can't stand it sometimes."

The bells again. The waitress took that as her cue and we placed our order. Izelle spoke a little menu Japanese and I didn't mind listening to it, but I was a little surprised. When we were alone again those big eyes pointed back at me.

"So you're a messenger of some kind? At least they sent a handsome one."

"Thanks," I said warmly. "There are a few things we need to discuss. Nothing big, of course." I lowered my voice to barely audible, leaning in. "I'm what you call tier-one security. Very specialized. I know all of Tommy's secrets. I'm who he calls in the middle of the night crying, if you see what I mean."

"And that man can cry," she said softly. It was then that I began to officially think of her as a she. Izelle was that convincing. And it was easier for me.

"You actually have no idea," I said, "but we'll file that away with Butterhole, okay?"

Izelle made the lip-zip motion. I nodded and continued.

"So a lot of things have come up this week. Some good, some not so good. There's a great opportunity for you and that's why I'm here. To go over the facts and present you with an offer. No strings attached. You can take it or leave it."

"Save it for now," Izelle murmured. "My place is right down the street."

"I know. I'm the one who drops him off half the time."

Her smile broadened. "We'll go there for after-dinner drinks and you can lay out Butterhole's proposal. A little more private."

"Please don't call him that," I said, still smiling.

"What? Butterhole? Why?"

"Because he'd probably have me killed if he knew."

Her smiled faded a little and she looked back out at the rain.

"I can see that," she agreed.

✳

WE GOT BACK to Izelle's apartment half drunk, but my perpetually fragile buzz was already fading after the short walk. Her place was a lavish three-bedroom, full of extremely tasteful H. D. Buttercup furniture, splattery impressionist paintings, and of course a piano. I flopped down on the sofa and rubbed my face, then took my coat off and straightened my suit. Izelle hung my coat next to hers.

"So the after-dinner drink," I prompted. "What are the options?"

"'Bout anything and everything."

"Scotch?"

That got me a wink. "Two good ones coming right up."

While she was busy at the dining room bar, I scanned the living room without getting up. It was all very clean, as in maid clean. It smelled like perfume and polish and Izelle, but also there was a three-day-old undertow of the scent Christophe had described. It was mixed with a little bit of mingled fear sweat and two kinds of blood, and something else I couldn't put my finger on, but if I had to, I'd say it was how it smelled ten miles downwind of a massive convention of business people.

"So," Izelle called. She emerged with two crystal glasses filled to double. The high heels were on the floor in front of the bar. I took my drink and sat back. Izelle took a seat in a comfortable-looking leather chair across from me. We smiled at each other.

"So," I returned. "I'll get right to it. If Tommy had to, say, leave the country for a year or so on business, would you go with him? Nothing illegal, nothing like that. Just business. But I don't think he could make it without you. That's why I'm here. He has no idea, but, Izelle, listen to me. It would be super bad for everyone except you if you said no. He'd make my life a living hell, for one thing. Mine and about a thousand other people, but especially me. So tell me, would you go? And if the answer is no, what can I do to change your mind? Money? A yacht? Slaves? A small army? An island? Name it. I can make it happen."

"Butterhole knows what I want." It came out dark. The booze was sinking in.

"And?" I waited, as breathless as I could fake. I took a huge sip of scotch.

"I want my hole punched."

I smacked my forehead. "Oh no. Not that again. Jesus weep." I covered my eyes with one hand, massaging them. I had absolutely no idea what she was talking about.

"He told you?" It was little more than a whisper.

"It's all he ever talks about when we're alone. I can't believe this." Izelle snorted. The next part came out as a hiss.

"They can do shit in Thailand no one ever dreamed of even a year ago. I get clipped and get my pussy, we got a deal. No pussy, no Izelle. And you can quote me."

I sat up, wild eyed. A sex change. "But, but . . ." I stammered. Izelle gave me the shame look.

"I hope you aren't trying to be funny, Kevin. Dildos and strap-ons have been around since the beginning of time. He isn't going to suffer from neglect."

Ah-ha. It was time to whip out the coke. I did and unfurled the bag. Izelle's eyes lit up. I studied the Peruvian. One line of it and I'd kill half the neighborhood. The first and last time I'd done it was in 1974. Body count: fifteen. Motorcycle gangs didn't sell coke in Fresno for an entire year after that.

"Since we've moved into the realm of deadly secrets like Butterhole and hole punching and the history of dildos, we'd better sober up a little and hash this out."

"I'm game," Izelle said. "What the hell. You only live once."

I dumped a generous pile on the glass coffee table and rolled up two hundred-dollar bills, then looked up. "Business card, something disposable we can line this up with?"

"*Women Today* has those renewal cards." The magazine was in a little brass rack next to the sofa. I opened one and took out the renewal form, lined up two big fat lines. Then I held out my empty glass. As soon as Izelle had sashayed into the dining room and was pouring, I fingered one line onto the carpet and made a long snorting sound.

"Ghah!" I croaked. I dropped the bill and leaned back, holding my nose, eyes closed. I heard my glass clink down on the coffee table.

"Pure as pure can be, but my sinuses are chapped. Indoor golf. The heaters suck all the moisture out of the air."

That purr again. There was a long snort followed by a delicate cough. I opened my eyes as Izelle fell back into her chair, a smile plastered across her face.

"Yummy."

"Yeah, yummy is right." I sipped my new drink. "So let's make a deal, sweetheart. Right now. Can you put the hole punch off until the South American thing is over? I'll be there the whole time. We can pal around, take up surfing, go dancing, get drunk all the time, and fly around on the jet. It'll be a blast. C'mon. We're friends now. I know about the whole Butterhole thing, you know about my coke habit. We have secrets on each other."

"Secrets can be a powerful thing." The languid blink followed by a coke shiver. "I'll tell you another secret."

I held up one hand. "I think maybe not. We're already—"

"He hurts me. My long skinny dick. He makes me hurt him, too. I don't know if I can take that man for a whole year, even with you along for the ride. So here's your deal. I get my hole punched, he agrees to keep the raw kinky to a dull roar, and then we talk."

"He was just here a few days ago," I protested. "You look fine! More than fine!"

Izelle's jaw hardened. "The limp went away this morning. So did the blood in my piss."

"Ah shit. Shit." I carved out two more big lines and drained my glass, handed it off. "Put something that works in there this time."

I repeated the same routine while Izelle fixed me another drink. The coke in the carpet was a neat trick. When she came back, I was gacking and holding my nose again. I heard the snort of the other line going down and then both of us were making the sound.

"Okay," I said finally. "Let's negotiate. I think I can get us what we both want, as in my head stays on my neck and the rest of the internal staff stays off the chopping block of Tommy Butterhole. You get to visit Thailand and get your hole punched and we all live happily every after." I opened my eyes. Izelle had me cornered and she knew it.

✳

I PARKED THE Lincoln about twenty blocks from my house and walked slowly through the rain under the cover of my umbrella, in no great hurry. It was twenty past eleven when I finally got to the Demmings'. They were asleep again. I leapt the fences, close to tired, but the twenty blocks had sobered me up. Fuckin' booze wasn't good for shit. When I finally landed in my backyard I sniffed and listened. Nothing. I went through the back door and froze.

It was dark and quiet, the air still and warm. No one had been inside. I stripped off my jacket and shirt, and after I'd taken off my shoes and socks I picked up my cell phone. Eleven missed calls, all from Miss Misery. I cautiously peeked out at the street. No cars with people in them, and all of them were local. Whoever was watching my house was hiding somewhere down the street. I lit up a smoke and stepped out onto my front porch to get a better view. The cold wind felt good on my naked torso. My cell phone rang almost instantly. I answered on the first ring.

"Where the fuck have you been?" she snapped. "Christophe has lost his fucking mind! I'm lucky to be alive, damn it!"

"I left right after you did. I guess your spotter wasn't in place. Maybe he was taking a leak."

"Then why has your car been in the driveway all day?"

"I was dealing with Izelle. I can't have a target ID my ride. Are you fuckin' nuts?"

"Don't slip your guards again. Don't. This isn't a game. When did you get home?"

"Just now. Your spotter needs a bath. And a refresher course in paying attention. Lucky I didn't just go on a recreational killing spree, but it's my street. Great news, though. I'll have our man in the bag two days ahead of schedule. This Friday."

There was a long pause.

"I'm coming over." She hung up. Angry and on the way.

I'd actually have him on Thursday, but details, details.

CHAPTER

TEN

I'VE SEEN MANY extremely pissed-off women in my time. A handful of them I had loved in my own way. Many more of them I'd sort of half-loved. Most of them I was just attracted to, but otherwise found either dull or downright repulsive on some level. And then there were the Izelles, who made good neighbors because there was absolutely no chance I'd ever want to see them naked.

Whenever I let a woman get at all too close to me, the fury usually happened in them, but seldom on the nuclear level. Miss Misery evidently deemed we had bonded enough over two dinners, with a minor stabbing thrown in for good measure, to be on the inside track. I opened my front door on a woman with rabies.

"You fucking piece of shit," she foamed. She charged in, swinging like a pro. I caught the first punch in the palm of my hand and yanked her inside, kicked the door closed, and dropped her with a sweep. The second she hit the ground I was on her, still as calm as a mountain lake. She spit in my face, so I punched her.

Unconscious, she looked ten years younger. I rose and pulled her pumps off, then padded over to the wine cabinet and took down one of my favorites, Château Margaux. This whole thing was costing me a fortune in wine alone. After I uncorked it and poured myself a glass, Miss Misery stirred a little and let out a soft moan. I sat down at the dining room table and looked through yesterday's mail. No bills, but there was a new *Scientific American*. I always loved to hunt for the super weird ads in the back.

"What the fuck?" she mumbled. I put the magazine down.

"I had to knock you out," I said evenly, in what I considered to be my most soothing bedside manner approximation. "It was either that or kill you. The whole killing thing seemed too messy, so . . . wine?"

She slowly sat up. Her hair was a tangled bird's nest and her glassy eyes were slow to focus. She stared at me blankly. I wagged a finger at her.

"There's no excuse for that temper, Linda. My excuse is hardwired into my genes. You're just a bitch."

She looked around as if only just registering where she was and what was happening. She rubbed her jaw. I handed her my wineglass.

"Here. I'll get you some Advil and a bag of frozen peas."

She took the glass and absently drained it, childlike. I got the Advil out of the bathroom cabinet, then crossed to the wine rack and got down a second glass and picked up the bottle. I gave her three Advil and refilled hers, then poured myself a new one. She remained sitting on the floor, her legs splayed out in an unladylike position. After a moment I handed her the bag of peas and she held it up to her jaw.

"You might have a mild concussion," I said, "but I don't think so. It just takes a minute or two to fade back in. I got hit by this car once? I was naked, don't ask me why. I really don't remember. It was probably around moon time. Bumper. Right in the melon. Man, that hurt. I was in and out there while I beat him to death." I thought back, shaking my head. "Who hits a naked guy in the rain?"

Linda just stared. I wiped her spit off my face and sniffed it. Bile. Lipstick. Gum. Salad dressing. I smiled, faking a sad one.

"You get hurt a lot, don't you?" When she didn't reply, I took another sip of wine and picked up my magazine.

"You . . . you . . ."

I looked up. "Yes . . . yes . . . ?"

"Fuckin' help me up."

I looked back at the magazine. "Nah."

She lurched to her feet and made it to the couch. Amazingly, she didn't even spill her wine. She put her head back and moaned again.

"If you're going to keep making baby whale sounds, maybe you can do it out on the porch. Call someone and have them come get you. I can fill Christophe in on my delivery schedule tomorrow morning."

She clammed up, and few minutes later it seemed like her shit was coming together. She was still a little wobbly, but measurably more stable when she walked over to the dining room table and dropped into the chair across from me.

"So what happened?" Still putting it together.

"What. With you getting knocked out, or are you finally ready to talk business?" I had to admit, I was enjoying every minute. All in all, I'd had a pretty good evening so far.

"The tranny."

"Don't call Izelle that," I chided, putting the magazine down. I sipped my wine. "Remarkably sweet creature. A little gullible, but I can be pretty convincing."

"Izelle." She closed her eyes.

"It was all very fascinating. Thomasini likes it hard in the ass with a painful reach around. Clips. Then he recharges with some coke and a Viagra and returns the favor. All very disgusting, but what can you expect. Anyway, Izelle wants her hole punched in Thailand. I've never heard the term before, so it's probably what Thomasini calls it. That's where ladyboy gets the chop and has a phony cooter installed. Supposed to be almost as good as the real deal these days." I paused. "And I can remember a time when they didn't even have penicillin . . . Anyway, Izelle is afraid he'll move on to more dick-positive transvestite action. Maybe have her killed. I convinced her that he would indeed be in the mood for murder, that he was in love, and that love can go bad fast in his world, the two dead wives, bla bla. Izelle bought it because she half believes it already. It was all there in the fear sweat and the pulse, and then the anger and the paranoia. I left her with enough carefully speedy coke to drive a team of horses mad. When Thomasini comes over on Friday, I'll be waiting. A little trank, I'm thinking roofies because they're my new thing, I bag him and drop him out the back window into a rental truck, drive him over and freight elevator him right up into Christophe's office."

"And that's going to work? You're sure?" She was sold. I could see it.

"Totally. I can't believe I'm getting paid so much for this. You people are idiots."

"Well, thank God at least something is going right. I think you chipped one of my teeth."

"Open up. Let's see."

She craned her mouth open and I leaned over and peered in. Her tongue was red with wine.

"Naw. You little baby. Just hold the peas on there or the swelling will kick in. There is one other little thing. I told her I'd pay for the operation."

"And?"

"I'm not. You guys are. It's eighty grand for the place she wants and I need it by tomorrow. Cash is king. It's not that much to pay, considering it's buying her total cooperation and our bag. She calls him Butterhole or something like that. I know you keep files."

Miss Misery sighed. "Fine."

"Good!" I felt tired but light. It was time to sleep and maybe dream of the woods, or food. "Now finish that wine and get the fuck out."

She took one final sip and rose to her feet, firm now. After slipping on her shoes she turned back, hand on the doorknob.

"I won't forget this," she said evenly. Part threat and part something else.

"I hope not. Then we'd have to do this all over again. Just be a little worse next time."

＊

I DREAMED ABOUT Germany, about the fires, about how it had satisfied me for enough time to forget, even for a brief period of months, who and what I am. I also dreamed about a woman

I'd known in St. Louis more than fifty years ago. Roberta. Long black hair eventually streaked with white. She'd made good food, and I'd eaten twelve years of it. Biscuits and gravy. The tomato garden. She'd painted eyes on the headboard. Our cat Margo had made it to fifteen. I hid eleven bodies in a fig grove. The river had so many things in it. Fade to running water, slow fade to black.

✳

I WOKE AT dawn on the couch, fresh and rested. After I stoked the fire and made coffee, I finally got around to stripping off yesterday's clothes. Flashes of the day before skittered through my head, vivid every time I blinked. Insect Lady. Izelle and the hole-punch operation. Miss Misery on the floor with the bag of peas. That made me smile. A woman can really beat some shit out of you if they think you're the kind of pussy who won't put the brakes on it. Unpleasant yet surprising advances for everyone all around. I felt constructive, even morphine-esque, but it was a natural high. I padded into the bathroom and turned on the shower, and while it slowly heated I brushed my teeth and shaved, then got in and washed off the fine silt of northern rain grit and the haunting, lingering hints of the perfume I'd picked up from Izelle's sofa.

I dressed in a wool suit, brown and almost drab in a bohemian sort of way. With my thick raft of hair, I looked like a twisted journalist or an adjunct professor of something obscure and vaguely wrong, like semiotics as applied to the cladistics of culinary verbs, or an esoteric branch of some largely forgotten and worthless history of the damned. I smiled into the mirror. The final touch was there.

My Very Special Pen was out as an accessory, and considering I was about to rip off Christophe, something bigger was called for anyway. The opposite option was nothing at all. I studied my reflection and popped a few Xanax and a roofie. Bullshitting seemed to be the order of the day.

I went to the closet in the library and considered my coat collection, finally selecting a brownish wool knee-length that completed my daily disguise, but on studying my reflection I was briefly deflated. I needed some fake horn-rims and a worn and overstuffed leather satchel with a broken shoulder strap, and I didn't have either one. It wasn't the better sort of omen.

It was raining when I left, but it was turning to a heavy mist that smelled like seaweed and wet grass. I casually looked around and spotted a car just down the street with two men in it. The windows were tinted, but I could hear their breathing and scent them more than a little. It was Steroid Hemorrhoid Dude and his partner, Mr. Toothless. The Meat. I lit my first cigarette of the day and waved at them. Nothing.

After locking up I went down the stairs and got in my car, started it, and turned the heater on high. As the engine warmed, I scrolled through the radio dial. I'd left my three new phones inside a carved-out chunk of a Stephen King book and brought my normal one. It rang after about a minute. Miss Misery.

"Tell your boys to back down a block," I answered by way of greeting. "Their grunting and bodily bubbling woke me up. Those guys are like walking sewers with massive hair clogs."

"My jaw hurts," she said shortly.

"I'd say I'm sorry, but I try to tell a minimum number of lies per hour and I don't want to waste one straight out of the gate."

"Your money is at the office. Christophe wants to see you in person." She sounded muzzy, like she'd taken something stronger than Advil when she got home last night.

"Gotta stop for breakfast first. Care to join me?"

She hung up.

She was obviously in a sour mood. I took another breath of morning air and car smells. Then I got out and left the engine running.

The Meat's lights flicked on and the engine turned over as I approached, but it was too late by then. I knocked on the driver-side window and it slid down. The two huge body builders glared out at me. Their suits were rumpled and a smell wafted out that was part chemical and part bean burrito. Bloodshot eyes. Nasty all around. They'd been watching me sleep all night, which would put anyone in a bad mood. I looked at the driver's bulging pecs with open admiration.

"Nice tits." I gave him my best smile. His face fell from ape to crocodile.

"It's a job, kid," he said sharply. "Fuck off."

I leaned in a little. "Here's the deal. I ever see you or any of your people on my street again, anywhere in my neighborhood, for that matter, and I grenade your big asses. Chunks everywhere. Crows be busy for days. Or maybe I'll just light your car on fire and then light you up when you try to run. Then again, welding the doors closed and introducing you to a few hundred starving sewer rats is charming. Or snakes. I know I have some somewhere." I snapped my fingers. "Just remembered."

Hemorrhoids in the passenger seat leaned forward. Big gun. Shoulder holster. I grinned hugely. He made his fierce ex-commando mask and I frowned. They just don't make them like they used to.

"So listen," I continued. "I'm heading out for breakfast. Little place on Kerney. Just follow me. You guys should come in and wash your hands, at the very least. I won't tell your boss that I made you this easy, but there's a price."

They looked at each other, then back at me.

"What?" the driver spat.

"Well, either I kill you, Christophe kills you, or you buy me breakfast. We can chat and make friends. So it's A, B, or C. You can also elect D, very Swiss, as in none of the above, but that pretty much reverts back to A in this case. What's it gonna be?"

The window rolled back up. I walked back to my car. The first omen of the day had been reversed. I was back to a clean slate.

The drive had that magical quality I've always loved about the Pacific Northwest. The rain kept the stench down and muffled the sound, too. Once in a hotel in Arizona I'd gone half-mad because I could hear every heartbeat in a three-block radius, and I could smell every little detail about the heart owners themselves. Rain was good for me. Probably for Christophe, too. No doubt that was part of the reason he was in Portland.

Weekday traffic was light. My little caravan made it to The Hill just off Tabor with parking to spare. The Meatbags pulled in behind me. I'd heard snippets of their conversation as we commuted to breakfast, mostly tones and the like. Angry. Vulnerable. Blustery. Confused. I hadn't been concentrating, mostly because I didn't really care.

Toolie's was at the top of my second-tier breakfast places, but it would probably be added to my file, which sucked. It was ultimately worth the sacrifice, considering what I was about to coax out of the morning blackmail. When they pulled in and parked in the small lot beside me, I motioned for them to follow.

There was a brief sunbreak, the kind where buttery light falls down through a canyon of clouds, and for an instant the wet parking lot swam with millions of goldfish. I stood mesmerized as the Meatbags flanked me, very smelly. I ignored them until the window passed, then slapped 'Roids on his meaty arm, maybe a little hard.

"Mind your manners," I cautioned. "And keep your fucking fingers away from my mouth while I'm eating."

I entered. They silently followed.

The inside was quintessential Portland breakfast dive. Mismatched tables, sticky floor, whiny jukebox, and a hairy waitress. Even the coffee cups came in a deliberately haphazard collection scored from the Salvation Army. It would have been cheaper to buy them from a real supply outfit, but Stumptown Retro had a code. The rulebook also included the jelly jars they served water or wine in.

We took a greasy four-top in the corner. The boys were quiet, clearly out of their element and sitting across from someone they had probably been warned was extremely volatile and exceptionally dangerous. They barely fit in their crappy picnic chairs and they didn't touch the table.

The waitress arrived and wordlessly dropped off our menus, which stuck where they landed. The big men across from me glanced at them, but otherwise did nothing. They were still wearing their sunglasses. The waitress looked our unhappy group over.

"Coffee?"

Toolie was from France. His daughter ran the front of the operation and Toolie and his skeezy nephew Jacque ran the kitchen. Both Toolie and Jacque were ex-cons of some kind, delivered to American soil courtesy of longshoremen via Greenland and a single-prop airplane. I never did figure out what they'd done, but after getting drunk with them one night three years ago, before I'd met Lemont and I was sounding them out as a possible uplink to get rid of a truckload of miscellaneous hunting equipment I'd stolen, I'd come to the conclusion that they were as utterly useless as most French criminals, except when it came to food. I smiled at the furry waitress.

"Three duck-egg omelets. Gruyère and potatoes. Coffee, the house red, and maybe some bread. My buds here need to carbo-load. And tell Toolie I said hi and to keep his fucking cigarette ashes out of my food."

She smiled knowingly and wandered over to the kitchen window to hang the ticket. The Meat Boys glared at me.

"Duck eggs?" Both were openly skeptical.

"What's Gruyère?"

I was having a little trouble telling them apart. Not because they looked all that alike, or even smelled the same. I decided to differentiate them by naming them formally. Roids and Dentures. I liked it.

"So listen. Roids. Dentures. I made you guys and you almost got killed. Then I lured you here, to a place run by French ex-cons who would allow me the use of their dumpster and a mop for a fifty-dollar bill. So that's, like, a double error. Now that I have the royal flush, it's Q&A time. Nod if you understand."

They both turned red. One by one they nodded.

"Do either of you two idiots know what an auction house is?" I watched them closely. They remained red. I continued. "I do. Let me give you a good example. Christie's and Sotheby's. The two fat girls at the opera. Now, not too long ago they got popped for fixing prices and some other assorted bullshit, so they were essentially ripping off rich people to get richer themselves."

That got a little reaction. They stirred in unison. Fear sweat. They thought I was crazy.

"So stock prices plummet. But then guess what happened? I bought in at half price. No way I was going to lose out on a deal like that. See, no one had the infrastructure to compete with those fat girls, so stocks rebounded and bam! Six months after they molested the other rich people they were back in biz. Nature of the beast."

The waitress set our drinks down. I nodded at her pleasantly and plucked up my wine. Jelly jar, a tiny bit of crust on the rim. I drained half of it while the two across from me watched.

"What the hell are you telling us this for?" Dentures asked finally.

"I was wondering if either of you had any idea where you fit into that kind of equation." I watched them think it over. Painful. Roids finally touched his chin.

"We're like . . . auction houses?"

"No." I sighed. "You're the crap that players swap back and forth to fuck over everyone else. I'm an auction house. Salt Street Development is the other auction house. You two are the cows we're trading this morning." I took my cell out and showed it to them. "One phone call to Christophe and you won't even see the watery smear of sunset. So I won't get the meat, but I don't eat people anyway. Too greasy. I suspect he does, though. Probably goes straight for the liver and the 'nads."

Roids went to chalk white pretty fast. The fear sweat bloomed hard across his zitty back. Dentures started wringing his hands, blooming as well. Roids looked out the window with his mouth open.

"Know the fastest way to get off the auction block?"

They both gave me stares that mixed horror with deer in headlights. I drank the rest of my wine and held up my empty to the waitress, who nodded from behind the register, where she'd been picking at something behind her knee. I leaned back with Roids's wine jar in my hand.

"Pick a side. Now, Christophe will kill both of you before you can blink, and you know it. If he knew that we were sitting here right now, both of you would be in a BBQ pit by noon, probably still alive. I might kill you as soon as we walk out the door, or maybe even right here at this table, like a few seconds from now, but I go for the neck snap. Dumpster. I'm sure you read about it in that fancy file."

They said nothing.

"So what's it gonna be? You answer some questions off the books, or I tell your boss that I made you, lured you into a trap, and then made you buy me breakfast."

They thought about it. But not for very long.

"Cards on the table," Dentures growled, looking at his hands, his expression almost boyish. "What is it you want?"

Right then our omelets came. The steaming beauties. Toolie had even put little spirals of strawberry on the side for color. Our hairy waitress thoughtfully tried to brighten the mood at our obviously pensive table.

"Toolie said he kept the ashes out, but he may have gotten some mice droppings in there. He said watch for raisins."

"Noted," I said brightly. She giggled and went back to the register to pick at herself some more. I dug in and chewed, thinking.

"Nothing right now," I said finally. "You guys stay on your night detail, but no more reporting in to the home office with hourly descriptions of my movements. From now on it's more like you say I'm in there reading or cooking. Got it?"

They both looked at their omelets.

"That was a yes or no question, boys. Nod now or forever hold your peace. You clam up, you definitely die today. It's neck or flayed alive. Choices choices."

Duck eggs are more rich and buttery than chicken eggs, and no surprise, they taste a little like the smell of birds. Toolie had a good touch with them, too. A cheese and potato duck omelet must not have been on the Meat Boy's menu, but I decided to bully them a little.

"Eat, fuckers. Don't piss off the French man. He might start crying or chuck a spatula at you. And take the sunglasses off."

They took their shades off and picked up their forks. My wine came and I grazed for a while. Outside it was sprinkling again. Real rain was on the way.

They ate with reserve for the first few bites, then laid in like it was their last meal. Dentures even sipped his wine. Roids got some hot sauce off the next table over and doused away. I finished mine and pushed the plate back.

"So what the fuck are you two sandbagged dimwits supposed to do for the rest of the day?" Fun time was over. Dentures answered first.

"Supposed to follow you into Salt and then check out until the night shift, get some shut-eye."

I nodded. "Who's my day tail?"

"Korean guy," Roids answered, chewing. "Has some Euro name like Stephan. Weirdo."

"Weirdo," Dentures agreed.

"Be more specific." I waited. They both looked thoughtful. Their eyes were tired, defeated, washed out and already dead.

"Skinny," Dentures said, "like you. But not like you. No energy, has this terrible cough. Likes guns. Old, but it's hard to tell with the slopes."

"He just sits there without moving," Roids added. "Staff meetings, people almost hang their coats on him."

Invisible. Interesting. Old. Useful. Works alone, so more dangerous than they were. Coughs. Bonus.

"What's he drive?"

They both shrugged. I waited.

"Car pool has about fifteen vehicles," Dentures said. "He usually takes this little white Miata."

"And he picks me up when?"

"Right after you exit the building," Dentures replied.

"And you guys come back on at . . ."

"Fuckin' nine." Roids didn't seem too happy.

"Till whenever," Dentures added, surly himself. "The money's good, but all the car time is murder on my lower back."

"Bummer," I said. "Okay, kids. Last question. Who's working me on Thursday? I need the entire schedule."

"We got nights all week steady," Dentures said. He was almost done eating. "The Korean has the days, solo. We go on at eight."

"Till just after dawn or whenever you go into Salt."

I thought about it. On Thursday Thomasini would be arriving at Izelle's at 9:00 PM, so the two across from me would be my trackers.

"Good. On Thursday I have some other business to attend to. General crime shit, nothing that concerns you or Salt, but I don't need to be blackmailed if they find out. I've been working on this deal for over a year and I have one and a quarter mil on the line. You boys like cash?"

They looked at their wineglasses.

"Thursday you sit outside of my house and report that I'm cooking and reading, waiting for Friday, when this Thomasini shit is going down. If my investor reaches out, I'll be out on the town for a few hours finishing my deal. Twenty Gs cash for each of you at the end of the month after I convert the currency. And you get to stay alive. How you like that deal?"

They looked at each other, then back at me. Both of them nodded. I rose.

"I have a date tonight and I expect the same thing. No way I want anyone to know any more about my personal life. So I'll probably leave right after you guys are in place. Park in the same spot. I'll bring you dinner. I'm gonna smoke a cigarette out front while you two settle up. Then we caravan down to the office."

Dentures looked like he had something to say but was unsure about it. He shifted and frowned and his guts burbled. It was possible the duck eggs were disagreeing with his man drugs.

"What," I prompted. He frowned, uneasy, unsure of everything.

"Well, we ah . . . see, there might be more people following you soon. I mean real soon." He looked so guilty that I almost laughed. Roids suddenly looked betrayed, like he had been waiting to say this first, or maybe he was surprised that he hadn't thought of it.

"Why?"

Roids jumped it. "See, about three or four times a month, usually right around your kills, we lose you for a few hours. It has to do with your use of the trains and the cab relays. No one can figure out where you're going. The first couple of times people got fired. But—"

"But then they didn't care so much," Dentures interrupted. "They figured you were hiding money or ditching tools. But then we dug out the safe, so—"

"So now the . . . the," Roids spluttered helplessly.

"They want to know," Dentures finished.

Lemont's. They were talking about Lemont's, the one place I'd been pathologically cautious about. I could never risk even the slightest chance of being tracked there, or being followed after leaving, so I'd made it as close to impossible as I could.

"So probably a three-man tag," Dentures continued.

"Probably right after you pick up Thomasini," Roids added.

"Probably right after you get paid," Dentures clarified.

"Well, shit." I rose. "Settle up and let's blow."

While they paid I stood under the awning by the trash can and lit a smoke, watching them through the windows. Roids went to the bathroom while Dentures dealt with the waitress. I took cell number two out and dialed Lemont. He answered on the first ring.

"Momma? Don't need to be hearin' 'bout them ankles, damn."

"Be there around ten tonight. Got my Verber?"

"Aw baby, Lemont done you solid. Ten it is, homie."

I hung up and tossed the phone in the trash can.

ELEVEN

CHRISTOPHE WAS SEATED at his desk, looking out at the gathering storm, his back to the room. I'd poured myself a drink and settled into a comfortable slouch in my now customary chair. The briefcase with the new pussy cash had been sitting next to it when I walked in.

"People are so disgusting these days," he said. "Have you noticed?"

"Yeah." I sipped my expensive bourbon. "It's only going to get worse, too."

"My thoughts as well." Christophe sounded pensive. I thought about offering him a roofie but decided not to. He had his own drugs. "So you hit her and knocked her out. Why?"

"She's a bitch," I said to his back. For a long moment he didn't respond. We both looked out the window.

"No more beating on the help, Verber. You've already stabbed her, and now this."

"Yeah yeah." It was all I had to say.

"Your transvestite cash. Snip snip. An interesting development, Mr. Verber, considering what you're calling yourself these days. Preposterous irony, or just a genital variety coincidence in keeping with the intransigent degeneracy of the day?"

I thought about it. "I'd have to say a little of both. I mean, who could have predicted?"

He thought, too. "Maybe we've entered another new era, where everything is a comedy draped over pornography."

I sipped and scowled. "I sure as fuck hope not."

Christophe sighed and stretched. Even at rest he seemed fast. I sensed that our meeting was already over and finished my drink.

"Don't lose your cell phone again," he said softly. "It's how my people track you."

I shifted a little. "I don't have a damn thing to do until showtime. Plus I'm sure you have eyes on me. I'm going to stay home and read. Marinade some ribs. Maybe make some posole."

Christophe chuckled and finally spun around. His pale eyes were bright and had a sharp quality, like he could see into my pores. "What is it with you and the cooking? The pots and pans and whatnot?" Genuine interest.

"Don't tell me you're a utilitarian eater," I said. He shook his head.

"No. I just have other people make it for me."

✳

THE WHITE MIATA picked me up about a block away and hung pretty far back, occasionally disappearing altogether. The Korean was good, I had to give him that. If Roids and Dentures hadn't tipped me off I never would have noticed him, which is saying something considering how paranoid I am. I wondered how long he'd been working for Salt. It could be the answer to exactly how long they'd been spying on me. My current estimate was less than two years, but I could have been wrong.

I stopped at the City Market, one of my favorite grocery stores, and picked up supplies. Pork ribs, pork shoulder, pomegranate juice, corn tortillas, honey, chicken stock, three cans of green chiles, two big cans of hominy since I was too lazy to soak the corn myself, some cheeses, a few New York steaks, and the wine special of the week. As an afterthought, I tossed in some mixed greens and a lemon.

The checker was a mousy little thing named Mary. I'd taken her out once, but she'd smelled funny, like bleach and hazelnuts and wart remover. A pleasant evening nonetheless, but I'd dropped her off with no more than a peck on the cheek. Luckily her boyfriend had moved back in and there was no tension between us.

"Charlie," she gushed, as bubbly as ever. "How's your horoscope?"

"Full of empty houses and empty buildings, same as always." I smiled back. "You?" That's when I smelled it. Mary was—

"Pregnant. Todd and I are moving to Cleveland."

"Congrats. Family there?"

She shrugged. "His parents. I actually don't know shit about babies."

I paid and gave her my best wishes. At the back of the store I heard a phlegmy, terrible cough, but I didn't turn. If it was my guy, he was good enough to notice if I made him.

The white Miata appeared a few minutes later, about five cars back. I took the scenic route home, stopped for smokes at a convenience store, and finally wound up in my driveway. The Miata was nowhere to be seen. I sat there for a moment, listening to the rain. I hadn't been able to map the sound of the little car's engine yet, but it could have been muffled with steel wool and asbestos if Christophe knew what he was doing, which he almost certainly did. I reasoned that it didn't matter anyway. The night watch was in my pocket. I'd do something about the day shift later.

Once inside, I stoked the fire and peeled off my coat and my shoes and socks, then carried my goods into the kitchen. I set the pork shoulder in a pan of water with whole garlic cloves and salt and put it on low heat for later shredding. The three racks of ribs went into a pan with the pomegranate juice and more garlic. At that point I had a few hours to kill. It wasn't even noon, so I lay down on the bearskin in front of the fire and stared at the books.

At first, I'd resisted learning how to read. It seemed at the time like the kind of thing I could easily get away with never getting around to. The sole teacher at Mama Heads had beaten me for it several times until I finally bit her, and that was when I was entrusted into the tender care of Laurence, the handyman. Somehow just the thought of my file, sitting on the buffet in the dining room, was bringing up memories I hadn't visited in decades. A century.

Laurence would have none of my childhood antics. He was a big man, very white, with a doughy face and large, sweaty hands. He always wore the same faded denim bib overalls and he liked to show everyone his ring of keys, his symbol of power. Laurence kept me away from the other kids, so I ate alone after them under his watchful eye. He knew what I was supposed to learn, and he made me do it by any means necessary. There was no way I was going to live if I didn't, and I knew it. So I learned. He thought that his inability to leave permanent scars on me was a sure sign of possession. Even the burns always faded after a few lunar cycles. And there were other things, and it all got worse as I started puberty. Laurence had every reason to believe I had a demon in me. Beating him to death with a hammer had brought me no real joy. Only a sense of relief. Vague, but real. Satisfying, but ultimately only in a small way. It was like I'd always known I was going to do it, and so had he, so in the end we were just acting out our roles.

It hadn't been like that with Gelson Verber. I'd wanted him to die in the best possible high-speed horror I could generate, and when I did, when I swallowed his life, his future, when I'd cut his gene line and his breath, the animal in me had eclipsed the thinking ape. I'd watched from behind and to the left of my own being, blurred with motion, howling, my heart vomiting laughing flowers in some ecstatic hallucination, and that, that had been too much, an overdose that effectively scrambled reality, when the world became so bright and so much more real than real that no memory was possible. And the moment faded. Maybe it only came once, like birth, and then diminished into a horizon.

The crackle of the cherrywood fire. Rain on leaves. I sighed. The neighbors were out, probably at work. Across the street someone was watching TV, but I tuned it out. The mailman hadn't come. He smelled exactly like you would expect a mailman to smell in the first stretch of a bad winter, a mixture of plastic from his bag, the plastic from his rain slicker, wet paper, metal. Some Small Fear. In the distance, a block or so down, I thought I caught a muffled cough, but I didn't get up. The fire was making me drowsy.

Laurence. I thought back to the last minute of his zealous life. The strange noise he'd made, like a kitten, and how wide his small eyes were, his thin eyebrows clowned back, making something of his face I'd never seen before or again, a mute look at his imaginary god, a divine witness recording his final seconds on earth through my inappropriate eyes. My clothes were clean that day. That detail seemed oddly large as I drifted off into a serene nap.

✳

WHEN I WOKE up it was just after 6:00 PM. The fire was red and low, so I tossed on two fat logs, grabbed my smokes off the counter and padded through the kitchen, and went silently out the back door. I scented, sounded.

Scents were easily lost in the rain, but not as badly as most people believed. After a century, I'd learned how to huff my way through a constellation of climates. The trick was to breathe, slow and even, nostrils flared with ears tuned, head rotating to catch the air and the sounds at different angles. And then there was the slightly more challenging sorting and filtering of the background. Filtering was one of my advantages over a thing like Christophe, because as near as I could discern, the selective suppression of sensory background was a purely human thing. And he didn't have that much of it in him. The herd around me could work in cubicles with people chattering all around them. Ride a bus and think about getting laid or what was on TV. Listen to music and dance and never hear the accordion solo. Dream impure things and spend the day harassed by their profound assessment of someone else's problems. Et cetera.

The randomness of rain faded and the evening came alive as I flexed my head. The neighbors were home. Spaghetti sauce from a jar and poorly boiled noodles, no parm. Garlic bread. The boy was getting a C in math and no one was happy. Next. People were generally quiet across the street. A few TVs were on. Next. Some cat down the street was whining and scratching at a screen to get in. Huh. Leaves. Nice, moving along. A few other fireplaces were going. Pine. Crackling sap. Someone other than me was smoking a cigarette no more than two blocks away, puffing hot and fast, pulling hard to get back under a roof. I dialed the leaves back.

It was time. I reached around inside the door and grabbed the bag of coals, then dumped a generous amount in the hibachi and fired them up. They were the good kind, with wood grain. I watched the slowly spreading flame and thought about music until they began to fall into a flickering orange heap. Then I put the grill back on and watched as it burned and sizzled with a thousand spices from days gone by. When the hissing had gone away and the metal was glowing under thin ash and runs of lightless carbon, I went back inside.

The ribs were easy. I trimmed the three racks and basted them in molasses, brown sugar, and sea salt, then took them out and slapped them down, lidded the operation. It gave off just the right kind of spluttering, with horns of aromatic smoke that curled away at speed through the open vents. Back inside I extracted the now tender pork shoulder, shredded it, and drained the pot, added the green chiles and pork, butter, and the chicken stock. Then I fried out several corn tortillas and crumbled them in with cumin and salt. Not posole, which would have pressed me for time after the pre-slaughter nap, but green chile stew, just as good. I kept it on low heat and let it bubble while I opened a new bottle of wine from the refrigerator, Santa Rita Reserva, a Chilean white.

With all ingredients cooking, it was time for an inventory check, so I laid everything out on the dining room table with persnickety precision. Piano wire, cut from high in the right side of an antique grand in a dead man's house in Boston. The short, curved gutting knife. Two trashable cells. A wallet with the fake ID I was about to shelve after meeting with Lemont. A briefcase full of cash that had been extorted from a blackmailer and promised to a transvestite, but would instead neatly pay for the Detroit identity of a dead German. Keys to both cars. Smokes and a lighter. Pills. A small vial of rat poison. It was enough.

After showering quickly I flipped the ribs and basted them with the same mix as before, stirred the stew and checked the time. My flipped Meat Bags would relieve the Korean in less than an hour and a half, so I shaved and dressed. Black suit jacket and slacks, long-sleeve black V neck, and tight black patent-leather dance shoes, perfect for kicking the soft parts. Then I fucked with the ribs a little and smoked. The night was quiet. I was just washing down my drug cocktail when my real cell rang, so I went back in and looked at the number. Miss Misery.

"What," I answered.

"Where are you?" Terse. Strained. Angry. I yawned.

"At home cooking ribs and green chile stew. You aren't on my porch again, are you?" I added a little more cumin to the stew.

"I'm at home with an ice pack on my face, asshole."

"Mmn." I stirred with my favorite wooden spoon. "You're missing out." I sighed, feigning boredom. "I have to build another bookcase tonight. I bid on a semi-rare collection of Octavio Paz and it should be arriving Monday. I wish I could learn how to build a chair."

"Spare me the boring details of your nerd side, psycho." Definitely high on something.

"Fair enough. I think Christophe wanted me to apologize for popping you."

She waited. "And?"

I hung up.

Outside, I flipped and basted and let the rain run over my hand for a while, smoking and thinking. Lemont wanted something. The timing was bad, but even closing on five million if I counted all of my secret stashes, there was really never enough. In the early eighties I'd almost gone completely broke after being shot through the lower spine. It had taken three years to heal and another two to get up to speed, then one more to get really dialed in. By the time I was ready to hunt big game I was a homeless skeleton with two dollars and clothes that didn't fit.

When the ribs were done, I carried them inside and opened two bottles of Bordeaux. Then I fed. The ribs were excellent, perfectly tender. The green chile stew was smoky and spicy and so delicious that I ate three bowls. I drank half of the first bottle and let my mind wander, sitting in the darkness that wasn't dark to me, listening to my inner critic. Nothing important came up, except that I had forgotten the garlic in the stew.

When I was done, I washed up and went down to the basement. In the pantry area I had several Tupperware containers and a basket of plastic sporks for long surveillance, so I took out two of the bigger ones and two of the fanged spoons and went back up. I ladled out two generous portions of green chile stew and topped them with some of the cheese I'd purchased, in this case a type of herbed cheddar from England, and a little minced red onion. Then I cut one of the remaining racks of ribs in half and put one on top of the chili in each container. The warm tortillas I rolled and wrapped in foil. I put both containers in a paper bag and then recorked the second bottle of wine and put that in as well. It was fifteen minutes after eight, so I stepped out onto my front porch and made a casual sweep with my eyes. No sign of the white Miata. The Meat Boys were in place just down the block. Shift change was right on time.

I finished my cigarette and went back in. The rain wasn't too bad, but I didn't want to get my suit wet, so I put my coat on, picked up the grocery bag, and headed out.

If they were surprised to see me, they didn't show it. Dentures's window zipped down as I walked up. I leaned down a little to get a good view. They were set for the night. Two big gas station coffees, a *People* magazine, a bag of sunflower seeds, and Rolaids. I passed the bag in. Dentures took it without opening it.

"Pork ribs marinated in pomegranate juice with a molasses glaze, green chile stew with tortillas, and a fuckin' three-hundred-dollar bottle of wine. Enjoy."

Dentures opened the bag and sniffed. He and Roids exchanged a look. Dentures peered up at me. "Thanks. I guess."

"Least I could do. Now, I might go out for a little bit later to deal with that thing I was telling you about. I might not." I passed Dentures my cell. "My handler got kinda beat up last night and she sounds like she's taken something, plus I told her that I was staying in to work on home crap. If she calls, tell her I'm passed out drunk on the front porch, sleeping under a bearskin on one of the chairs. You came up to make sure I wasn't dead, but you were afraid to try to wake me up. I was snoring and growling. She'll buy it."

They exchanged a look again. Dentures smiled in a bad way. "We heard about the incident."

"People clapped, is what he's saying," Roids added.

"Good for me. When's the shift change?"

Dentures answered, looking into the bag again. He was hungry. "Six AM. The slope again. He just checked in downtown about three minutes ago."

"Then I'll see you a few hours before he gets here to pick up my phone." I left them unloading the bag. A stakeout is especially tedious for really big guys who can never get comfortable. Some good food, a little wine . . . Projecting friendly to get their guard as low as possible . . . Any little edge could make a difference later.

Back inside, I took the money out of the briefcase and stacked it on the table with my gear. Then I studied the briefcase itself. The GPS locator was stitched into the handle. I left it where it was, active. Then I went through the bills, thirty bundles of them. There was one more locator, a very advanced wafer of a thing I'd never seen before. I put it in the briefcase and put the briefcase under the dining room table, then loaded up.

Everything went into a different pocket. The money went into a black duffel bag. I stepped out the back door and listened. Quiet. Everyone had either had dinner and was watching TV or getting ready to. The rain wasn't too heavy. I went down the back stairs through my yard and hopped the fence, landed in the grass, and casually strolled out onto the sidewalk. I made it to the Lincoln in ten minutes without a tail, free until dawn.

TWELVE

FIRST STOP WAS the 7-Eleven to get more smokes and more phones. I bought three little lurid pink cells with a month on each, and four packs of menthols, and as an afterthought I tossed in a handful of beef jerky and a six-pack in case I needed a snack. In front of the place I unwrapped the phones and threw away all the plastic and the two phones I'd already used, then took the cherry scenic route to Insect Lady's.

Her swanky street was pretty quiet and her little car was in the driveway. No ping from the engine and it was wet, so it had been sitting for a few hours at the very least. Not much of a social life, I mused. The lights were on in her living room and I could pick up tiny flashes through the curtains. She was watching TV. I cracked the car windows and closed my eyes, listening.

It was television, but not what I'd imagined. She was watching surveillance footage, clicking from camera to camera, live feed. All of it from Salt. Some late-night office workers were haggling over a legal document involving a tiny segment of the waterfront that had zoning issues, a woman was on the phone talking to her husband, bitching about having to stay late and complaining about her constipation, Korean Miata was coughing in a room with lots of echo, then silence, then the sound of an electric floor waxer. I settled back. A flushing toilet. Random buzzing. Fingers on a keyboard, quick. After about twenty minutes I hit minor pay dirt.

"—ble to reacquire the entire sum early next week." A male voice I didn't recognize. "I know, so shut it down. Just temporarily reallocate the sixty thousand and we'll write it off as—" Next screen. I started the engine and slowly drove away. Apparently Insect was already in the loop on the nature of the conversation.

Interesting. The exact sum of money going to Izelle was to be reacquired in one week. So they'd never planned to pay Izelle, either. Someone was slated to track the cash down via the wafer and the GPS and take it back after I delivered it, which very likely meant that Izelle would end up at the bottom of the river at the end of the transaction as the tidy courtesy of whoever was sent to recover the funds. It made me wonder about my own payment scenario, of course. I was stealing from everyone. It was business. But I didn't like being in the same kind of business as Salt Street Development. I didn't like it at all.

Izelle Tatum. Bought and paid for by Thomasini, then evidently tortured in a fashion so clever that she would let it happen again and again. And Salt and I were jockeying for position to steal her only way out of it. An ugly, irrational fury worked its way into my hands and my jaw. Everything was a symptom, suddenly. The world was tightening. With revelation came the smell of ozone, copper in my mouth, blue light at the edge of my vision. Izelle was the tip of an iceberg that was as large and heavy as a lead mountain and as cold as the dark side of the moon. Her death had almost certainly already been planned, for early next week, as in Monday morning. Intuition told me that I was on some calendar, too. I could feel it, like someone staring at me through a crowd.

After several twists and turns, about an hour later I ghosted up to a warehouse a block down from Lemont's with the lights out and the engine dead. I scanned the street, but there was no activity at all, other than a few rats scrabbling around under a dumpster two warehouses down. I got out and sniffed. Rain. Moss. Organic garbage, rust. Distant fear. New plastic. A dead pigeon. Lemont's warehouse had the security lights down, which was odd. In two years, I'd never seen the place running all the way dark. I called him from across the street and he answered a fraction of a second through the first ring.

"Yo, homie, hit the gate."

"Right outside."

The gate had been oiled and it slid back silently, just wide enough to admit me. The gate guy was especially bulky, with body armor that had new-car smell under his huge puffy Raiders coat. He had an M5 with a suppressor slung over his shoulder and he looked especially grim. He smelled like gun oil and curry, and he was the source of the fear stink I'd picked up. We nodded at each other and I slipped in. Once I had passed, he peeked up and down the street and silently slid the door closed and remained looking out through a peephole, one hand on his gun. I walked alone into the warehouse, duffel bag over my shoulder, left hand in my pocket wrapped around the gutting knife.

Lemont was sitting in the dark at his desk. His ever-humming computer was off. A match flared as he lit a cigarette. His face was sweaty, even though he must have been cold to the bone. My eyes went straight through the deep blackness, scanning. Other than his desk and the dormant computer, the entire warehouse was empty. It was never, ever empty.

"Lemont offer you a drink, but . . ." He shook the match out. "No glasses. Or bottles."

"What's the story, Lemont? Why the whole lights out? And what's up with your guy wearing armor and packing the big stuff?" I remained just inside the door.

Lemont opened his computer and hit a button. The screen flared, shedding a cool blue over his desk.

"You got money, Lemont got the new you, deluxe ride."

I walked over and gently set the duffel bag in front of him. He took the money out and counted it in the dim blue glow while I waited. When he was done he opened one of the desk drawers and took out a manila envelope, handed it to me. I opened it and unceremoniously dumped the contents on his desk.

Driver's license. Very good, even real. Two credit cards. Social Security card. A veterinary practitioner's license.

"Cards have two hundred on 'em already, so call in the morning and set somethin' up for the payments. The whole vet thing came with the package, don't even ask." His voice was strained, just around the edge of each word. I pocketed everything.

"Thanks."

"So now you got a name other than Way Fuckin' Spooky White Dude. You welcome, homie. You welcome."

I turned to leave. Whatever was going on was none of my business.

"So you runnin', baby?" His voice was quiet enough to be telling. The level of wrong was palpably in the red zone, beyond a simple Fed raid coked into inspired superstition. I stopped. My new identity was too new for any problems from the provider. For a week or two, the minimum amount of time needed to switch the trail around and cover Lemont's track, his problems could blow back on me. He'd called it a weensy, teensy-ass problem, which could mean anything. But the empty warehouse, the paranoia, the body armor, and the darkness all pointed to something bigger.

"You won't be seeing me around anymore, if that's what you mean. But it's been good for both of us. Good luck, kid." Bait. It worked. Instantly.

"Wait." His whisper was lower and desperate. "Mr. Verber. Lemont got somethin' to say 'fore you go. I told you I need somethin'."

"Talk." I didn't turn. And he had stopped referring to himself in the third person, at least for the moment. The truth always comes out when you aren't looking for the action.

Lemont cleared his throat. "Ever wonder why Lemont in this rainy damn town? I tell you, case you did. Detroit, that one mad-ass fuckin' hell pit. I got real estate, most of it shit. Game. But the game up in Hades be fierce. Here in P Town? Like the wide-open prairie for an advanced nigga like Lemont."

He went quiet. I waited, perfectly still.

"See, I could have made grade A in Murder City, but there wasn't the time. Big fish start to nibble my baby kingdom. Had to blow town. But . . . on my way out, maybe I wasn't as graceful as I shoulda been. Didn't show respect." Respect came out clipped and with flecks of spit. He put his voice into the rest. "And now? They done found Lemont, and the man they sent to teach me my manners be about as spooky as they come."

"What does this have to do with me?" I was just a silhouette framed in black to his eyes.

"I was gettin' to that. See, the address on that driver's license? I own that house. S'nice. Kinda crappy neighborhood, but it got a fireplace and hardwood floors. Market what it is out there, it worth maybe twenty grand tops. Probably way less. I know that. But it be big, homie. Old-school big. Even got a garage. And you goin' out that way, if I'm right." He let that hang.

"So you'll give me the house and all I have to do is make the dude with the manners pamphlet disappear?"

"Well, yep." He had some kind of hope he was hiding. My paranoia ramped. Secrets around the clean ID already.

I thought about it. Lemont's eyes glittered in the soft blue light, unblinking. There was no possible way he could know that I could see his pupils.

"What other houses do you have out there?"

"Mostly crap. My sister up in one. So's my mama. Got a run-down cabin 'bout an hour out of town. Got a warehouse, roof all fucked up. Got two—"

"Cabin."

Lemont's smile flicked on and off.

"Deed's in your pocket. Once the deed is done."

※

BEHIND EVERY GOOD plan is an equally good backup plan, and built into the backup plan is an escape hatch that leads to an equally good third plan. I left Lemont's with everything I came for, plus a potential house in Detroit, located in a marginal neighborhood, and a cabin in the woods that even he admitted needed serious restoration. I also had the name and photo of a nasty-looking mutation named Leon G, and a list of his possible locations in the city and the kinds of things he went in for, like expensive weed, crack, and skinny Asian hookers. Lemont had also enclosed Leon G's employer's name in case I fucked up and became nothing more than retribution for his death, and he'd given me a sawed-off pistol-grip twelve-gauge and extra buckshot in case Leon was already waiting outside. Promising.

I walked back down to the Lincoln and rolled away unmolested. Two blocks down I turned on the headlights, wove around back streets and alleys for a while and finally hit the main roads. On impulse I took one of my pink cell phones out and called my real cell to check on the new recruits. Dentures answered.

"Uh, hello?" He sounded both scared and uncertain. Not my favorite combo, but it was evidently the theme of the evening.

"It's me," I said. "What are you guys doing when you get off work?"

Silence while they conferred. Muffled whispers. "Why?"

"I might want to hire you. Nothing you need a gun for. Strictly just sitting around a few strip clubs looking for this guy I have to track. Drinks are on me, three bills a day cash, two-day minimum, plus a moderate expense account because I understand you have to stuff bills up the dancers' asses and get the occasional blowjob."

A long silence again as they conferred.

"When do we start?" He was more certain now.

"Noon. Give you some rack time. I'll drop the cash and a photo with some stats when I pick up the Tupper. You guys dug that green chile stew, didn't you?"

"Aw yeah. What kind of wine was that?" Dentures was downright convivial.

"The expensive kind, like I told you. Catch you in a few hours. I'm almost done."

"You . . . you're not inside?"

I hung up and tossed the phone out the window.

The freeway was relatively quiet as I motored and switched lanes at random, just roaming. I turned on the classical station and lit the first in a chain of cigarettes, all autopilot and going nowhere not too fast, granny driving and watching the rearview.

Freeways had changed over the years, as much as everything else had. Sometimes I wondered how people who participated in society could even stand it. There had been a generation of Americans who as children had gaped at gritty newspaper prints of the Wright brothers taking flight. That same generation saw a man walk on the moon with their grandchildren watching next to them. There was a time when there was almost no way to drive across the states from coast to coast unless you were lucky or desperate. It was train or possibly horse, if you didn't mind the extra year and the occasional Donner Party. Now, I could make it to a place like Detroit without a road map.

Christophe. Miss Misery. Bug Lady. Korean Cough Guy, probably Christophe's best. Thomasini. Izelle. The Meat Boys. Lemont. And brand-new Leon G. My life was getting cluttered with people. Uncomfortably so, and it looked like the list was only going to get longer. I needed to thin the herd. Fast.

The Meat Boys would find Leon G or they wouldn't. If he was any good, he'd hit the streets hard, and there was only one area on Lemont's list of possible locations where he had one-stop shopping. The edge of Chinatown had it all. If I planted

Dentures and Roids there, a seasoned pro would probably pick them out and they'd wind up missing, but that was their problem. There was a chance somebody might just get it right. And if they did go the way of the body bag sooner than I had planned, it would still put me on Leon G's trail.

My plan to make the grab on Thomasini a day early and stash him still needed work. For one thing, I still hadn't decided where to put him. My place was out. A hotel was out. I needed him to have access to a computer so I could rip him off for saving his life, even though if it got too hairy in the aftermath I'd just turn him over anyway. But only after he put some money in an offshore account for me. I didn't really like the guy and I'd never even met him. I doubted my first impression would change a thing. I put his safe house's location on percolate in the back of my head.

On to Insect Lady. She was the key to something, but I couldn't tell what. Something was roiling under the surface in my mind, a suspicion that was ready to break. And I was down to forty-eight hours, give or take ten, to settle everything and get back to my normal life of hunting and gathering. The entire situation was cramping my style. My flow was off. In truth, I'd even lost interest in whatever I had forgotten I was interested in.

I saw an all-night Kinko's coming up, so I took the off-ramp. The parking lot was mostly empty, but I parked at the edge anyway, and after making sure my new gun was safely tucked in under the seat, I put Leon G's photo and his personal sheet in my coat and went in.

The fluorescent lights were overly bright and the entire place was heavy with the scent of carpet, plastic, and toilet paper. The clerk looked up and smiled vacantly. Young hipster girl, predictably stoned. She was making a collage out of random tabloid articles. I nodded and went to the color copy machine and zipped out five Leon's and two personal sheets, carried them to the register. Her nametag read "Kim."

"High Kim." It was an inside joke. Other than weed, she smelled like gum and a two-day-old uniform fresh from a bathroom floor. She had a male cat.

"Hi. Five colors and two regs?" She seemed glad to talk to someone.

"Yep. Stale night, huh?"

"It's a job." She shrugged as she tapped the register screen. "I get to monkey around doing shit I'm not supposed to be doing."

"I do the same thing," I admitted.

After that I passed by Bug Lady's one more time. It was after eleven and she was still up and watching something. I paused down the street to listen. Porn again. It sounded like the same movie, but there was a good chance they all sounded the same. I listened to the moaning and computer-generated music for as long as I could stand it, and then I headed downtown.

Chinatown is a pretty crappy place, and not because of the Chinese, who seem to have been slowly condensed into one block, but because of what had happened to their former turf. Surrounding them in every direction was a collection of shitty dive bars, strip clubs, and crackheads. Hookers, of course, but at least half the streetwalkers had been shifted to other points in the city to ensure the trick profits of the strip-club bathroom workers. I parked and walked to Siamese, the really nasty Asian pole-dancing joint. It wasn't going to be pretty. I like naked women a great deal, but I never went into strip clubs unless I was tracking a target. It wasn't a moral objection in any way. It was vanity, pure and simple. There was no way I was ever going to pay to see a naked woman unless she had a map to some kind of treasure written on her stomach.

The place had a peculiar and awful reek that smacked me deep in my sinuses as soon as I walked in. It was a solid, stagnant wall of layers of old stale beer and cheap wine, rotting everything, bad teeth, sweat of every kind, jizz, Dollar Store deodorant, hair spray, and urinal cakes, to name just a few. Worse still, it was packed. I almost ordered a beer, but decided that touching anything at all would taint me in some way. I had to move fast, before the vile soup sank into my coat too deep for anything but fire to remove. I pushed my senses out and eavesdropped at high speed, flicking from conversation to conversation. It took forty-five extremely long seconds to get nowhere.

The bartender was a weathered hag named Jo Jo, but she had an intercom that connected her to the scrawny junkie DJ and the back room where the strippers argued, snorted coke, made fun of the bums in the front row, and talked at length about their genitalia and a regular named Brian, some "juicy" young piece of unfortunate man meat they'd been taking turns on for the last month or so. I found him without even trying. He practically bumped right into me. Coke, pussy, and disease rolled off him in cigarette-laced waves.

"Brian," I said. He looked at me, a little blurry. Then he smiled. "Hey dude."

"A guy with lots of money wants to show you a picture. Take one sec. Let's smoke outside."

I led the way and he followed. The street had people on it, so he knew he wasn't getting robbed, and cokeheads with strippers needed money like fires needed oxygen. Once we were out, we stood under the awning and lit up. I reached into my coat and took out one of the Leon G copies, handed it to him. He squinted at it in the light of the club's neon.

"I'm supposed to know this guy?"

"Maybe. Maybe not. But here's the deal. A friend of mine wants to talk to him. Nothing illegal, just talk. But I'm busy as fuck and I understand you hang here a lot. The ladies love you. Et cetera."

He looked at me, calculating. "Home away from home."

"Call me if you see him. Five bills." I gave him a slip of paper with the number for cell phone two written on it. "Flash it to the girls, especially the Asian ones."

"Five bills?" He seemed to think that was a little low. I shrugged.

"I'll throw in an ounce of blow. How's that?"

Brian smiled then. "Dealio. See the black man, call the number. Show the Asian hoe hoes."

"Correct."

He nodded and went back in. He had a bowlegged amble that reminded me of a bad horseback rider. I flapped my coat to get the stink out as I walked to the next club on my list. It was beginning to seem like a house in a bad neighborhood and a ramshackle cabin had not been a negotiation high point for me, plus I was getting hungry and cranky in general. I needed food and drink and pills. And someplace clean to decompress. It occurred to me that I still had the key to Vinnie's, or whatever the hell his name was, rapist's upscale house, and that's when I knew I only had a few more strip clubs in me.

By last call I'd put two more scumbags like Brian on the potential payroll, though of course none of them would ever see a dime, and I was finally on my way home, smelling like a rest-stop toilet in spite of my best efforts. I parked in a slightly different spot, just around the corner from the dry cleaners by the health food store where the hopefully suicidal checker worked, took Lemont's gift gun out and stowed it in my stinky coat. There was still thirty grand in the trunk, so I quickly peeled a flap on the stash tire open and took out five and locked up, then walked through the rain with my head down. I was a little tired and sticky and the downpour was steady but not pounding. I kept my nostrils flared and my ears perked out of reflex, but when I finally bounded the fence into my backyard and landed in the tall, wet grass, I knew there was trouble, instantly. The lights were still out in my house, but there were big footprints, fresh, wet ones, leading up to the back door. I drew my knife and skulked forward low and slow, just a dark blurry thing in more darkness, and then I scented it. Green chile stew. Denture glue. The Meat Boys had been snooping around.

I went in fast. The house was empty. No wet tracks, no new smells.

I slipped my shoes and socks off and padded silently into the living room, then slipped out the front door. They were still down the street. Something caught my eye on the porch, right next to the front step. An empty wine bottle and my cell phone. It was go time. I glanced at the clock on the mantle. Just after three in the morning.

I hit the Meat Wagon hard, a high-speed blur of black and teeth and flashing metal. Dentures lost his dentures as I ripped him out of the car. Roids broke wind, low and big and bubbling moist. Dentures had a pleading look in his eyes as I tucked the knife into his groin.

"She's coming," he gasped. I paused.

"What?"

"Fucking Linda! She just called. We told her what you said to say. She said she was on the way. That was like five minutes ago. I planted the bottle and the phone on the porch. It was all I could think of!"

"Oh." I helped him up. "That gives me about four minutes." I took the envelope with the money and the Leon G photo out of my coat and thwapped him in the chest with it. It dropped into his hands. "Good then. Tupperware?"

Roids passed them out, shaking violently. They both looked stunned.

"Okay then. See you guys tomorrow. Sorry about the mix-up."

I sprinted silently back to my house while Dentures picked his teeth up and got back in the car. Back on my porch, I kicked my cell phone and the wine bottle farther down as I passed. Once inside I hung my coat up, put the Tupperware under the sink, poured a new glass of red and quickly dragged the heavy bearskin out and laid it down about ten feet to the left of the door, right next to the phone and the empty. Then I took a big pull out of the glass, rubbed some on my face, and spilled the rest. I flapped the edge of the skin over me and went limp. Then everything was silent. I waited, listening to the rain. After a minute I found that playing dead on my own front porch was actually extremely relaxing. The sound of the weather and the fur and fireplace scent of the bear hide all combined in a pleasant way. I closed my eyes and thought about Thomasini and Leon G. Hunting imagery, my favorite soporific.

Down the street a car came to a stop and I heard a car door close, then the click of heels on wet pavement. Closer. Closer. I recognized the stride. Linda was in a hurry, and it wasn't just the rain.

THIRTEEN

AT LEAST SHE had the common sense not to kick me into a waking state. I let her stand there, confused as to how to wake me, before I finally rolled over and ended her tense deliberation.

"Miserable Cretin Woman," I said pleasantly. "To what do I owe this already lame late-night encounter?"

She scowled impressively. "Late-night drive-by had you rolled up on the porch. You're an asset two days from go time, so I thought I'd come and make sure you were dead."

I sat up and rubbed my scalp. "No such luck. How's your face? I mean the part I punched."

"Swollen." She crossed her arms.

"Good," I said warmly. I got up and looked at my phone and the empty, the spilled glass. "Can you get that crap for me? Gotta drag the bear back in."

Cursing, she followed me with the garbage. I put the bearskin back in front of the fireplace and tossed a few logs on the coals.

Then I sat down in front of the fire and watched them catch while Miss Misery watched me.

"Why are you here bothering me?" I finally asked. "Again."

"What kind of wine do you like in the middle of night?" she countered.

"Scotch. No ice. You know where it is."

I listened while she poured two glasses. A moment later she settled heavily next to me, just out of arm's reach. The flickering light played over the bruise on her jaw. I wondered what the hell was eating her so bad that she'd become an early-AM boozer like me.

"Swelling isn't that bad," I commented. "I told you the peas would work."

She stared into her drink. I could have sworn she looked depressed. Since I didn't care, I sipped scotch and looked at the fire. She decided to tell me anyway.

"Did Christophe tell you why he wants Thomasini so bad?"

"I assume he knows I could give half a shit, so no, he didn't."

She sighed. "Thomasini runs one of the larger telecoms. Inroads into Mexico, Brazil, Argentina . . . He's beginning to take up some real estate here in the US. Stepped on Christophe's toes."

"Thomasini is on the fat side, but I can't imagine it hurt that bad."

She sipped. "It wasn't pretty. He torched and scorched some valuable property. People died. We delayed the IPO. But Thomasini just kept coming. He's too guarded for Christophe to get to and come out alive. Salt is under constant surveillance. Thomasini's people know his every move. They know he's a killer, so his people are focused on Christophe in a very intense way. Hence you."

She was lying. It was in her heartbeat. I listened anyway.

"That's part of why this is so important," she continued. "Why I can't have you sleeping drunk in the rain."

"I wasn't drunk," I protested weakly. "I like sleeping outside. What the fuck time is it?"

She glanced up at the clock on the mantle. "Almost four."

"Close enough to breakfast," I said, rising. "You like ham? Eggs? Salmon?"

"Not hungry."

"Suit yourself."

I went into the kitchen and within a few minutes I had two thick slices of ham sizzling, six eggs cooking over easy, and salmon poaching in white wine with capers, a minced shallot, and unsalted butter. I went back out into the living room and she glared at me. This time my apron didn't get anything close to a smile. I refilled my glass.

"So you're trying to tell me Christophe is upset about the dead people. And you had the whole drive over to think up something more convincing." I took a seat at the dining room table.

"You can believe whatever you want, Verber."

"I always do."

"Amazing." She was openly disgusted. "Not everyone is as much of a cynic as you are. I have to say, you've achieved an exceptionally rare level of assholery."

I went back into the kitchen and flipped the ham and the eggs. Salmon poaches fast, so I sprinkled some salt and dill on it and plated it, then the ham and the eggs a moment later. Forks, knives, napkins, and I carried the plates out to the table.

"C'mon," I prompted. "At least watch me eat."

She got to her feet in a tired way and sat down across from me, stared at the food in front of her like it was poison. After a minute she took a small bite of salmon and discovered she was hungry. We ate in silence. When our plates were clean, I took them back into the kitchen and put them in the sink, then plucked up my scotch and lit a smoke, headed for the tiny back porch. She followed and sat in the doorway.

"Coffee?" she asked.

"Only if you make it."

I stuck my hand out into the light rain and let it run over the back of it. I was tired and I still had to go stalk Leon at some point. I needed to call Lemont and tell him how I was rolling and how many eyes I had on the street before he had a heart attack. There were still a few things I needed him to do to get my emergency escape plan in order, just in case I need it. I had to get rid of Linda. There were taco supplies to consider. The day was stacking up.

"Black, right?" She handed me a steaming mug and sat down in the doorway again. I sipped and kept fooling with the rain with my other hand, cigarette between my lips.

"Finally ate breakfast with me," I commented.

"The whore from the other night would be so jealous," she said with a touch of wry.

"Probably. I'll take her out Saturday. Steak tartare at Foza. Oysters here. Caviar off of each other's abdomens upstairs. Champagne out of her belly button."

She snorted. "I just ate, Verber. Don't make me hurl all over your pathetic little porch."

"If you do, try to angle into the grass."

We listened to the rain for a while.

"You didn't read your file, did you." It was more of a statement. She already knew the answer.

"Please. Don't start. Just don't."

A gust of wind blew the rain in sideways, spraying me. It felt good. Clean. I needed a shower after the strip clubs. The whole crappy vibe and putrid stink of the mice holes had left me in a weird mood. I felt like shooting for a serious buzz and taking a short nap or a long bath. I didn't feel like Miss Misery's sorry-ass company in the least.

"Go home and get some sleep. Take a vitamin." I turned. "You look like shit."

She smiled, very tight, and the expression didn't touch her eyes. "Think I'll stay here and read. Keep an eye on Christophe's errand boy. I have the day off. Some asshole punched me, so they're calling it sick leave."

Which is why I slipped a fat, greasy roofie into her next drink. Twenty minutes later she was drooling on the bearskin in front of the fire, completely gone. I put a blanket over her, took all my phones and my gear upstairs, showered until I smelled clean again, which took longer than it did after a really bloody killing or a gun battle at the dump, and then fell sound asleep just as the sun was showing the first sign of putting in a cloud-smeared appearance.

✳

AFTER FOUR HOURS of deep sleep I felt much better. Relaxed, even. It was after shift change for the guard duty outside and the Meat Boys would be sleeping for the next few hours before they began bumbling around with the three scumbags looking for Leon. It was a little after eight-thirty. With Linda's car out front, Korean Miata would probably have his guard down.

I took another shower in the upstairs bathroom and changed into my ghetto wear. The faded orange canvas jacket over a long-sleeve black tee, baggy black jeans, and scarred engineer boots. I loaded all my stuff into the jacket pockets, this time with a few items I rarely brought along. Wire, knife, Verber wallet with two grand, extra smokes and a lighter, three phones, and my keys. The extras were a roll of duct tape and a loaded disposable .22 with a suppressor, ten cross tops in the clip. Then I went downstairs to check on Miss Misery.

She was resting peacefully. One of her legs was sticking out and the house was cold, so I tossed a few logs on the fire and used the bellows to get the fading coals hot, then made coffee. While it brewed, I did the dishes and then carried a cup out and really looked at her, studying without the distraction of her personality.

She was pretty in the way some mean, calculating women can be when they've relaxed their society mask. Even in a drugged slumber, when most people looked like children, the faint lines on her relaxed face painted an existence of concentration and anger, ambition and focus. No laugh lines, just traces of frown and squint. Some good scowl, too.

I shook my head. The world was pumping out so many faces like hers. Climbing the ladder into an ugly place that ripped the juicy parts out of their minds, higher and higher into a scouring and frozen storm of sand and blood dried to shrapnel, and all to shit on the rungs below them to make them slippery for the mass of eager sufferers on the same path, climbing as fast as they could and clawing apart anything they could get a piece of. The modern corporate climate had created an army of wasted lives, of hard-sleeping faces. Looking at her I couldn't help but think about the difference between wolves and hyenas.

I bent down and sniffed her from head to toe. Her camo scrub was wearing off and her scent was finally coming through. Oranges. She ate lots of oranges. Something bitter, like the taste of the brown papery tissue around peanuts right out of the shell. An acrid whiff of medical. Bleach and more complicated chem. I stuck my nose into her hair and scented her scalp. She went to the gym. Plastic, cotton, yellow padding foam, aluminum, and her real hair smell, scraped out twice a day but blooming now. Toasted sesame oil. Dust. Root beer. Unripe cherry tomato.

I sat back down at the dining room table and finished my coffee. It was beginning to look like I had a hostage, at least for another six hours. I took another roofie out of my supply and ground it up in a shot glass, poured some scotch in and stirred until it was a cloudy mess. Then I dumped it down her throat. She spluttered weakly a few times, but swallowed when I plugged her nose, and then she was as limp as a rag doll. I covered her up and turned her on her side in case she puked, then went and sat down and thought for a few more minutes.

I finally decided to take a roofie myself while they were out, and washed it down with some of the leftover wine. As it sank in I pondered. Then I went through her things.

She'd brought the gun I'd smelled before, a Lady Smith, fully loaded with one in the chamber. Her car keys. All the same shit I'd found in her purse the first time, plus some heavy-duty pain pills. I pocketed the gun and the pills and considered. I had a day and a night to hunt Leon G, provided I could ditch my guard. I was wondering how to do that when one of my disposable cells rang. I clicked it.

"Found your whack job." It was the scuzzy kid Brian, jittery with speed and the joy of money on the way. "He's staying in the same motel as half the bitches at the club. The one next to Tiny Ed's on Lombard with the big burned-out neon Christmas tree sign. Has some Asian hoe in there with him. He's big, dude. Just went to the vending machines in his underwear and it's like about getting ready to snow. So he has superpowers."

"You're sure it's him?"

"Oh yeah. He's driving a wicked-cool Lexus. Coal-black, tinted, gold rims."

"What about the plates?"

There was a pause. "Michigan."

Leon G. "Okay. Hang way the fuck back. That guy is a serious pro killing machine. You get a room number?"

"Nineteen. When do I get my money?" He was on full bubble bath.

"I'm on my way. I'll meet you at Tiny's in thirty. I want you to keep an eye on that car. He leaves, you call, but don't let him see you and don't try to follow him. Got it?"

"Cash, right? I don't do banks."

"Cash."

It was time to move. I swept up Linda's cell and looked through the contacts. There were only two oriental names. I picked the one that sounded male and texted. "I think he made it past you, idiot. Go check HIS office. Don't call OUR office or we're all dead. Await further instruction at that location. I'll wait here." Then I watched through the blinds, listening. The white Miata appeared at the end of the street and made a fast three-point turn, then sped away. I pocketed Linda's keys and went out into the rain.

Ten minutes later, I was across town with no tail. Izelle answered the door before I knocked. She was wearing a black glittering mini, a pink bra, and a black fur coat. I got the oddest look before she recognized me.

"Mr. Message Man? What the fuck are you doing in that outfit?" She giggled. "You look like some kind of lunatic punk savage."

"Get your purse," I said. "We gotta run."

Izelle's hand went to her throat and the ladyboy let out a delicate gasp. I pushed past her into her place. The door closed behind me. I looked around like I was looking for something.

"Where are we runnin' to? And why?"

I turned. "Thomasini hired the only hit man we know, this psycho named Leon G. I'm about 99 percent sure he's here in town for you. He might be in the mood to meet me, too."

Another gasp. Izelle sat down and looked at the carpet, then up at me. I sat down next to her. When our eyes met, Izelle's were full of tears. The fear sweat was mingling with coconut body lotion.

"What are we gonna do?" Izelle whispered.

"Jump the gun, so to speak. Everyone on the top floor is freaked out. So you and me, we're going to pay Leon G a visit and get your walking papers. And I'm afraid I have to set my boss up for blackmail at the same time. You get the cash for the deluxe hole punch and enough to live off of for the rest of your life, and I get enough to get the fuck to Belize or wherever and start a new life. But we need dirt. On tape. On camera. You got an iPhone?"

Izelle nodded.

"Good. So you record the entire thing. I'll do the rest. Got a gun?"

Izelle shook her head no. I handed her Miss Misery's Lady Smith. She took it and stared at it like it was the key to a door she'd never seen in her apartment.

"Know how to use it?"

Izelle nodded. "Wasn't always just a lady in a fur coat." Her eyes were sad, soft, lost.

I smiled cheerfully. "Get your shit. We have about ten minutes to get across town."

"And then what?" Izelle got up and quickly put on her fur coat, a really big one that looked real. Mink. A beautifully nasty little creature, perfect for the occasion. She slipped the gun into the right-hand pocket.

"And then we get to see exactly how clever we are."

FOURTEEN

L EON G'S CAR was still in the parking lot when we pulled up down the street. I nodded in its general direction. Izelle's eyes narrowed as she picked it out.

"Let me guess. The Lexus with the gold rims."

"This might even be easy." I turned to her. "Let's go over the plan one more time."

"All right!" Exasperated. "I knock, tell him I need my hoe back in the stable or longer green. When he opens the door you cruise in from the side and clock him, we tie his ass down and get the facts while I record. Then we pay his room up for three days, hang the 'Do Not Disturb' sign, and go back to life as usual after you buy me caviar blinis at Five One Five." The blinis were a new addition, circa three seconds ago. "We bust Tommy with the bad news on Thursday, and then Friday morning I'm on my way to Thailand via none of anyone's business but mine."

"Bingo," I said. "Let's roll."

The morning was cold, bright, and wet, with big patches of open blue sky between the fat black clouds. Izelle's coat rippled in the wind. Her hand was in the outer pocket, but she was remarkably calm. Izelle more than suspected a setup, so it was agreed on the ride over that the first thing she would do if that looked like the case was shoot me in the dick. Then the head. I'd agreed, but the thought of having a paranoid, trigger-happy tranny with a gun on me had undermined my confidence. Just a little.

We moved across the parking lot, me as silent as a snake in the grass, Izelle clipping along as quietly as she could. Room nineteen was on the second floor. The sleeping motel had a pervasive crappy quality to it. Everything looked dirty, the kind that only a bomb could fix, and even then it might leave psychic stain. Izelle knocked, dainty knuckles rapping it out with real sound. She drew Miss Misery's Lady Smith and pointed at my crotch. I rolled my eyes.

"What!" The voice was deep and angry and loud.

"Mona Tyrona," Izelle improvised. "I need longer green or my bitch back. Now."

"Fuck off."

"Ain't no fuckin' fuck off. Open up an' let's see me some money."

I caught the scent right then, wafting out from under the door. Death. There was a tiny click. Safety. Handgun. A grunt.

I swept Izelle's Lady Smith aside and shouldered her hard as the perfect bullet went through the eyehole. Then I kicked out hard, knocking the door open. Leon got off one more shot, which ripped like fire across my side, and then I was on him, snarling and rolling. I tore the gun out of his hand and delivered a head butt that smacked his brain around and he went limp. Straddling him, I took the roll of duct tape out and put a generous strip over his mouth. Izelle stepped in, gun sweeping back and forth, in shock. I turned to her.

"Close that fucking door," I snarled. She used her heel to slam it, her gun trained on me. Together we surveyed the room.

The Asian hooker was dead. From the smell I could tell it had only been about three hours. Leon was wearing boxers and one white sock. He was indeed one meaty guy, with an old bullet wound high on his left pec and a few long slashes, still pink after five years, stitched across his abdomen. Missing part of one ear. Gold teeth. Dim future, even before I met him.

I picked him up and taped him to the room's only chair. Then I turned to Izelle, who was still frozen.

"Keep the gun on him," I said. She swiveled and pointed it right at my face. "The next minute is going to be ugly. Slowly use your other hand and get your iPhone out. Let me know when you're rolling. And point that fucking gun somewhere else."

"He killed that poor bitch," Izelle whispered.

"I can see that. The plan has changed a little. Tomorrow night that would have been you. Right after Thomasini ripped you up one last time."

She lowered the gun and with a trembling hand took out her iPhone and started recording. First she took a long, detailed shot of the hooker, who was not only dead, but remarkably dead. Leon had done some very bad things to her. Then she turned the phone on Leon G. I slapped him a few times, and when that didn't work, I unzipped and peed in his face. He spluttered and Izelle gasped. Leon's eyes opened and a muffled curse came through the duct tape. His eyes focused and I stepped back, then drew my gun slowly so Izelle wouldn't shoot me. The bullet slash along my side burned like a string of red-hot metal. And my orange jacket was ruined.

"We know why you're here, Leon," I said in a low growl. His eyes flicked to Izelle. "And by looking at your target like that, you just gave yourself away. In case we had any lingering uncertainties."

Izelle spat. The fear sweat was turning to cold fury. Ladyboy's heart rate was slowing a little as the blood began pooling in her core. She was ready to kill rather than run. I beat her to the punch.

"How much was Thomasini paying you to whack this mighty creature behind me, and exactly how nasty were you going to be about it? Like that? And was I on your cleaning list?" I gestured with my gun at the dead Asian woman, contorted and bloody. "You like your work too much, Leon. It was never supposed to be a hobby, too. I was going to let you go after a long and detailed confession, but after seeing this, I just can't risk you coming back. But at least you got your jammie up one last time." I raised my gun. Izelle stepped forward, her gun now trained on Leon, who looked at her with hard eyes.

"Allow me," Izelle said.

"Wait." It came out flat and hard. She paused. "No silencer." I took a pillow and put it over Leon's face, then motioned her forward. I was moving a little too fast for the average person's happy level. Not that it was a joy-filled situation. "Put the gun right up on it. No spray back, less sound. And remember. Measure twice, shoot three times."

Without any hesitation Izelle put the muzzle of the Lady Smith up to Leon's head and fired, a tight triangle. Brain and bone sprayed the wall behind him. I turned to her.

"Look away," I said. She shook her head.

"Naw." Izelle sounded different. There was a hard freeze in her. "Take that pillow off."

I did and she made a close-up sweep of Leon's ruined head with the phone. We both stared at it for about ten seconds, and then I handed her Miss Misery's car keys. She put her phone and the gun away and took them.

"Take the car over to our caviar blini place. And take the scenic route. I'll meet you there in forty-five. Gimme your phone." She handed it over and I gave her one of the unused pink cells in return.

"What are you gonna do?"

"Quick sweep. We were never here. Now go. In spite of all this I'm getting hungry, and I need a drink. I'll ditch Leon's ride and take a cab. And don't lose the gun. I need it to drive the point home with Thomasini."

Izelle nodded and calmly walked out, closing the door behind her. As soon as I'd heard her *clip-clip* to the bottom of the stairs I went through the room, fast.

Leon's wallet was in his pants, which were on the floor on the other side of the bed. I took it without opening it. His car keys were there, too, and a cell phone. I pocketed all of it. Then I peeled open my coat and lifted my shirt. The long bullet rip looked like a welt that had burst open. It had scraped along one rib, entry and exit. The rib was probably cracked and the blood was bad, but not terrible. I ripped off a piece of duct tape and closed both ends, then went quickly into the disgusting bathroom and wetted down the only hand towel, stuffed it into an outer pocket. On the way out of the destroyed motel room I turned back.

"Thanks, Leon. I mean that."

✳

THERE WERE NO sirens in the distance as I climbed into Leon's car. It smelled like five mason jars of cologne, menthol cigarettes, and the money in the trunk. Some gun oil and plastic. Afro hair product. Crab killer toxins for pubic hair. The engine purred when I started it and I rolled out quietly.

I was marginally fucked. Bloody coat. Stolen car. A dead body I didn't dispose of. But only marginally. Other than the normal number of glitches, things were going my way. I rooted around in my pockets and came up with my smokes, fired up and made for Lemont's warehouse. A block away from the motel one of the pink phones rang. It was Brian, the scuzzy guy with the reportedly juicy penis. I answered on the second ring.

"Yo, kid."

"I'm still waitin', dude. Got places to be." He sounded a little desperate. I cleared my throat. "That you goin' in and out? With the hot chick? You taking that ride?"

"He's dead," I said shortly. "You will be, too, if you don't leave town tonight." Then I hung up and broke the phone in half, tossed it out the window. I took out a fresh one and dialed Lemont. He somehow answered before it even rang.

"This better be my number-one homie."

"It's Verber. And I better be your number-one homie after this morning. I'm driving your guy's car since he doesn't need it anymore. Plus I have an interesting vid for you, as in interesting like I hope you didn't eat a big breakfast. Open the gate, because now it doesn't matter, and turn the fucking lights back on. I'm there in ten minutes."

Lemont crowed. "Doin' it now."

I broke that phone in half and threw it out the window, too. Ten minutes later I pulled the Lexus in and the gate guy closed up behind me. Lemont was standing in the doorway wearing his huge fur coat, beaming. He even did a spastic little jig.

"Two grand on the ride, minimum," I said, getting out. "And I get to keep whatever's in the trunk."

Lemont rolled his head back and forth like a blind piano player on futuristic happy powder. "C'mon then! Lemont need a drink an' it look like, it look like you need the first-aid kit."

I followed him in. "And a new coat. A shirt would be nice, too."

The warehouse was still empty. The gate guy came in and found me a folding metal chair. He was smiling, too. I handed Lemont the phone and had a seat. He found the home movie and watched, the huge smile still in place.

"Who's the crazy bitch?"

"Friend of mine. Long story."

"Lemont like to take her to the movies. Maybe hit some clubs."

"You probably wouldn't." I winced as the tape gripped me. There was no way I was going to remove it for a day or two. "He's a boy, man, something. About to be a woman courtesy of some clinic in Asia."

Lemont looked confused. "You run in a strange crowd, Mr. Verber."

I shrugged. "So, a coat. And a shirt."

"Fur be good?"

"Yeah, I guess. Try to make it match the one my pet tranny is wearing in the video. I also need that phone back."

Lemont snapped his fingers. The gate guy came to attention. "Homie. Go upstairs and get Mr. Verber here a nice fur, one of the long ones, and a silk shirt. Red."

"And some aspirin," I added. The gate guy pounded up the stairs. Lemont played the video over again, as happy as a kid with his first Xbox. I took Leon's crap out of my pockets along with my stuff and lined it up on Lemont's desk. Lemont's eyes flicked to Leon's pile for an instant. I picked up the dead man's wallet and opened it. A little over two grand, which I took. The rest was credit cards and a few business cards. His license read Vernon Brown. I tossed it next to Leon's phone and pushed it all over to Lemont's side of the desk.

"Trophies," I said. "Enjoy."

"Nasty," he purred. When he was done with the third viewing he handed me the phone back, then opened a desk drawer and pulled out two property deeds and two grand. "Wanna go see what this dead-ass killin' machine had in the trunk?"

"Yep."

Together, we walked out into the bright cold and I popped it. A briefcase, a rifle in a weatherproof jacket, two suits still in the dry cleaning plastic, and nothing else. I took the rifle out and hefted it. Some kind of sniper thing. I handed it to Lemont.

"Consider it another gift. It was meant for you, after all. And I have a bunch of this kind of crap already."

"Thanks, baby," he purred, snuggling the heavy thing to his chest. "Lemont treasure it like a pet poodle."

Then I took the briefcase out. It was heavy. I turned it around and sniffed it while he watched. The sniffing didn't seem to faze him.

"Let's get out of this wind," I said.

We went back inside and sat down at the desk again. Upstairs, the gate guy was rummaging around, humming softly. I took my knife out and popped the locks on the case and opened it. Lemont came around to inspect it with me. The contents were chilling for him.

There was a photo of a slightly younger Lemont on top. The three photos beneath it were of warehouses, addresses written on the back. The third photo was of the warehouse we were sitting in. The rest was cash, around forty thousand, give or take. Lemont whistled and I looked up at him.

"Looks like you had about ten hours to spare. Good thing I was bored today."

Lemont patted me on the shoulder. In two-plus years, it was the first time he'd ever touched me. We'd never even shaken hands. He took the photos out and went around the desk, sat back down.

"Looks like I still owe you, homie," he said quietly.

"Depends on how nice the coat is," I replied.

His smile came back on, all one thousand watts of it.

✳

THIRTY MINUTES AND two cab rides later I walked into the Five One Five, an upscale place on the upper west end of the Pearl District. I was draped in a long, thick fur coat loaded with all the crap from my last one and carrying a new briefcase Lemont had given me since I screwed up the locks on Leon's. Izelle was seated at a two-top, staring into a tumbler of brown with cubes. I settled quietly across from her and met the waiter's eye, pointed at Izelle's drink, and held up two fingers. He nodded.

"Hey, baby," I said softly. I needed Izelle to hold it together. She looked up with dry eyes, toyed with the tumbler.

"That was one fucked-up morning," the ladyboy said.

"Could have been way worse," I replied. "How do you like my coat? We're twinsies."

That got me a sad smile.

"More good news," I went on. "Turns out you were worth forty Gs. I have it right here in the case."

"Keep it." Izelle had no interest in blood money that she thought had been pointed at her.

"I'll keep half, but listen to me." I slid her phone back just as the waiter set our drinks down. He politely vanished. "Some money is worth more than just the number printed on the paper. We have proof. Tommy is going to pony up a few mil for each of us, but this, what's in this case, is worth more than that."

Izelle looked up, listening. I drained my drink and picked up her second one, as she hadn't finished her first.

"This money has your soul printed on the paper. So use it to buy something you never, ever thought you could touch."

Izelle thought about it. I turned to the waiter and held up two fingers again. When I turned back Izelle was still lost in thought. The silence went on for a long time, long enough for the waiter to drop off the next round and wander back to the bar.

"What would you spend it on?" The question came out low and husky, with a hint of growing enthusiasm. I leaned back and smiled, raised my drink.

"Cooking stuff, probably. Hard to say."

Izelle's laugh was like bells again, throaty, loud, and graceful all at once. My smile became genuine. We drank.

"So," I said. "Caviar blinis?"

"Hmm. I'm watching my girlish figure, but for some reason I feel like seeing this whole plan through down to the last detail. So caviar blinis it is. And some fucking oysters."

"I like your style, Izelle," I said, meaning it. "If you throw up, I'm sure I can carry you."

✳

ABOUT AN HOUR later, with Izelle safely tucked in on her couch with a bottle of champagne, a huge joint, and the TV remote, I drove Linda's car back to my house and parked where she had left it. The neighborhood was quiet. The white Miata was nowhere in sight. The Korean was still at my office, watching, and very probably irritated.

The fire was low and the roofied Miss Misery was still out. I hung my new coat up in the downstairs closet and took her cell and her gun out and put them back in her coat pockets where I'd found them, slipped out of my shoes and socks, and poured myself a glass of wine. I stowed the briefcase with my share of Leon's kill cash under the table.

It was shaping up to be a boring afternoon. I added a few logs to the fire and then took her cell out again and texted the Korean to come back and take up his position. I included that the fuckhead Verber had been in the basement the entire time and that he'd better just keep his mouth shut.

With not much else to do, I went upstairs and showered. The five aspirins were working about as well as they ever did, so when I got out, free of blood but with a big strip of super sticky gray tape on my side, I popped a Thorazine and a few Xanax, then dressed in a casual black long-sleeve V-neck and black cotton slacks. The chemical combination needed some hard liquor to make it bite into my fresh bullet holes, so downstairs I poured myself a scotch and sat down at the dining room table. I had everything for tacos, but I'd made a real pig of myself in the whole blini and oysters affair. I sipped and considered as the throb in my side ebbed and flowed. I'd been shot many times of course, and I healed fast, but it was always such an itchy process, and I'd have to wait for the next full moon to get all the way through it. In the meantime, it was going to be like two bee stings, a whip stroke, and a second-degree burn all in one, and all on top of a crunchy, more-than-slightly-grindy rib. Booze and pills helped, but there was a clear limit on what they could do to my system. Ether worked pretty well, but it always made me hallucinate, which could get messy.

It was getting close to late afternoon. I glanced at Miss Misery's phone. No missed calls. That was good. I looked at mine. Same. Also good. I fired up a cigarette and stepped out onto the porch, stretching with my good side. My neighbors to the left were home, making a snack for the kid and watching TV, talking about some bullshit in the papers involving politics. I didn't even know who the president was. I tuned them out and casually glanced up and down the street. The white Miata was back in place. I sniffed, and even at the distance of a block and a half I could smell the radiator. Fresh arrival. I took one more drag and pinched the butt out, then went back in, my body language projecting utterly bored, which was easy.

I had no experience in waking someone loaded on roofies, but now that my morning was done I wanted the wretched piece of corporate suckdog on my bearskin on her way. I sat down and considered my options. None of them seemed biochemically sound, but they all had an element that could serve to spice up the afternoon, at least until taco time.

Option one: There was some coke stashed in a bindle in one of the throw pillows on my bed. I used the stuff as part of my barter system. Hand over mouth, coke under nose, let her breathe and then stand back. Potential for an extremely bad reaction: unknown.

Option two: Toss the bitchy thing into a bathtub of extremely cold water. Potential for hypothermic reaction: unknown, but given her spa-membership percentage of body fat, possibly high.

Option three: Pee on her face. Instinctually satisfying, but there was the bearskin to consider, and I didn't want her to have a sample of my urine, even if it was just in her hair. Discard.

Option four: Slapping. With a possible hairline fracture to the blue-stained jaw, unfortunately out.

Option five: Proceed as normal. Ignore the drooling mess and read.

I went into the main library room just past the bathroom and took down a couple of books on the Middle East and carried them out to the couch. The *Scientific American* was there on the end table, so I picked that up first and read all of the articles. When I was done, I added two more logs to the fire and went to the kitchen to begin taco prep for one hungry me and two big meatheads with a dull night in store. Whatever happened, even if I had to combine options one and two, the wasted Miss Misery was going to be on the road to somewhere else before dinner. If she wrecked on the way home, so much the better.

Once the huge hunk of beef was simmering in spices and wine, I sat down at the dining room table again. I was lost in thought, mostly wondering why I hadn't picked up any cilantro, when the one remaining pink phone started ringing. I padded over to where I'd hidden it and looked at the number, even though it could only be one person. It was Izelle, using the other pink phone, which was supposed to be for emergencies only.

"Who and where are they," I answered.

A languid sigh. "I'm bored. Adrenaline crash followed by a bottle of Chardonnay."

I sat down at the table. "It happens. Actually, I'm bored, too. I just read the new *Scientific American* and now I'm watching this awful woman I roofied half to death. She's drooling on my bearskin rug."

"You got a bearskin rug? Is it nice?"

"Yep. Grizzly. Huge monster of a thing. Me and an old friend of mine took it down years ago. Alaska. The final frontier."

"You sure know how to party. Bear hunting in the land of mosquitoes. Helping a lady blow some brains into wherever brains wind up once they leave the head." It didn't come out as an accusation. Izelle was lonely, and maybe a little scared. I glanced over at Miss Misery. She hadn't moved in hours. It was throwing my game off. I sipped my drink.

"It was fun at the time. My friend got a bad . . . scratch, but he was okay. For a while."

"Hmm. How's your bullet hole?"

"Holes. It went in and out, right along one of my ribs. I've injured myself worse just dinking around changing a flat tire."

The bell of laughter. "I've never changed a tire in my life."

I laughed, too. "With those fingernails I'd say it's too late to start. Plus, after tomorrow you'll be able to afford triple A."

"I already can." Her laughter came and went again. "But I don't have a car and I don't really want one. A cab is just a lady's phone call away."

"I always lose my cars," I said. "Especially the ones with flat tires."

"I decided on what I'm going to spend my blood money on." I heard the twinkle of wine hitting goblet.

"Tell me." I sat back, took another sip of scotch.

"Well, first I'm going to take you shoe shopping. And I get to pick out the shoes. Something to match your fine new coat." She sounded pleased, even playful. The playback phase was on her early. I was the distraction.

"That won't even make a dent in it," I replied. "You still have a whole huge stack to consider."

Izelle sighed. She was a real Oscar winner when it came to the sound.

"The rest . . ." she paused to sip. "The rest I might just blow on a fine collection of wigs. Does that sound stupid?"

"Nah." I was smiling like Lemont had been earlier. "I mean, yes, but it's your cash. Wigs it is."

"You see the irony, right? A wig collection, Leon's head? Is that sort of . . . Mostly blond, I think. Maybe some chestnut brown. Long, flowy. And I think I might need a really cool gun. Small and with purple inlay on the handle thing, maybe rosewood. And something alligator. Alligator house slippers, silk lining, custom made."

"A rockin' plan if there ever was one." I got up and refilled my glass. It was closing on eight and the shift change. The Meat Boys would be out front soon.

"What about you? What are you going to use the money for?" There was something in her voice that needed a good answer. I thought for a minute while she listened to me think. The fire crackled. Miss Misery let out an impatient snort.

"I was thinking I might chip in on your wig fund. And I was also going to maybe, just maybe, get a parrot. I can't seem to get along with dogs too well. They tend to, well, they tend to clam up and just hide. But I knew this woman with a parrot years ago. Damn thing loved the hell out of me."

She laughed again. The bells. "That's an expensive bird, Mr. . . . What the hell is your real name?"

I glanced over at my file, sitting on the hutch. My birth name was in there. My birth name, and the name of my mother and father, where I was born.

"Verber," I replied. "Gelson Verber."

"Gelson Verber," she repeated. "Is that German or Yugoslavian or what?"

"German. But I'm not really German. It's one of those names that mean something other than where it came from."

She sipped and smacked her lips. "Same with Izelle."

I thought about that. I thought and sipped and looked at Miss Misery, who had shifted a foot and burped. She was getting ready to come around.

"Izelle, I might have something for you. You need a rock-solid fake ID? I mean the kind that you can take to the bank and not break a sweat? New name, new cards, the whole nine yards? So solid you can get a passport off the package? Might be a better use of Leon's donation than a wig collection."

Silence.

"Izelle?"

"Bless you, baby. I most certainly do." She sniffed.

"Fella with the tools owes me one, so we can get the kind of discount you need. Think up a good last name."

Sniff. "I'll take all night. Gelson, I'm glad I met you. There are so few gentlemen left in the world today. You aren't my type, but I see no reason to not buy you a birthday present every year until we're both too old for tearing tape."

"ID photos the day after tomorrow. Namewise, maybe pick something French."

Silence as we both drank. She finally cleared her throat, composing herself.

"So what's a roofie-doofie doing laying on your bearskin?" She had only casual interest, I could tell. After killing someone, the average person, even a transvestite, apparently, had only a passing curiosity about that kind of thing.

"This deal I have going on the side. She's kind of a stalker, really. Heavy-duty corporate type, real attitude. You know, swinging the world around by the dick. Minor blackmail. She's actually associated with the whole Thomasini deal. I had to shut her down while we took care of business."

"I see." Izelle was quiet, pondering. "Want me to come over?"

"Nah. The hard part is over," I lied. "I think we have clean sails after tomorrow. But Miss Roofie here is a cakewalk compared to this morning. It looks like she's ready to wake up, too."

"I read somewhere that if you stick an ice cube up a junkie's ass they come right out of it. I'm always happy to help." Izelle was serious, but a bark of a laugh escaped me anyway.

"I'll put that at the bottom of the option menu."

"Well then, good night, baby. I'll see you tomorrow. You like bacon and eggs, or are you a chicken and waffles man?"

"All of the above. I'll bring the wine."

"Nighty then. You know I don't chef it up, so bring the ingredients and I'll watch and cheer."

It made me smile. "Like I'd let you touch a stove. Night."

I hung up and realized I was still smiling. I'd made a friend. The first one since my last one's suicide. John Bridger would have smiled, too. He'd always maintained that the only way to make a friend was to find someone as isolated as we were. By isolated, he'd meant someone hiding something in plain sight, though he hadn't use those words. I sipped my scotch and for the first time in two and a half decades, it felt warm in my chest, like breath, or a perfect bath. Then I walked over to Miss Misery and savagely kicked her in the side.

FIFTEEN

MISS MISERY COUGHED and I smelled the preamble to puke. I looked around wildly. Her coat seemed like a good buffer between her and the bearskin and my house in general, but my gun plant was in it. I tore my shirt off and just got it under her face as she jetted. It was a vile mix of bourbon and something that smelled like tuna, mixed with stomach acids and pharmaceutical spit. I gave her a ringing slap on the forehead.

"Wake up, big drinker." I projected an air of absolute disgust. She looked up at me, dazed. "Off my rug, into the bathroom."

That got me nothing more than a blurry stare. I grabbed her arm and dragged her into the bathroom and she didn't even whimper. When I propped her head over the toilet, she spewed again and held on to the basin for dear life. I swept the shower curtain aside and plugged the drain, started the bath.

"Okay, party girl. Your pain pills and the half a bottle of booze you drank knocked your ass into next week so hard that half the weeds in your yard are dead. Keep puking and don't drown. I'm going to clean up the mess in the living room and then throw your gross ass into the tub to get the big chunks off you."

She moaned and then set into the dry heaves. A sheen of sweat had broken out all over her and I got a good bead on what had been under her scrub downs, far better than before, and it made me frown. In addition to what I had picked up earlier, her natural scent had a heavy base of a kind of mossy algae thing, with a hint of spotted grape leaves and sweat-worn leather. Earthy, but not in a good way.

Because far underneath all that . . . I leaned down and sniffed her left armpit and there it was. A curling tendril of burning doll hair, mixed with a kiss of the black mold that grows underneath refrigerators down south. A moist pop of the smell of a fake blue feather fresh from the plastic bag. Sun-dried hair spray. Lymphoma. Cancer was just knocking on her door. And yet there was no trace of doxorubicin or carmustine, which I could detect even after cremation. An MRI couldn't have found it this early, but Christophe could, and he evidently didn't think it was important enough to share. I didn't consider it for a second.

I went back into the living room and quickly bundled up my ruined designer shirt and tossed it into the fireplace. The smell was awful, so I opened the window and the front door. Then I grabbed my smokes off the dining room table and lit up and stepped out onto the front porch. I could hear her retching behind me. Some people.

The rain had come back into play along with the shift change. The Meat Boys were just down the street, Miata gone after a long, confusing day. I smoked in silence, listening and taking in the cold air. I'd managed to spare the bearskin and all it had cost me was a two-hundred-dollar shirt I'd had for less than a day. It was going to take another few minutes to burn the stink down, so I dropped into my Cambodian monk crouch and rocked on my heels, thinking.

I had another not-so-sleepy night in store if I didn't haul ass. I needed to dig up my body armor and the rifle in the neighbor's yard, and that was going to be muddy and slow and obnoxious. But I was still high on Izelle. Until that day, I'd never really understood how isolated I'd been for years. A friend. The concept had become foreign to me.

It was hard to say why I even liked her at all. A part of me felt that since I was being cornered, I was looking for backup. But that wasn't it. The Meat Boys filled that role, and metal for hire was as easy as a trip through downtown. John would have pointed out his isolation angle, but he might have tossed in that Izelle had never really judged me, in the hard and narrow and common way. Bridger had meant something to me. I'd taught him about cooking, and he had shown me new things to cook. I'd explained Dickens to him, and he'd shown me a way of unlearning what I projected into books. It made me wonder, briefly, what Izelle had to say, and even though I was curious, I didn't wonder for long. I couldn't. I didn't have time.

I finished my smoke and chain-lit another. If I wanted the breeze to run through the place, I had to open the back door, plus I needed to add bubbles to the tub so I could interrogate the drugged and heaving thing before she came to her senses and at the same time spare myself from seeing her naked. I took one last big drag off cigarette number two and pinched it out, took a deep breath and went to work.

Holding my breath, I sprinted to the back door and opened it. The gush of rainy wind picked up power almost instantly and the air started to clear. A little of the beef on the stove began to peek through the burning vomit and designer fabric roiling out of my fireplace. Destroying any external evidence that I'd drugged her had been a smelly split-second decision. From the bathroom, I heard Miss Misery moan. I went back inside and tossed a few more logs on the fire to really fry Miss Misery's stomach out of the air. The place was beginning to smell like books and cooking again, so it was time for the really dirty part of the evening. I padded into the bathroom and closed the door behind me.

Linda looked up at me with bloodshot eyes. The bathtub was almost full, so I dumped in some bubbles so I wouldn't see her dried-out, unused pussy. I flushed the toilet for her and tossed my head at the tub.

"Get in," I said. "Take your clothes off first." I turned my back to her. It took her a solid minute to rise before she began shedding her sweaty garments. Then came the splash. Groan. I sat down on the toilet and looked at her. She had her eyes closed and her nose was running.

"Did you rape me." The question came out flat and toneless.

"Of course not. Feel yourself if you don't believe me."

She actually did and then sighed in relief. "So what happened?"

I leaned back on the toilet. "You came over, already pilled up on whatever, and then you drank too much. And then you kept going. I think you might have stress-management issues."

She didn't have the power to open her eyes and glare at me.

"Then you passed out," I continued. I inspected my finger-nails. "Drooled impressively. I tried to wake you up, but it didn't work. A friend of mine suggested I stick an ice cube up your ass, but I decided not to."

"You have a friend?" Her first jab. She was coming around.

"Yeah. So anyway, your phone rang. It was the guy in the white Miata, the Asian. I texted him and told him to go stake out my office, that you had me covered. Something like that. So I covered your back and you might even get paid overtime. You can thank me later."

"Jesus," she whispered.

"Just look at the sent mail. I covered your collapse pretty well. Can you . . . can you rinse the puke out of your hair? I have a sensitive snout."

"Don't look at my tits."

"It would blind me if I did. You need a tan or some kind of spa treatment. Snap to it. Shampoo is behind you. Use the conditioner, too."

I turned away and listened to her grunt her way through the bathing process. When she was finally done I blindly held out a fresh towel. She snatched it and stood, started drying herself off. I kept my eyes on the door.

"What time is it?" Linda Misery sounded a little less miserable.

"Around nine. At night."

"Holy shit." She stepped out of the tub, drying faster.

"You were out for, oh, maybe twelve hours. Twelve hours of sitting there watching you so you didn't drown in your own vomit like those rock kids in the seventies."

"Huh." Not even a thank you, even though it was a lie.

"I'll make coffee. If your underwear is all moist and streaky, I have a few things upstairs that might fit. The small dresser, last drawer down. Since you already went through my place you know where it is."

I closed the door on the steamy bathroom on my way out and padded into the kitchen. After I got the coffee brewing, I poured myself some scotch and put a tin-foil-wrapped pile of tortillas in the oven. As I chopped onion and tomato, I heard her upstairs, cursing and rooting through my women's walk-of-shame stash. When she finally came down she was dressed in pink sweats with "Go Go" across the butt and a flannel shirt.

"Nice," I said, imitating Izelle's purr.

"Fuck you."

I handed her a cup of coffee and sipped my scotch. She glowered.

"I can't believe you can drink this early," she said, disgusted.

"It's nine o'clock at night," I reminded her. "And you're not driving anywhere until you can get that down. Sit."

She went to the dining room table and crashed down into a chair. I carried my drink out and sat down across from her. It was interrogation time.

"So Thomasini. How are we getting rid of the body?"

She shook her head. "None of your business."

"It is my business. I make the grab, I handle the cleanup. It's how I work."

She burped. "Ask Christophe."

"I'm asking you. I'm . . . volunteering. For a quarter mil, the least I can do is make sure some moron pillhead drunk and a psychopath don't blow the operation. Pot calling the kettle black all around, I know, but last night you proved something to me. You can't handle your shit too well, Linda. And your boss is crazy. We can at least both agree on that. In situations like this, when I'm the one who has his shit dialed in the most it alarms the fuck out of me."

She was silent as the coffee churned in her empty stomach. When she finally spoke, it was little more than a whisper.

"Plan is to get him on a computer and have him make some transactions. Then wrap him in plastic. No blood. Then he disappears."

"Hmm. Totally rookie." I was improvising at top speed. "I've made a shitload of bodies disappear, but none of them were like Mr. Big Boy. You have to leave a ghost trail for the police right from the beginning, or the bloodhounds from downtown will just keep looking forever."

Miss Misery looked up. Her bloodshot eyes were unfortunately focused.

"Keep going," she said. I got up and went to the hutch.

"Remember that dude I killed when we first met? The rapist guy."

"Vince Percy."

I snapped my fingers. "Right." I opened the top drawer and took his keys out. "We use his house. That dude's trail is as cold as it can get. We cook up a cell phone record, plant the body in a closet, maybe use the guy's credit cards to book some bus tickets or whatever. You get the idea. Rape guy did it and split. We get to point where anyone looks."

She thought about it. "Ghost trail," she finally murmured.

"I might as well be worth what you're paying me," I said cheerfully. "Plus, I like to avoid cages. Something in my temperament."

"Give me some details." She sipped her coffee, still watching me. I sipped my scotch.

"I deliver him, you guys do your deal, then I wrap him and take him on a short ride in what's-his-name's car. Hump the carcass into the house and dump it in the bathtub. Torch the face, but leave the fingers and the teeth for ID. Rough the place up a little, then park the car in long-term at the airport. A few days later the stink flares up. Mailman gets nosey, no pun intended. Maybe a neighbor. Might take up to a month before the paint starts to peel and everyone on the block begins to zero in on dead body. Bam. A ghost trail. And of course that might not even be what I do with the body. Think plausible deniability. As long as it vanishes from the earth. Just like rapie guy. Shift the line of inquiry."

I finally got the glare. "You are one creepy fucker, Verber."

"But I'm on the payroll now. So pay attention."

I sipped scotch while she deliberated. Her face was so pale it reminded me of mayonnaise. When she finally looked up, I knew I had her.

"Ghosting it is," she said in a monotone. "Christophe will go for it. I'd commend you on a job well planned, but I can't stand you, so please forgive me."

"You love me, liar," I said. "Who else cleans up after you?"

She shook her head.

"I don't want a toothy blowjob or a dry and painful freebie or anything like that, but I do expect a bonus for officer thinking. Cash. In the morning. Send it with the Korean you have spying on me. One hundred grand."

I got the glare again. I shrugged.

"I have to rent stuff. I have to bribe a guy to run a credit trail across the face of the earth to make it look like Vinnie killed Thomasini and panicked, I have to smuggle a body around, I have a ton of shit to do that wasn't in the original agreement. So do it. I want the cash at 9:00 AM sharp and I want you to make sure no one is following me. If I pick up a tail, then the trail goes as cold as a locker at the county morgue."

She rose and rubbed her face. I remained still. Deep inside, I was glowing that I finally had her scent. And her confidence, however bitter.

"The money will be here." She walked slowly into the living room and put on her coat and her shoes. Then she gave me one last red glare. "And I really don't like you, Verber. Read your fucking file, psycho. I did. No one could ever even—" She left it at that.

And then she was finally gone.

❋

IT DIDN'T TAKE long to make the tacos. I shredded the beef and then stewed it in a little red wine and bacon fat, cumin, sea salt, garlic, and smoked paprika. After I ate a drippy dozen I plated two dozen more, grabbed a bottle of red, and headed out into the rain wearing my new fur coat. The rain was light, but cold as it could get without turning into hard pellets. The Meat Guys were expecting me.

"What the fuck happened?" Dentures asked as I passed the bag and the bottle in.

"I had to roofie the crazy bitch so I could take care of that shit I was telling you about. Plus I made tacos. No guacamole. Me and the avocado are on the outs."

Dentures passed Roids the bag. Roids sniffed and began taking them out.

"So," Dentures said, "we staked out the clubs for about six hours. A few people had seen your man, but no one knew where he was. Apparently he picked up some zitty Asian hoe."

"He's all wrapped up. I'll get you guys some dough by the end of the month."

"Cool." Roids handed Dentures a taco. "So you roofied the queen. Points for style, Mr. Verber." He took a huge bite and nodded at the pure goodness of my cooking. I smiled.

"It was pretty fun. She puked a lot when she finally woke up. There's a good chance she might wreck on the way home."

"We can hope," Roids said, chewing.

"Yeah. So I'm not going out tonight. I might visit my next-door neighbor, Barry. We play chess. Keeping up appearances. So take it easy. Tomorrow I have to go do a cash pickup and deliver it to my currency guy. Take about a week for him to do the shuffle. You guys good?"

They nodded, eating.

"Right on, then. I'm going to go clean up the rest of the bitch puke and play Mr. Rogers. I have a bunch of books if you guys are bored."

"We got magazines," Dentures said.

I nodded and went back to my house. Behind me, I heard the window zip back up.

Once inside I tossed another log on the fire. It was about to get cold. The temperature never really bothered me, but a good raging fire was a commodity I had gotten used to at about the same time I got used to good cooking knives and copper-bottom pans. It was the little things that often counted the most. I went to the basement and got my spade, then stripped and put my clothes on top of the dryer. It was time to visit my neighbor

Barry. Except we weren't going to be playing chess. I was going to be digging up his backyard.

✳

THE FIRST RULE of disrupting soil while naked in the cold rain at night is to make sure no one is watching you, because it looks outwardly odd. I scented and listened on my dark back porch for a long minute. Barry was watching TV. His wife Charlotte was already asleep upstairs. The kid was on his computer, faking homework again before bed again. None of the occupied rooms had windows facing the back, but I'd still have to be quiet.

Shovel in hand, I hopped the low fence. Ten steps in from the third fence post, then five steps to the right. The second rule of naked nighttime digging in the rain is careful sod management. I used the edge of the spade to cut a completely irregular shape in the grass and then carefully rolled it up. A square could be detected by a chimpanzee. A strange blemish could be attributed to anything.

Once the sod was rolled up, I began digging. Quietly. Every shovel load was about one cup. I kept the pile of fresh dirt on top of the exposed dirt rather than the grass. About thirty minutes into the operation I hit the top of my package, a waterproof box enshrouded in plastic. I gently pulled it out and refilled the hole, then rolled the sod back into place and patted it down. One hop and I was back in my unlit yard. I stood under the rain gutter and sluiced myself off, parcel in hand, shovel against the wall. Once I was relatively clean and my box was clear of mud, I rinsed the shovel and went inside.

After pouring myself some coffee, I stowed the shovel back in the basement and went upstairs. The drippy plastic-wrapped box was on the kitchen floor, so I used Linda's spent towel and wiped it down, took the plastic off and trashed it, then carried the box over to the fireplace.

After four-plus years, it all still looked good. M1 sniper rifle with a not-so-modern scope and subsonics, and my body armor. The armor was as thin as they made it, circa 2007. Military grade, but still not very pleasing when it came to the profile of my boyish figure. I carefully inspected every inch of it, and when I was finally satisfied I put it back in the box. Then I cleaned the gun.

I'd never really liked guns all that much. As a weapon, they absolutely sucked when compared to bombs or poison. There were so many better things than bullets. But sometimes it was necessary to dumb things down. It was a shame, really. Bullets took the inventive edge, the actual fun part, out of the equation.

Thomasini would be at Izelle's in sixteen hours. I'd have to be there in less than eleven. My money would arrive in nine. I showered and dressed in what I considered pajamas, stowed the armor under my bed, chewed up a roofie, and dropped into a blank trance on the bearskin in front of the fireplace. It wasn't quite sleep, but I still had dreams. The bearskin smelled like Linda.

SIXTEEN

A T EXACTLY 9:00 AM there was a soft rap on the door. I was already dressed and eating breakfast. Ham, three eggs, two tacos, and coffee, with a short scotch and a few Xanax on the side. I opened the door without looking through the blinds.

The little wet Korean man with the briefcase looked gray. Behind him it was raining, not hard, but not soft, either. I motioned with my head for him to enter. He did, and took his shoes off without my asking. Polite.

I sat down and got back to work on my breakfast. He stood until I pointed at the chair across from me with my fork. Then he sat.

"How did you make me?" he asked quietly. He had a San Diego surfer accent. Raspy smoker's voice. I shrugged.

"I never kiss and tell." I speared a big chunk of ham. "Got my cash?"

He put the briefcase on the table.

"Open it," I instructed. "Facing you. Then turn it slowly."

He did. I put my fork and my knife down. My rib was itching so badly I wanted to claw at it. I popped the pills and drained the scotch, then looked at the money.

"How many transponders are in there? Don't lie. I'll know."

He gave me a poker face people would pay hard soul currency for and said nothing. I shrugged.

"Two," I guessed. "Dump the money on the table. You leave with the case."

He did as instructed while I ate and watched. He smelled like generic cigarettes, dandruff shampoo, sadness, and zucchini. When he was done he set the briefcase on the floor and wiped the rainwater off the table with the sleeve of his gray suit, then stared at me. I kept eating.

"Hungry?" It was the least I could do.

"I'm a vegetarian."

"Figures." I finished. "You drink?"

"No."

"Huh. What's your name?"

No response. As fast as I could, which was very fast, I leaned across the table and slapped him. Not hard enough to break anything, but hard enough to get his attention. The fear sweat bloomed in an unexpectedly controlled way and a distant fire flickered for an instant in his eyes. I settled back.

"We're on the same team now, you dumpy old ninja wannabe. So get it through your flat head. In the next forty-eight hours I have a ton of shit to do for our mutual employers. Now, I don't give a shit what they told you. I'm in charge of this stupid-ass operation, so here are the rules. I got people to pay and things to set up. If you follow me, I'll kill you. Then I'll cut your eyes out and rob you of your fingertips, find out where you live, and start working from there. I have some kind of file floating around, so you may have some kind of inkling as to whether I'm bluffing or not."

He bowed his head.

"Smart. Now, I'm going to go through these bills and get the tracking crap out. Then you are going to go home, take a sleeping pill, watch a kung fu movie, and pass out. Your best hope is to just say yes, we're going, he's moving, et cetera. They already know I'm on pre-run errands, and they also know I'll kill you if you try to follow me. They may think you're worth a pinch of belly button lint, and you probably are, but to me you're just a car and a carcass I need to get rid of, which will put a kink in my day. Nod if you understand how expendable you are."

He reluctantly nodded.

"Super duper. Don't even move while I debug the bills. I really mean it. Hands on the table, eyes forward."

He complied. It took me twenty minutes to go through the bills three times. I found two wafers. I put them both in the breast pocket of his shitty suit and he never moved, not even his eyes. But there was no more fear sweat, which made me a little uncomfortable.

"Okay then. Take the bugged case and fuck off. Remember what I told you about the whole you being dead thing."

Without a backward glance, he picked up the briefcase and walked out. On the porch he lit a cigarette and then went silently down the stairs.

He was going to be trouble.

✳

GETTING THE BODY armor on was a bitch, just as I remem-
bered, but at least it still fit. The first step was getting the tee shirt
and the underwear on. They had to be tight. Then buckle the
semiflexible chest piece to the semiflexible back piece and tighten
them. All slow and uncomfortable. Then snap in the crotch
piece, twenty snaps in all, and them snap in the thigh plates,
which had to be slotted into grooves first. All this without catching any of the undergarments. There were Kevlar pads that went
into my boots and flared up the shins, and the kneepads had to
go on before them. The whole thing took the better part of an
hour. When I was done, I put on black cotton slacks to keep my
heat down, a thin black silk button-up shirt, and then marched
downstairs, twenty pounds heavier and still a little cranky after
the nap I had taken once the ninja split.

I took a roofie and four Xanax and washed them down with
some wine, then selected a nice bottle from the top of my collection and put it in the duffel bag with the hundred grand and
the broken-down sniper rifle. Then I put my new fur coat on and
called Izelle. She answered on the first ring.

"Low?"

"I'm on my way."

"Good. I'm bored as hell. Can you stop and get us something
to eat?"

I thought. "You like tacos? I made them myself. They seem to
be a big hit in the neighborhood."

"Mr. Verber, I absolutely adore tacos. But no cheese, please."

"'Kay. See you in twenty."

I fixed ten tacos and added them to the wine bag, then left.
Four hours until Thomasini showed for his weekly torture ses-
sion. I briefly studied the cold, blustery night. It smelled like

snow, but a light rain was all that was falling. I got in my car and started it up, then slowly pulled out. As I passed the Meat Boys I slowed to a stop. Dentures zipped his window down. I did, too.

"The currency guy called. I'll be gone for a few hours." I opened the duffel next to me and took out a five-grand bundle and tossed it into their car. "Walking-around money. If anyone calls and asks why I'm not answering my phone, which is still in my house, tell them I'm in there sleeping. I looked drunk and I played chess with the neighbor for a few hours."

"Chess. Neighbor. Drunk. Got it."

"See you guys in a little. You need anything? Soda? Comics? Snacks of any kind?"

Dentures showed his dentures. "Still chawing on those tacos. Fucking miracle. But I do like Spider-Man."

Roids leaned in so I could see him. "Vanilla ice cream. If it's easy."

"Okeydokey." I zipped the window up and headed for the Lincoln.

When I got within range I parked and walked the last few blocks, listening and scenting. If anyone was following they were silent and invisible and unscented, so I considered it possible. When I got to the car I stowed the cash in the trunk, which was getting cluttered, and then I took the scenic route to Izelle's.

Neighborhoods all look different in the day than they do at night. Mine was dark and quiet. Izelle's was loud and full of people and light. Wonderful. I watched the thick parade on the sidewalk in front of her place until the car behind me laid on the horn. A quick drive around the block revealed no parking spaces, so I had to improvise.

The parking lot behind her building was full, tenant parking only, but there was a dumpster abutting the building. I studied it for a moment and calculated. Then I cut the headlights and slowly rolled up on it.

Dumpsters were familiar objects to me. Some of them had wheels, some of them didn't, but if the pavement was wet it didn't really matter. I nosed up to it and made contact with the Lincoln's front bumper, then slowly eased some gas into the monster engine.

The dumpster shuddered and slipped a quarter of an inch. I gave the car a tiny bit more gas and the dumpster began to slide. It took about fifteen seconds, but I moved it ten feet without making too much noise and in doing so procured myself a parking space. When I was done, I got out and looked around. Nobody. I quickly took Lemont's sawed-off and tucked it deep into my fur coat, picked up the tacos and wine bag, then walked back and popped the trunk. I took the thirty grand and put it in with the fresh cash and the broken-down rifle, locked everything up, and then strolled over to the front of the building. I buzzed Izelle's number.

"Izelle Dellafortuna?"

"You picked Italian?"

There was a buzz and the door popped. I went in, heavy with heavy stuff. When I got to the second floor her door was already open and she was leaning out, smiling.

"I adore that coat," she purred. "You didn't forget my tacos, did you?"

I held the bag out. "I brought a few other things, too."

Once inside, I sat the duffel bag down and she took my coat. She was wearing a canary-yellow silk robe and ballerina slippers.

Her apartment smelled like she'd made cinnamon toast some-time in the last few hours.

"Let's bring the coat into the kitchen," I said. "I need to get some stuff out of the pockets."

"Drink?"

"Oh yes, please. Red wine or brown booze."

I followed her into the kitchen and sat down, then began unloading the coat while she poured us a couple of big bour-bons. I laid everything out like a display, all precisely aligned. Duct tape, gutter knife, a tight coil of wire, tin snips, smokes, a lighter, two grand I had forgotten was in there, a Glock with a suppressor spray-painted a dull black, my pink cell phone, and a pill jar with no label, contents full. Plus a lock-pick set, just in case, and the sawed-off. She looked at it all while she fished out the first taco.

"That's a ton of shit for a fur coat," she commented. She took a dainty bite and her plucked eyebrows arched. She nar-rowed her eyes at me. "You part Mexican? This is goody-goody gumdrops."

"I might be," I confessed. "I actually have no idea."

"Me neither. I think I'm pure American mongrel. Shake my family tree and about a thousand varieties of beautiful ape come raining down." She ate with more enthusiasm. I sipped my drink. While she was chewing she looked over at me and her brow fur-rowed, as much as her facial products would allow.

"Did you gain weight in like, the last day?"

I tapped my chest. "Body armor."

"Huh. Did you bring me some?"

"Nope. You won't need it. I did bring you this." I patted the sawed-off. She looked at it without touching.

"Looks like it could hurt more than one person at a time."
She didn't seem pleased or displeased. It was a simple evaluation.

"It could. Put it under the couch and bring me that duffel
bag, will you?"

"Tacos get more expensive every day." But she did. A moment
later the duffel bag was on the table and she was on taco number
three. I unzipped it and took the rifle out, then carefully reassembled it as she watched. When I was done, she finally spoke.

"What's that for?"

"Well, Tommy usually has a few guys down the street. This
has subsonic rounds, so it sounds like a dog sneeze, basically. If
they get touchy I'll drop 'em."

"Aw. That sounds mean." She didn't mean it in the least.

"Yeah."

Then I took the money out and stacked it in a neat cube.
When I was done, it was pretty large.

"What the hell . . . how much is that, and why is it here?"

"I might need to use it to prove to Tommy how much his life
is worth. He has to answer some questions and make a seriously
better offer to walk, which he won't be doing, in any event. He's
going to transfer a bunch of funds, and then this pile is yours.
When people help me, I generally make it a rule to either kill
them or pony up."

Izelle stared at the money, remembering something unsavory,
and then her eyes met mine. "It was almost worth it."

I winked. "The night is young. This is just a drop in the
bucket. And it's a really big fuckin' bucket."

After a long stare down she winked back. I watched as she
rose and poured herself a glass of wine. White. Into a coffee cup.
When she sat back down she seemed calm and composed.

"Is it okay if I kill him?" She asked the question like she was asking if she could borrow the Lincoln. I shrugged.

"If you want to. But there are rules."

"Like what?" Again, casual.

"Well, first we get the money. It gets transferred offshore. Then we wait for confirmation. Takes about ten minutes. Then we have to use your shower curtain and the bathtub, wrap it up and clean everything. I guess you'll do the cleaning part. Then I weigh the package down and dump it in the river after transport. I'm not sure if the escort guys know exactly where Tommy's headed, so time is on our side."

"The escort. That used to be you."

I toyed with my glass. "Yeah. I, uh . . ." I trailed off.

Izelle stared off into memory. "It was the kind of thing . . . you know, money is important in life." She focused on me. "Did you grow up poor, Mr. Verber?"

"Gelson. And yes. Very. Like it was a different time."

"Hmm. I didn't. My daddy was dead by the time I turned two. My momma went drunk, but not wild drunk. More sofa than dancin', if you see what I mean. Daddy's pension was good. So I raised myself, only child, middle class."

"Sounds boring."

She smiled. "It was. That was in the old VCR days." I had to smile at that. "I had one. Watched it over and over after school until it wore out. Damn thing played for years. Same movie. I had lots, but I only watched one."

"What was it?"

"*The Sound of Music.*"

We sat in silence. Two hours until go time. I drank. She drank.

"What about you?" she asked finally.

I considered. There was a good chance I was going to be dead in the next forty-eight hours. A very good chance. A supremely good chance. As insane as it sounded, I decided to tell her the truth.

"Well," I began, "I have to preface the entire thing by telling you that I'm a liar, a thief, and a killer. It's a design flaw on a genetic level."

"Interesting beginning." No fear sweat. Just a perplexed curiosity. I held out my glass and she refilled it. Then I opened the pill can and shook out four Xanax, a roofie, and a Thorazine. She looked at them with mild alarm and let out her girl gasp when I popped them and washed them down with the bourbon.

"I know. Drug habit." I pulled my shirt up and unbuckled the chest piece on my body armor. The duct tape made her wince. I steeled myself and ripped it off in one smooth stroke. The bullet holes were round and pink. The welt was gone. She leaned in and stared.

"That was one shitty bullet," she whispered. I rebuckled and pulled my shirt back down.

"I was born somewhere around 1860. Maybe a little later, maybe a little earlier. I don't know what my name is. Gelson Verber is a guy I killed in World War Two. Bit his package off and he bled out. I've had hundreds of names. My grandfather was a werewolf, so I'm a watered-down version of the same thing. I'm being blackmailed by a development company called Salt Street, and they want me to abduct Thomasini, so they can torture him for reasons they didn't feel like sharing. I can't really tell you more than that until the whole thing shakes out, but I think I've proved at this point that I'm not out to kill you. Pretty much everyone else, yeah, but . . ."

Izelle stared at me like she was staring at a warped, destroyed, utterly insane asylum escapee. I took a sip of my drink. Her eyes flicked over the guns and the pile of cash.

"I think I'm a woman," she said softly. "Even gettin' my hole punched." She looked back at me. "Maybe we can get you some fangs."

Her eyes were the eyes stolen from the photograph of a child who had accidentally killed a beautiful bird. It was a rare variety of sad that unfolded from nothing into existence and was never accompanied by tears, because it was too late for them to offer any release. I'd seen those eyes before. Always been pointed at me.

✳

THE NEXT TWO hours were awkward, to say the least. Izelle put the sawed-off under the couch, as much for Thomasini as for me, and then sat over it, surfing cable TV. I sat in the kitchen and drank, thinking about how the evening was going to unfold, but mostly thinking about why I was so sure I was going to die soon, and why I had bothered to talk about anything other than the weather. I was deep into contemplating the finer points of blowing up Disneyland when the door buzzer sounded. I leaned back and looked down the hall at Izelle, who was leaning forward on the couch, looking down the hall at me.

"Showtime," I whispered. Maybe she just read my lips, but she got up and buzzed Thomasini in. In the distance I caught the sound of his slow, heavy tread on the stairs. Izelle looked at me and then looked at the door, trapped between two madmen. I'd taken my shoes and socks off already, so I padded up to her in complete silence and leaned in. She was either too brave or too scared to move.

"Play the game like usual," I whispered. "Don't blow his shit away until I'm done."

Izelle nodded, once. The tension flowed out of her and she became fluid. I backed down the hall and picked up my painted Glock, then put the duct tape roll on my left wrist like a bracelet. Then I backed around the corner of the kitchen and closed my eyes. I just listened, and that was my first mistake, because what I heard made me really, really mad.

"Bitch," Thomasini spat as he entered. There was a ringing slap. Izelle fell, her hard body hard on the floor. "New sugar for you. It has pearls on it." Something big and rubbery smacked into his palm. He'd brought a toy to the party.

The door closed. My mind closed. Reality hung up the vacant sign and my essence jumped into the garbage disposal. But I remained frozen, just to savor the moment and let it build. The spray paint on the Glock smelled like sand.

"Butterhole," Izelle purred. It was a voice I had never heard before. Deep, smoky, and dangerous. "I'll see those pants now."

Zip. Shoes clattering on the floor. Izelle turned up the TV. I took the clip out of the Glock and set the gun down on the stove. The clip went into the toaster. I picked up my gutting knife and flipped it open. It was hair-shaving sharp and only two inches long, but everything you ever really wanted was really only two inches away from skin.

"Big bad Butterhole," Izelle murmured. She was as calm as a monk. "You bring a car battery?"

"Hook it," he moaned.

Snap.

I slid down the hallway like a waft of nothing. Izelle looked up at me, an unreadable expression on her face. She was holding a hybrid cattle prod/dildo with big bumps on it. Thomasini was bent over a chair for the sexy, sexy preamble of the evening, pants around his ankles and butt up, reared. Waiting for what I assumed was butter. I flowed the last twenty feet faster than the eye could register. The Thorazine wasn't working. The Experiment was just another happy rest stop on a broken car's scorching rampage to the outskirts of Tulsa. I put the gutting knife to Thomasini's left eye and dug a sweet but shallow groove, all blindingly fast, inhumanly fast. Time had slowed to molasses. He let out the beginning of a whimper and a snarl escaped my chest. Without thinking I grabbed his left hand and bit his pinkie off. The clock on the end game, though I didn't realize it then, had started running at triple time.

SEVENTEEN

I ZELLE GASPED AND dropped the dildo. I spit the pinkie into her wineglass and hit it dead on. Thomasini took a deep breath to scream and I punched him in the back of the skull, right at the base, just short of a kill. He went lights out. I took the roll of duct tape off my wrist and turned to Izelle, who was paralyzed.

"Sorry," I said. "Please don't scream. I'm sorry."

"You . . . you . . ." she stammered. She'd turned into a white woman.

"Bit his pinkie off and knocked him out, I know. I have behavioral issues. I can admit that. Right now, I need you to focus." I wiped blood off of my lips. Izelle remained frozen.

"Focus," she repeated.

"Focus." I looked at Thomasini. Pants down, bleeding, a dildo on the floor, his pinkie in a wineglass. There was no way anyone could have predicted such a perfectly unsightly disaster. Even me. "Here's what we do now. We make it up as we go along. I'm going to tape his little nubbin off and then tape his hands to his belt. You go get me a cup of ice for that finger. He might want it back. Toss that dildo thing in the trash before I freak out again, and then get me a drink."

"Ice. Dildo. Drink." She reeled it off like a grocery list recited by a tired, half-drunk transvestite in shock. Totally in character. I began ripping tape.

"Snap to it, Izelle. This is no time for a breakdown."

She disappeared into the kitchen, wineglass with pinkie in one hand, dildo in the other. I taped Thomasini's fresh stump and then put a second rip across his mouth, because he was going to wake up screaming. Izelle was fumbling with ice cubes and making tiny puke noises. I sat down and looked everything over.

I'd pretty much fucked up. There was blood everywhere. An extremely rich guy had lost a finger before I'd even introduced myself. My new tranny pal was dry heaving. I considered.

"I need your laptop," I called.

"Laptop." Little more than a whisper.

"And paper towels."

A little more dry heaving. Thomasini stirred, but remained out. I pulled his pants up for him and then not so gently tossed him onto the floor. People bleed a little less in vertical. Then I turned off most of the lights. Izelle appeared with a roll of paper towels and two glasses of scotch. We sat down on the couch together and watched Thomasini for a minute. Izelle was getting a grip on the situation. I could smell it. I went into the kitchen and brought back my pink cell phone, sat back down, and dialed. Lemont answered on the first ring.

"Don't you ever sleep?" I asked. He chuckled.

"Sleep is for white girls, homie. What you got?" Back to business as usual.

"I have a really rich fat man with a missing finger. I need a hole to put him in for about forty-eight hours. Also have a pal of mine who needs to go to ground, but I like her, so food and water, etc. She has class, so keep everything in your pants. I also sort of need them to be kept apart. She might try to kill him. Plus she needs an identity as good as mine and she's paying cash. Michigan is fine if we get the same discount."

I looked over at Izelle to see if she had caught the compliment. She was staring at Thomasini's blood.

"Uh-huh," Lemont said slowly. He was calculating. "And Lemont's end is . . . what?"

"Whatever you can squeeze out of a super rich guy with a missing finger, plus the ID roll." It was the first thing that came to mind.

"Hmm." He thought it over. "No dice, homie."

"Okay." It was my turn to think. "I'll up it. You deal with this, keep the rich pervert alive and put a roof with caviar over my asset, I clean out the rat nest in Detroit that sent Leon after you. So no more Leons."

"Deal," he said instantly. "When you comin' and what kind of ride?"

"About an hour, give or take. Long Lincoln."

"I send my boy out to get some vittles."

"Fatso here is a bajillionare, so think white anchovies and truffles, basically anything you think costs way too much. Greasing the hostage is good diplomacy."

"Mmn. Lemont see the opportunity. We dig you, baby."

I hung up and turned to Izelle, who was still fixated on the pool of blood. Her drink was half gone. I drained mine.

"So," I began, "essentially what we have here is a pig's breakfast. I just talked to an associate of mine. You'll like him. He's a real card, sort of like—"

"I heard," she whispered.

"Yeah, so here's what happens now. The fat boy is going to wake up. I do some extortion. Then we go to the safety zone. There you lay low, watch TV, make friends. I go deal with the people who blackmailed me into this whole fucked-up situation. Then you take all your dough and go do the entire hole thing. I . . . it looks like I'm going to split town."

"Detroit?" She finally looked at me. I nodded. She shook her head.

"Shit hole."

"That was before air-conditioning, baby." I got up. "Let's get to work."

"I'm glad you bit that pinkie off, Gelson." Her voice was firming up. "I just wish I'd done it."

"He still has another one," I said, projecting cheerful optimism. "But I doubt your teeth are up to it. Let's wake him up. If he's super rude we can find out."

"I'll do it," Izelle said. She started to get up. I stood back, just to see what would happen.

There are times when people surprise you. After uncounted years, it becomes a rarity to be savored, essentially because the rare combination of artful whimsy and justifiable revenge in tandem is unfortunately uncommon in the world anymore. Not so for Izelle. She whipped out a surprisingly large dick and peed on Thomasini's face. She was imitating me.

Thomasini spluttered and his eyes opened. Missing finger, angry big-dick tranny peeing on his face, duct tape over his mouth, restrained. He tried to scream, just as I predicted.

"You have one huge bladder, kid," I commented casually. I yawned. My rib hurt. "Let me know when it's my turn."

Another muffled scream from Thomasini. Izelle flicked the last drop and lowered her robe. Then she turned and smiled at me, and I had to smile back. She was absolutely adorable in that instant, a newborn thing that had slipped some kind of metaphysical bond that the imagination conjured from the rude elements of social engineering. Izelle was finally free. It made me feel oddly parental.

"Take a bench, sharpshooter," I said. Izelle sat down on the couch and picked up her drink. Her eyes never left Thomasini. It was a bad kind of eyes. I pulled the rich man into a sitting position and gave him the long, hard stare of a thing that had just snapped one of his fingers off. He got it.

I never liked the water too much. As in swimming. Low body fat equated to poor buoyancy. It was a purely random thought, but a useful one. In an interrogation, it was generally a good idea to let the itinerant babble rise to the froth at the top of the kettle. It scared the shit out of people if you immediately gave proof of total insanity.

"I bet you float real good. Tommy."

He let out a muffled curse. I started pacing in front of the couch, slowly, distracted as I listened to my own inner dialogue.

"Fat is tasty. Not human fat. I don't really eat people, but if I had to, say like in a really bad famine type of situation, I'd only eat women. I've already thought about it. And I'd start with the ass."

Izelle's evil chuckle was like the perfect spice. I continued.

"So I don't want you to get the wrong idea about your finger. I didn't swallow it. Too gay, and this is the wrong group to make that kind of confession, I know, but since I don't care, it really doesn't matter."

"I'm not gay," Izelle stated. "Not yet." I turned to her.

"Do you really want to make this even more confusing? I wasn't . . . I mean." I flicked a thumb at Thomasini. "He's gay, isn't he? Not that there's anything wrong with it, but I'm totally in the dark on this one."

Izelle crossed her arms and pouted. I turned back to the fat man. His expression was unfortunate.

Rich fat men generally have a lot in common. One of those commonalities was that they tended to have gristle. Part of the reason why a human became a wealthy, semi-obese pervert was that they were surprisingly tough. Thomasini was just such a specimen. The difference between him and some impoverished ghetto monster was palpable, down to the smell, down to his heartbeat. Whatever variety of hell he had assembled in his skull to afford the shoes he was wearing was beyond my reasoning. I collected money out of paranoia. People like the nine-fingered man in front of me had far different reasons.

"Laptop," I said. Izelle got up and went into her bed-room. I steepled my fingers under my chin and stared deep into Thomasini's eyes. He stared back, predictably defiant.

"How many people are out there waiting to take you home?" I licked my lips. He blinked. Then I ripped the tape off of his mouth.

"I'm supposed to summon my driver when . . . no one is wait-ing." He was telling the truth. It was in his heartbeat and in the size of his pupils, his sweat smell.

"Izelle," I called. "Break that rifle down and put it in the duffel bag with the money. Little change of plans."

"I have extremely bad news for you," I began. "The situation is complicated, so I'm going to be honest so I don't have to remember a string of lies. I'm being blackmailed and paid at the same time to abduct and deliver you into the hands of torture and certain death. It's supposed to happen tomorrow night."

Izelle appeared with her computer, set it down, and went back into the kitchen, all without a word.

"So," I continued, "since I don't like any of this, I've made up my own game plan. I just want to be clear. I don't like being blackmailed. But I don't like you, either. When I blink, I see fire on the inside of my eyelids. But as much as I can't stand these little episodes of shit in my existence, for the moment, just for the moment, you're breathing. Minus one finger."

I let that hang for a minute while I gathered my thoughts. It was like gathering a basketful of grenades.

"So here's how this cookie crumbles," I continued. "You get to live. But there are conditions. First, the laptop. You're going to transfer double the price that's been tagged on your fat ass into an account I have set up. Offshore, blah blah. Greasy shit-bag weirdo like you already knows the drill. Second, Izelle here goes and gets her whole sex change deal and you never, ever see her or attempt to contact her again. Nod once if you understand that I will personally bite off all of your fingers and toes before I remove your eyelids if you even think about her after this."

He nodded, once. A few million and a tranny for his life was chump change. I nodded, too.

"Super. Number three on our list is a tiny bit more complicated. After you do the transfer, I'm taking both of you to stay with a colleague of mine. About forty hours. Then you get to go to a hospital and resume your creepy life. But while you're pecking away at the laptop and scheming up some kind of way to rip me off, I want you to focus on something else."

I knelt in front of him and clicked my teeth together. The sharp sound was loud in the stillness around us. He was stock-still as I leaned in and smelled his face, in rapid little nose sips from his chin to his scalp. Then I leaned back and slowly licked my lips, and a low rumble came and went in my throat.

"We're going to take a little ride in a few minutes, and when we get there, I want you to tell me why someone wants you killed so fucking bad. Start typing."

EIGHTEEN

"BUTTERHOLE," I SAID. "You fuck up one keystroke and the finger that touched the number is mine."

Thomasini was hands free and staring at the laptop. I had my shorty knife out and was standing over him. He didn't bother to say anything, just started typing. Izelle sipped her drink, pouting. I was getting hungry.

The entire money transfer took less than twenty minutes. I even learned a few new tricks while I was watching. Thomasini was clever, even under pressure. The way he navigated through blind accounts and formulated code was nothing short of brilliant. Any speculation as to his actual worth truly was actually worthless. He had pope-level cash. When he was done he looked up. I checked his work. Flawless.

"Now there's a good boy," I said softly. Izelle snorted. She was getting just a little too drunk.

"Babycake? Can you make us some coffee? I'm about to rip the tape off of this guy's face, so any pain pills and an adult beverage . . . plus I need a snack. All this whatever the hell I'm doing has me running on empty."

"A snack," she repeated. "Gelson, you eat more than the fat man."

"Another design flaw," I confessed. "But it has its perks. Sharp teeth. Immune to most everything. No cholesterol problems."

"When was the last time you had your cholesterol checked?" She crossed her arms again.

"About twenty years ago. It was good. I swear."

Thomasini looked back and forth between us, his eyes ever so slightly wider.

"Huh." She turned and went down the hall into the kitchen. I focused on Thomasini.

"It never changes. The nagging."

"I heard that," Izelle called. I gave Thomasini a mute shrug.

"That piece of fucking—" he began. I hit him in the jaw, once. He sagged back, dazed but not all the way out.

"I heard that, too," Izelle called.

"Fuck snack time," I called back. "I think my dude has a buffet set up by now."

Izelle appeared with three glasses. She handed two of them to me and sat down. "Good, because I don't cook. I already told you."

"I know. Stop with the—"

Thomasini interrupted me with a moan, possibly to stop our bickering. We drank in silence.

"So how do we get Butterhole out to your ride?" Izelle finally asked.

"Well, my initial plan was to throw him out your kitchen window into the parking lot. One of my cars is parked down there and I moved the dumpster under your window when I was making a parking space. But now I think we can just walk him out."

"I like the window plan."

"He could splatter. Plus, I really don't want to dent my car if I miss. When you see it I'm sure you'll agree."

We looked at each other. Thomasini was coming around enough to follow the conversation. His eyes tracked back and forth. Izelle frowned.

"You really didn't plan this out very well," she said.

"I was just telling someone about my planning skills the other day. Improvisation is kind of an art form, sort of like origami or painting Easter eggs. The thing is—"

"I'll walk," Thomasini interrupted. "I'll be quiet."

I rubbed my hands together. "Text your driver and tell him you're staying the night for a change. Then text your secretary or whoever and do the same thing. I'm going to check your work when you're done." He nodded grimly and I turned to Izelle. "Pack a bag, cupcake. Then grab the duffel bag and let's blow this taco stand."

✳

TRUE TO HIS word, Thomasini remained silent all the way down the stairs and on the drive over to Lemont's. When we were about ten blocks out, I had Izelle blindfold him and he didn't protest.

There was no choice but to pull into the warehouse. I couldn't risk Lemont's cover. If I did, and he thought my hostage could find his way back at some point, then Lemont would kill Thomasini as soon as I left and claim he'd tried to escape or steal something. The gate guy opened and shut the now silent operation and Lemont opened and closed the big bay door himself. When we got out, Lemont looked the three of us over, once again with his molar grin.

"Damn, all that fur is smokin'. Lemont never been to Paris, but this be what he be expectin'." He took in Thomasini after a second appraisal of Izelle. "You didn't say the motherfucker was fat fat. You just said fat."

"Lemondo," I began, giving him a forty-hour name he would remember, "he's just fat. Period."

"Whatever, homie." He went and sat down at his desk. The warehouse was filling up again now that Leon was out of the picture. Five racks of suits, a small stack of Mac computers still in the boxes, and about twenty unmarked boxes of anyone's guess. There was a fold-out card table with a nice spread on it, which made me uncomfortable. If the Detroit Rat Nest merited champagne, caviar, lox, and assorted goodies Lemont needed a consultant just to find, then I had made a deal with the devil. Again. It was true that if I survived, Leon's employers were the next people on my shopping list, my first lined-up score on arrival since I had a trail leading back to them and their assets, but Lemont had no way of knowing that. I almost frowned.

"Fur people, eat up. Fat ass, move your operation over here to the desk and Lemondo give you the rules that keep you out of the Drano bath and the pipes."

Lemont was a different kind of monster than me. Different from Thomasini as well. There was a sharp ring in his voice that made him sound much older than usual, and totally indifferent to the well-being of his new guest. Thomasini picked it up like a wet hundred-dollar bill on the sidewalk. So did Izelle. We watched as the rich man lowered his head in a final defeat and approached Lemont's yellow glare, a nearly pure predatory set of hooded eyes, flared nostrils, and wire lips, projecting at high luminosity from behind his metal desk, a thing which suddenly reminded me of an autopsy platform for students. I turned to Izelle.

"Hungry? My boy owes me for this sort of complicated deal involving a bizarre real estate . . . uh. Thing."

"I just need to sit," Izelle said. I nodded.

"Let's sit in front of the food."

I took her arm and we walked in an upright stride to Lemont's caviar getup. There were two folding metal chairs. We sat and I popped the cork on the bubble and poured. I never could stand champagne, but beggars can't be snipers.

"Cheers," I said. She gave me a tired pair of eyes with lips that matched.

"Can I just go home with you?"

There was nothing there. No sex thing, no angle, no profit, and no reason. Just a tranny in a fur coat with nothing to lose, because it was all gone. There was no reason at all to bring anyone home, especially when I was just about to get into serious trouble.

"Sure," I said. "But let's graze on Lemont's spread first. It's that or tacos."

Izelle took a thin wedge of rye bread and smeared a tablespoon of gray caviar on it. Bite. I scooped up half the lox and made a mouthful of it. We chewed and swallowed.

"You make me feel safe, Gelson." She said it in a way I didn't understand.

"All things considered . . . Izelle, have you ever seen a therapist?"

The bell of her laughter briefly distracted Lemont and Thomasini. Her eyes were bright with wet when she answered.

"You don't ever get to know. Can't remember anyway."

After that we ate and drank in silence. The conversation between Lemont and Thomasini was just out of Izelle's hearing range, but not mine. Lemont painted a very clear picture of the essence of gruesome. It was almost like Old Testament poetry. When he was done, Thomasini was convincingly shaken and Lemont was satisfied. And I had a question before I left. I finished a spoonful of some kind of meaty oyster concoction, which unfortunately involved spinach, while Izelle picked at things without any appetite. She evidently didn't care for champagne, either.

"Homie, I'm taking the gal with me, so give the fat ass the rest of this food," I called. "But first I need to talk to him and possibly bite off some other part of him."

"You sayin' you fuckin' *bit* this pinkie off?" Lemont looked horrified. "You never heard of germs, fool? Shit." He looked at Thomasini's hand. "I got a first-aid box be a little more advanced than duct tape. No spurtin'. Just sayin'. Got computers an' what not. And I need your woman's ID. Gonna use the photo. I put in the same address as yours."

I turned to Izelle, who still looked a little pale. "Go and wait in the car," I suggested. "This won't take more than a minute. And close your eyes. Take a nap."

She gave me a long, distant look, one that went straight through my head. Her hands were shaking a little as she took out her driver's license and put it on the table.

"I'm not going to do any biting," I promised.

"I feel sort of sick."

"It's natural. Just hang back. I know it sucks, but we need the Butter alive. He knows something I need to know. After he tells me, he becomes a poker chip, so we still need him."

Without a word, Izelle got up and went to the Lincoln. I motioned for Thomasini to join me. He rose and made his way across the warehouse like a man on death row, headed for the injection spectacle. When he finally sat in Izelle's still-warm chair, he looked at the food like it was ashes.

"So," I began. "You have a story to tell. These are the rules. Don't lie because I'll be able to tell and it will piss me off. I'm a walking lie-detector test, and you better believe that I'm good at it. So spare no details. The things you think might not matter may mean a great deal to me. You are going to paint one very big picture for me, right down to the final brush stroke and the signature."

"I got it," he said quietly. "Can I have some of the bubbly?"

I topped off Izelle's glass and set it in front of him. Just looking at it seemed to be enough for him, because he began without even tasting it.

"Communications is just part of what I do." He gathered himself, and a small measure of pride came back into his demeanor. That wasn't bad. When people brag, there is usually more truth in the subtext than when they lie straight out. "I can't even say it was really my fault. I take that back. I can say that I never really had any choice." He stared at the bubbles rising in the champagne flute. "It was a family thing." He looked at me. "You a family man?"

I shook my head no. He shrugged.

"Consider yourself lucky. I know how that sounds, but more than half the time it's true. I went to MIT. My brother went to prison. When I started my first company he had just gotten out. I was in motherboards and first-stage wireless micro. I hired him on as security. My model was tanking and he ramped everything by running heroin through my shipping conduit."

"Skip to the good part."

"So I finally get my feet under me. I start buying up radio stations and running my tech spin-offs. Profits go up, investors come in. And private auditors. The kind who don't really care where the start-up capital came from but are going to find out anyway so they can blackmail a dirty back door for their employers. The shit went on for ten years. I fired my brother and did my best to clean up his mess. He lives in Europe, and no amount of biting is going to get you his address."

I nodded. "Ten years is a long time."

Thomasini's face sagged. In one heartbeat he aged those ten years. "It is longer than you can imagine. I managed to dodge most of the private detective probes, but one of them hung on like a parasite. Nothing I did made any difference. Then the blackmail started."

"Blackmail," I repeated. At that point he drained the glass. I refilled it.

"About five years ago. Somehow they knew everything. They had pictures of my brother's house. His family. His kids. His dental records. And they knew every goddamned thing about my . . . hobbies. I had no choice but to pay."

My scrotum tightened. The hair on the back of my neck rose.

"Did you ever find out who they were?" The question came out raw. In my peripheral I saw Lemont glance up, sensing a shift. He couldn't hear us, but he could read our body language. Thomasini shook his head.

"No. A couple of months ago I hired two ex-Mossad and a former Spetsnaz team to track and sweep. I thought they were the best. They were delivered to my resort home a week later. Just their teeth. But I did get one thing out of them before they were taken. Two pictures. Each one cost me a million and change and I have no idea what to do with them."

"Where are the pictures?"

"In my safe, which was cracked. So those are gone. I had copies in the attic of my home. Those are gone as well. The digital copies were in my office on my computer, which is probably on the moon as of last month. But I still have one copy they never found." A tiny bit more pride, but the fear sweat was old on him.

"And those are where?"

"I'm going to reach into my coat pocket," he said. "Really slowly. You already know I don't have a gun."

"Slow means slow, big boy."

Thomasini took out his cell phone. I'd never seen one like it. About the size of my hand and all screen, with several access ports and some kind of mushroom with a fractal on it jutting from the side. He tapped the screen and called up an image.

"This is who runs the show. Fuckin' CEO bitch is a research genius. And this is her main goon. The guy who killed everyone who got me these. The guy who got past my security, cracked my safe, everything. She has something on him, I never found out what, but he serves her like she's royalty." He held the phone up.

Miss Misery. The CEO of Salt Street Development. And Christophe. Her blackmailed, murdering, safe-cracking slave dog.

PART

THREE

Lune

NINETEEN

T HE DRIVE HOME was a quiet one. Izelle nodded, half-asleep. My mind was racing and a grenade had hatched in my stomach. I checked my little pink cell phone. It was the Meat Boys' shift, so at least I could park relatively close. Izelle wasn't wearing the right kind of shoes for the rain that had kicked up, and she looked like I would have to carry her after two blocks even if she was.

"What are you thinking, Gelson?" she murmured softly.

"I'm just listening to my inner voice," I said truthfully. "Waiting for it to say something useful."

"Sounds bipolar." She was close to dreamland.

"Yeah, well."

I parked two streets away and we walked arm in arm to my house. Izelle woke in the brisk wind and near-freezing rain. When we passed my Meat Patrol they nodded politely. I ignored them.

"Those guys were checking out my ass," Izelle said, pleased.

"They can't help it. If they knew how big your dick was they'd probably commit suicide. They're coming over for dinner in about an hour, so try to keep your sense of humor in your dress."

She snuggled into my side. "I like your neighborhood. Nice trees."

"It never mattered before, but my house is bugged," I said, "so if you have any questions the people who are about to kill me shouldn't hear, we have about one minute."

"Why are people trying to kill you?"

"I plan on murdering them all. They usually try to kill me first when they find out."

"I see. Did Butterhole tell you something to spark this homicidal thing you have going?"

"Yep. The pieces to a very strange puzzle just fell into place."

"What's it look like? The puzzle?"

I considered. "Mostly red."

We stopped in front of my house. I sniffed and listened while she watched me. It was clean. Everyone was on standby until tomorrow night, which was going to play out very differently than expected. I didn't know exactly how, but plan B was forming.

"This is me," I said.

"You live in an old Victorian? In a residential neighborhood? I figured you for a condo man. White carpet. Blinds instead of curtains. Maybe a penthouse with chrome and plastic stuff. The kind of decor that always reminds me of office stuff. You know. Lean. Like you."

"That's actually the other guys. And you haven't even seen the inside yet."

She looked up at me and arched an eyebrow. "Am I about to be even more surprised?"

"Probably." I leaned in to her ear. "When we go in, keep it down for a few minutes. Brief tour and then you sit on the couch. I'll get dinner going and put on an opera to cover my sound situation until I clear it up."

"'Kay," she whispered.

Izelle's reaction to my house was nothing short of comical. She took in the living room with wide-awake eyes, her mouth slightly open. I hung my coat up and took off my shoes, then took her coat and did the same. She stared at the towering bookcases, the still-smoldering fireplace, the antique furniture, and the bearskin, then took a tentative few steps and peered into the dining room. When she finally turned to me she mouthed one word. "Nerd."

"Sorry about this whole hostage situation," I said evenly. "If it's any consolation, I'll take the tape off of your mouth before I feed you."

Izelle played it pro, making a muffled protest, her eyes smiling as she covered her mouth.

"Put your fat ass on the sofa."

She flipped me off.

"This might hurt just a little. Do you have to pee before I tape you in place? No?"

She sat down at the dining room table and picked up the *Scientific American*.

"Okey dokey. I'm in the mood for tacos, so I have some shit to do. Hold still."

I took my duct tape out and ripped several strips, rolled them into wads and put them on the kitchen counter. Then I dropped a few pounds of shredded pork shoulder into a pan with butter and went back into the living room. The old antique radio crackled to life and the classical station came into focus. I threw two logs on the fire and took my socks off, then glanced over at Izelle. She felt my eyes and looked up. I rose and held a finger up to my lips, then slipped out the front door.

The Meat Boys were close to being glad to see me. I didn't have anything for dinner, so that's why I got less than perfect enthusiasm. Dentures zipped his window down.

"Hi, guys," I said. "It's go time. You're invited in for dinner tonight. Pork tacos, refritos, some enchiladas, and BBQ salsa."

"We can't . . ." Dentures stopped, worried. "You're not mad at us, are you?"

"Not yet. But you are coming for dinner. I got us the money, so I need some data. But most importantly, I need you guys to gather up your bugs and put them in the basement. I have some classified shit going on and I don't need our boss knowing anything about it."

They looked at each other. Dentures cleared his throat before speaking.

"There's only three, but we aren't the only ones listening."

I dug my car keys out of my pocket and handed them in. "Duffel bag full of cash and gun parts in my trunk. Bring it in for me."

THERE WERE SEVEN bugs in all, more than I'd guessed, but ten would have made me feel important, so I was a little deflated. One in the living room in the bookcase to the right of the fireplace, one under a chair at the dining room table, one in the bedroom in the fire alarm, one in the basement behind a jar of tomatoes, one in the kitchen, carefully concealed on the underside of the spice rack, and one each on the front and back porches. It took the Meat Boys more than half an hour to find them all, even with the help of their detection wand, and then another twenty minutes to move them all into the basement and position them in different spots. When they were done they moved my radio to the top of the stairs and closed the door on it. Izelle finally spoke.

"You guys are pretty light on your feet," she commented. "Is that something you learned in spy camp?"

Dentures slumped into a chair. "YouTube."

Roids sat down across from him. "Chinese kid at Radio Shack."

"Izelle, be nice. These guys actually work for me." I almost crossed my arms, but using her own posturing against her struck me as overkill.

Izelle wrinkled her nose. Dentures and Roids exchanged a look of blunt confusion. I poured us all drinks and passed them around. Scotch, neat.

"Payment," I began, sitting down next to Izelle. "Twenty Gs a month plus bonuses, limited health, and dental. Two days off weekly and two weeks paid biannual. Cash and you stay off the books. Check, and then you get the whole W-2 and all the complicated shit that comes with it."

They were both silent. Izelle could sense their tension. It was reflected in her body coil. I continued.

"After tomorrow, Salt will be at the bottom of the ocean. Or we'll all be dead. So if we win, it's either me or something worse. Keep in mind my cooking skills and the general results of the 'Generate A Positive Work Environment' thing I read in the lobby at my last dental." I thwacked Izelle on the arm. "C'mon, kid. Let's give the new guys a chance to chat while we finish up dinner."

"I don't cook," she primly reminded me.

"You can be in charge of the can opener." No wink, but she could feel it. Some people are that good.

We went into the kitchen in single file. I could hear Dentures and Roids whispering. Izelle probably couldn't. We started whispering, too, as I clattered around with my pots and pans, creating a soundscape. They were discussing where to hide cash.

"You have a ton of cooking shit," she breathed, her eyes playing over all the brass and cast iron and copper-bottomed steel. I nodded.

Water running. Timer clicking. Metal on metal. Plausible dinner clamor.

"So what the fuck was that about?" She still whispered anyway.

I opened a sack of dried poblanos and dropped them in a pot and added a cup of water, fired up the stove. Then I picked up the smokes on the counter and tossed my head at the back door. We stepped out and I lit up, then gently closed the door behind us. My voice was as soft as the patter of the rain on the awning.

"Those poor guys have less than forty-eight hours to live. If the people who are blackmailing me don't kill them and they manage to survive, I'll kill them myself, because why the fuck would I want to hire anyone who would switch sides like that? Mid-game, no less."

"Jesus," she whispered. "How . . . why . . . I mean, what the fuck are they even doing here?"

"The people blackmailing me into abducting what's-his-name have them detailed to watch my comings and goings at night. I busted 'em down and took them in a similar smoke rub, but mostly I wanted data they're too stupid to get. Thomasini finally gave me the key. I know who their boss is now, even if they don't. But I need bodies in the worst possible way. Really big ones. I already got shot once this week."

"So they're cannon fodder." She didn't seem particularly concerned. I nodded.

"Yeah. Initially I was going to find some way to screw them out of whatever they could beg, steal, and borrow, but cannon fodder it is."

We looked out at the rain. Izelle held her hand out and let it get wet. She was thinking. I smoked, waiting, watching her. It was the most curious thing, seeing her cup her hand. Just like I did.

"So that's your job. Apart from this mess, this is what you do." It wasn't a question. It was a conclusion. I puffed on my cigarette. Eventually, I nodded.

"Part of it," I clarified. "I'm essentially a professional troublemaker. The pay is fantastic and the hours are unbeatable. Travel. Rivers of pussy. Just yesterday I got a new house and some kind of dilapidated cabin. And I made a cool mil today, and I've been ripping off some other really shitty people all week. Had to kill some guy and I don't . . . ah, fuck it, you did, too. The whole short-term memory thing for me is conveniently messy."

Izelle absorbed all of that without blinking. She finally plucked my cigarette out of my hand and took a drag. Still no blink.

"Does that sound, like, really bad?" I don't know why it mattered, but it did.

·   "Not really," she said, smoke rippling from her fine, fluted nostrils. "I just need an application form with a no cannon fodder clause."

Something cracked in my breastbone. I turned my face out into the night and cast my senses as far as they would extend. If I really concentrated, I could actually hear the clouds. An image of when my last friend dropped into his watery, shark-infested grave swam up in the blank meditation. The rifle I had, two clips hitting springs. When I dove in and stabbed until the water was too red to see. It was the year or two before that that I loved the best. I blinked and saw the fire. But I also smelled the rain. Izelle's wondering, intelligent countenance was focused on me, heartbeat, scent, pupils, galvanic, all anticipatory. I took my cigarette back.

"Charm those idiots while I finish making dinner."

She took my cigarette again. "Gelson isn't your name," she whispered.

"I already told you that."

She nodded. "My real name is Antonio. Lost, just like wherever the rain goes. Just like yours. So I don't know what to put at the top of my application."

I reached out and touched her face. My hands were always hot. She closed her eyes.

"I'm a lesbian, Gelson. I want pussy, but I—"

"Don't care," I interjected. "Go back in there and keep the Meat Boys busy."

Izelle nodded. Then she smiled. "What then?"

"Ah, well . . ." I took one last drag and fastidiously dropped the butt into the hibachi. "While I'm working tomorrow, I need you to whack this Insect Lady . . . thing. Same as Leon, but take the long gun. She might be a snake, so bring the .38, too."

"Why?" It was an honest question.

"Because she's number three, and I want nothing but ashes."

Izelle thought for a moment. The rain was soothing. She reached out and played with it again, mimicking me, but somehow it was real.

"She the wrong kind of bitch?" So soft it was a whisper.

"Number three in the domino chain is pretty much the end game. You take her down while I deal with rest of the party, disposable meat shield in place, and the horror show, even with all my fancy lies and fancy tools, is all for me. Your end is less than super nasty."

She deliberated for less than four seconds. "Gelson Verber. You're a glory hog."

"I know."

She touched my face. The hard, lean, warm flesh over the bone. Hers or mine. I couldn't tell.

"Take your hand off my face, you gay lesbian transvestite."

Her breath was frost. It was getting cold, fast. Snow was coming. Izelle remained motionless.

I sighed into a darkness only I could see through. "Okay." I sniffed her hand. Inside, I could hear the Meat buffing their resumes. Gold for the toilet rim. "Keep the kids high on their last meal."

Izelle winked her perfect one-eyed Vaudeville wink, where the open eye remained in perfect frame. I smiled. But there were the shark fins on the inside of my eyelid when I winked back.

"Let's do Last Supper," I said, rising. Our dinner guests had gone silent.

The chiles were soft and the kitchen was fragrant with them. I took a head of garlic out of the basket by the sink and popped off three cloves.

"Can you take that off the burner?" I asked, gesturing at the pork. "Without burning yourself?"

"Smartass."

"Be just a second, boys," I called. I seeded the chiles and put them into the blender with cumin and salt and the garlic, hit "blend." Izelle watched me work.

"My apron, please. On the hook behind you."

She passed it to me without a word.

It took two minutes to roll out the enchiladas and sauce them. The pork shoulder was almost ready. I tossed my head in the direction of the living room. Izelle nodded, but not before she leaned in and hit the blender one last time. Under the cover, she gave me the lip I knew was coming.

"A killer in an apron. Martha Stewart would be so—"

"Speak no shit about Martha," I interrupted. "That kind woman is a genius. So what if she did time for being held up as an example. Shame on all those hypocrites. But Julia Child . . . trash-talking that goddess is a straight-up invitation to a slapdown."

"Jesus."

We went back out and sat down at the table. The Meat Boys glanced at my apron, but it seemed to have a nervous effect on them rather than a comical one. Izelle picked up on it and refilled our drinks, smirking.

"So," I began. "What's it gonna be? Don't be shy." I waited. Dentures wrung his big hands. Roids looked into the fire. Dentures spoke first.

"Cash is good," he said. "But we need details. There's a little more to Salt Street Development than you know."

"Here's what I know," I said. "Your actual employer is posing as the secretary of the über-strange badass named Christophe. He's very likely being blackmailed, so he's one pissed-off, enslaved psycho. Exotic desk lady has a way about her, which makes me suspect she's your handler. Salt is a front for an operation that does nothing but extortion and a few other high-rent crimes, and you two are dead as soon as you find any of that out. Which you just did."

The Meat Boys exchanged a look. If there was even a shred of doubt left, it was gone.

"So," Dentures said slowly. "What exactly do you do?"

"Crime. But I don't hire people for anything but eyes and ears. So the risk factor is low. I do the messy stuff myself. And I know, *I know*, that I pay better."

They thought. It was like watching two broken hamster wheels turning.

"So, exactly, what is our job?" Roids finally found his voice.

"Tomorrow I'm supposed to abduct a really, really rich guy and deliver him up for something nasty. Instead, I'm going to deliver someone else, because the target in question is making friends right now with some nasty ghetto mutants in a warehouse. I snatched him earlier, a day ahead of schedule. At shift change tomorrow, you two will be there. This will be your first and last really gory job. I'm walking in, but basically killing my way out. You guys will be shooting, too. And you'll be taking my hardware in for me, because I can't get it past security. We'll be delivering me."

"The desk lady, no name, she runs the sweeps," Dentures offered. "Nothing ever gets past her, especially with you in the picture. Not after you stabbed Mrs. Morgan's hand in the elevator with that pen."

Izelle glanced at me. I didn't return the tell.

"Not tomorrow."

They had no reaction, so I went on.

"In the morning I tell the boss I have to get into position and wait, but I also bitch about the rain, ask for more money, whine about whatever else comes to mind, et cetera. As soon as I leave the house, you two call in and say I'm on the move and that you have me in sight. You won't. You'll be downtown, watching the Salt building."

"Watching for what?" Dentures asked. Roids nodded. Even Izelle seemed curious.

"To take a tally on who's inside. I need a headcount so we bring enough bullets. Plus, if they think you guys are on me, they'll give the Korean a little break. He's the fourth most scary guy in the entire equation, but he'll disappear once the brass is dead."

"Huh." Roids thought it over. In his own limited way Dentures did, too. It was the bare skeleton of a plan with a lot of improv. Or so it seemed. They didn't need the whole picture.

"Who's number one and number two?" Dentures asked.

"Christophe is number one with a big gold star and a plus next to every A."

"Number two?" Roids was slow, but he still had the math skills of a talented three-year-old, which was better than some people.

"That would be me."

Silence. And then a *ding* from the kitchen. I smiled.

"Dinner."

TWENTY

O NCE THE MEAT BOYS left, bloated, half-drunk, and with two large coffees, Izelle took a shower in the upstairs bathroom. I took the rifle out of the duffel bag and reassembled it at the dining room table. Izelle showered fast and was wrapped in half of my towels when she came back downstairs. She looked at the plastic-wrapped gun without expression. I gestured for her to have a seat across from me.

"This . . . it really doesn't matter. It's just a great big gun. Quiet, too. Low-velocity rounds. They kinda explode a little. This thing I'm screwing into the end keeps it down a little more. But none of this is enough."

"So I need what? Makeup? A new wig?"

I rolled my eyes. "No. Well, maybe."

"Your planning is out of focus again," she said. Her eyes were tired, but not slow or lazy.

"Not really. Once I call the Meat Boys, they call Salt. Salt calls the Insect Lady. She'll be in a hurry. As soon as she opens her front door, you put a few rounds into her. From my Lincoln, across the street. Once you plug your target, cruise for a dark spot and ditch the rifle, and drive right to the nearest megastore. Eat a muffin. Wash your hands about ten times. Leave the car and take a cab across town, then call a different cab company and have them drop you a few blocks away from here. Short walk. The spare key to the back door is taped to the underside of the big blue mailbox on the corner. If I live, I'll pick the car up later."

Izelle thought, her eyes smoky slits.

"So I get my hole punched and a ton of money. To shoot a woman I don't even know. And for risking my life and running the gamble on a bust for premeditated."

I'd seen it coming. "I just ran a hard burn on your former Butterhole. Cool mil. So an even 10 percent is yours, which is more than double the standard finder's fee, which, FYI, is only 2 percent or sudden death. Plus," and I held a finger up before she hissed, "I plan on burning the blackmail twat Linda Morgan for a sweet chunk of change before I get killed. Or I kill her. So I can yank down another fifty Gs for you. That is exceptional for a single hit. Even you know that."

Izelle gave me the very look that was on her fake ID.

"Not enough." She was firming up. I closed my eyes and settled in for a lecture.

"Money is funny," she said, enunciating with the sparkling diction of radio personae. "I pull the trigger, you get the storm on your end, fine. I'm betting a buck you pull your chestnuts out of the fire with some serious bank."

"And?"

"Let's say I go to Thailand next week. Two weeks there, then I have about, oh, some serious down time while my new razzle-dazzle heals into active duty."

"Sounds more than vaguely disgusting," I said, but I could feel my face, and it was wearing an expression I wore so seldom I almost didn't remember it. "And I mean that in the best possible way. I can toss in a few more bones, but then we go into the uncharted territory of—"

"I'm going to Detroit."

It stunned me, sort of like a Taser. I stared at her. Oddly enough, even though she'd been thinking it, saying it out loud seemed to have stunned her, too.

"What the fuck would you want to do that for?" It came out in a rush. I needed a drink. A different kind of pill. A nap. Maybe I just needed to run and never look back.

"What the fuck do I have here?" Izelle asked. She gestured. "Some dead bitch I don't even know. Two big boys in body bags. I don't even have a poodle, Gelson. I'll take that money, but I want the thing that matters the most, and I know you can feel what it is. I want you to take care of me while my shit grows together. And I know, we keep tight, I'll be returning the favor. You get fucked up all the time."

"Izelle," I began, using my sweet voice, which rang as flat as a dusty record, even to me, "sometimes I have these episodes, kinda makes me antisocial . . . I can't really go into it again because you didn't believe me the first time, but for your own safety and well-being, maybe—"

"Shut your pie hole," she snapped. "I believe you now, after what I've seen. Who wouldn't? So yes or no. It's a deal breaker."

"Well, shit." I stared at my hands. John Bridger, fast and clean. He'd smelled like pinecones in the fall. That odd smile that was always full of a haunting he never talked about, even once. Songs made him think of all kinds of things. The light, dimmed by a thing I'd known but never touched, fading from his eyes as he dropped into the water. Human beings have the illusion of faith to comfort them when the lights turn out and head touches pillow. The instant when the fire begins to transform into a red tornado on the inside of my face and splashed like a frothy Greek milkshake across the interior of my skull. If I'd ever had an altar, I'd left it in the basement of a different house sometime before I was conceived.

"Izelle." She was watching me. Watching the memory of John Bridger. The dancing sharks. "Izelle."

"Yes."

"Let's go over the scope."

"I haven't signed anything yet." She crossed her arms. I already knew what that meant.

"Okay. You do the dishes, I do the talking."

Izelle held up her fingers. Perfect, painted nails. I got up.

"Fine, fine." I felt my stomach rumble. She heard it.

"Shit," I said. It came out sour, even beaten. She smiled instantly and cradled her pointed chin. "You win. Detroit is a very reluctant go, as in I put Band-Aids and diapers on your newborn . . . Nah, I'll hire a live-in nurse. But I draw the line with my new life on a few points."

"Continue," she instructed.

"I'm sterile, but I do date. And I'm territorial. So hands off my Detroit one-nighters."

"All black anyway."

I sighed at that. "You can't be serious. What the hell is that supposed to mean? That can't be the racist observation of . . . you, to me, can it? I mean—" She gave me a half-drunk, dismissive flick before offering her rebuttal.

"I'm part black spooged out of a Puerto Rican. Might even be a Norwegian and a Hopi in the family tree. So you can keep your mongrel in the same place I keep mine."

"Fair enough," I agreed. "I also have to maintain a very strict control over home décor. The white carpet, the white vases, the glittery futon couch and the Jetsons tranny glitter lamps? All that shit stays somewhere else. You should never even go back there at this point, so I vote for long-term storage."

"Long as I keep my clothes. And I especially mean my shoes."

"Deal. Also, no touching my cooking shit."

"What the hell is it with you and the pots and pans?" She'd clearly been waiting for a good time to ask.

"Humanizing, I guess. I just lied about the other day, which is intensely human now that I think of it. But it's my inner ape. Loves all the shiny shit. And wolves are positively preoccupied with food. It all fits together for me."

"Can we get a dog?"

She was closing on relaxed now that her personal agenda was falling into place. I took her shoes off and covered her up with a blanket from the closet. She made a small sound and turned onto her side.

"No. Dogs don't care for me. I already told you that."

"The parrot thing again?"

"Maybe a parrot. And I get to pick the name."

"Long as it isn't . . . You mean like a big parrot? The screeching smartass kind?"

She was talking long term. I didn't say anything.

"All your books are old. You need some modern stuff."

"Maybe so," I agreed. "But you do, too."

Her eyes flicked open. She wasn't as sleepy as I thought. Big brown marbles of a short and confusing life. I rose and picked up the rifle. She stared at it like it was a skateboard or a lost toupee.

"This fucking thing is pretty much the bomb. I can't pull the trigger because this guy Christophe will smell it on my hands."

"Wonderful," She got up and yawned, started up the stairs. "That's why you had me shoot the lunatic at the motel?"

"Yeah. Sorry." I confessed without much of a voice. It rang true, which was sort of embarrassing. She looked back at me and yawned again.

"Night," I said. She smiled and went the rest of the way up the stairs. A few minutes later her breathing changed. I went into the library room and found a Sharpie. It was the lousiest pen ever, designed by a cretin who needed the very last shot at a discount Juarez veterinary clinic with a roadside taco stand and tomorrow's mystery-meat menu attached to it. I went back and pulled up Izelle's shirt. Then I wrote out the code and all the juicy numerals for the account Thomasini had made his donation to on her back, all in my old teacher's handwriting. There was a good chance I wasn't going to need it, and the Sharpie was only good in the end for one thing. Writing on people. It would last long enough for her to find it. I went back downstairs and thought about that until the fire was almost out. Then I tossed the pen into the coals for a final, shitty plastic flair, but it melted instead.

TWENTY-ONE

S LEEPING HAD NEVER really been my thing. Napping
was more my speed. Izelle was different, but I was hope-
ful that she could make a smooth transition between a
hungover pre-op homeless tranny about to pull a trigger and a
thing of peaceful, relative quiet. I dozed on the bearskin in front
of the fire, pleasantly drifting in and out until my internal alarm
clock went off. When I was done making coffee I carried two
cups upstairs and sat down next to her.

"Showtime," I murmured. Her eyes opened and I knew right
then that the show was going somewhere south of mathemati-
cally sound. Euclid and his fabled progeny had fled the building
without a map.

"Who the fuck are you?" Deep voice. Eyes like bathroom
slippers floating to the surface of a disposal pond. My hackles
went up.

"The guy with the coffee and the guns." I held the coffee out.
"It's 5:00 AM. Rise and shine."

Izelle grunted and staggered into character. She sat up and tugged at her rumpled clothes. Her hair was a wild mess and her lipstick had smeared a little. She took the coffee and scowled at me.

"Don't look at my hair," she commanded. There was not too much weight in it. I grinned back, forcing it.

"Hard not to."

She blew out a sigh and glanced at the clock.

"What the hell am I going to wear?" she whined, shifting from grumpy to petulant. "Did you think about that?"

"I did. It's raining, so a coat. Wear the fur one. In the leftover-from-one-night closet there's tons of women's stuff to choose from. Just don't take too long. The Meat should be here soon."

Izelle wrinkled her nose. "Don't call them that."

I got up. "You really aren't a morning person, are you?"

"Depends on what's in that closet."

I left her to make a wardrobe selection in private and went back downstairs. I could hear the shower turn on and then off, followed by the hair dryer. I laid the table and then finished suiting up, shoes and all, this time soft black loafers and a black Armani, and then I went over my supplies.

I was going minimal. Short gutting knife, a Luger, some piano wire, and one of those lighter-size torches crackheads used. I stowed it all, checked for unsightly bulges, and then went to the bottom of the stairs.

"Izelle!"

"What!"

"We aren't going to a fashion show! Hurry up!"

There was the sound of clicking pumps on hard wood and Izelle appeared, then vogued down the stairs in a black dress with a long white collar and a cinched waist, the black heels she had changed into before we'd left her place, a huge pink hat, and her tiny purse. She strode across the room and poured herself a fresh cup of coffee.

"I'm going with the fur coat, but don't think it has anything to do with your fashion advice. It looks cold outside." She blew across the top of the cup and sipped.

"Well, now that's settled, let's get down to brass tacks."

"Right." She seemed more adjusted after a shower and some coffee. I'd have to make a note of it in case I survived. "Find out where the boys are. Then I'll finish my coffee and see about getting a good parking spot for the Lincoln and the long gun." Her eyes were a little tired and puffy. "I don't need to go over the scope or the breakdown. Just show me where the safety is and make sure it's loaded. I can point, and I can get rid of a gun without any fancy technical advice."

✳

A HALF HOUR, six cups of coffee, one lonely roofie, and ten cigarettes later, I watched Izelle walk out into the cold, pre-dawn rain armed with a pink disposable phone, a pink hat, a neat floral ski bag containing a sniper rifle, and a flask of single malt. She also had the keys to my Lincoln, and I already missed it. While she had been sleeping, I'd crept out and gotten everything out of the trunk, and when I'd looked at the ride one last time, it had occurred to me that it was the first really tangible part of my old life to go. I wasn't going to pick it up. And Izelle also had all the digits and passwords to my Swiss account on her back. It dawned on me that I might never see her again and the revelation hit me in an odd way. What if she just . . . left? Or if the creepy front-desk Insect Lady creature turned out to be a more serious obstacle than I was anticipating? Or if Christophe twisted my head off? Change was getting harder every decade.

There was no point in speculating. Instead, I took one of my disposable phones out and dialed the Meat.

"Boss," Dentures said immediately. The phone hadn't even had a chance to ring all the way through. "We got five inside. Two security, and one of them is the Korean. Christophe is in his office with Linda. We're a block and a half south. Same car as last night."

"Good."

"Yeah." Dentures sounded tense. "We got about an hour and a half before the place starts to wake up."

"Right on. Izelle will be in position in about fifteen minutes. I'll see you guys in twenty. You two ready?"

Dentures cleared his throat. "Yep." He didn't sound ready. "You sure this is going to work?"

"Of course I am." I put a touch of scorn into it. I wasn't sure at all. "Two hours from now we're all rich, especially me, and you guys can take a long paid vacation in Belize or Slovenia, or wherever it is American bodybuilders go to hunt poon."

That got a tight laugh.

"Twenty," I said. "I'll be the guy in the fur coat. I'm going to call Christophe in a few minutes from my real phone. When I do I'll tell him I'm going to stop in for a brief chat before I get into position. Then I call you on the disposable, you call in and say you have my tail. Got it?"

"Yep."

I hung up and put on my fur. In the doorway, I took one last look at my house before I went out into the world. My house. I'd been happy enough in the place. It smelled like old books and vanilla, coffee and baked bread, furniture polish and clean linen. It didn't have very much in the way of other people. Izelle's lingering perfume was still in the air, as well as the cologne and nervous sweat of the Meat. It was a lonely house, I now realized. The small revelation had an omen quality to it, and something more. Christophe was more powerful than I was, more purely moonlit. He might have been able to smell the house on me, if it had been clinging to my hair and my clothes. My den had become so personalized. I'd never thought its scent would matter.

I closed the door. It was a quiet morning. The neighborhood was still asleep. I started my car and drove, letting my mind wander. Variables crept up and I swept them into the corners without much consideration. After more than a century of almost continuous activity, I knew something only the finest criminal minds ever divined, and I knew it well enough to work with it. Planning was good, though as I had learned time and again, improvisation was always a factor. But something else existed, on a higher plane, a place where most people never ventured. It was inside. I knew what I was, and even the moment when I had fully realized it. John Bridger had been like me, one-eighth werewolf, but the human, the pure ape in him, had been a good man. If the wolf had been taken away, he would have been a librarian, or maybe even a doctor. Without mine, I still would have been a criminal, and I knew it. He'd known it, too. Thomasini was a sociopath, by definition. I was seven-eighths something else, neither psycho nor socio, but in many ways just as bad. I lived in all of my lies quite naturally, but I had no choice, and in general cruelty was just another tool, not a reflex or a built-in characteristic. But I'd have been happier than Johnny without the wolf. I still was, even at that moment, driving toward a red question mark.

I put myself into blank pre-combat meditation mode and nothing came to the surface except for the occasional yip of the animal in my genes and the fire tornados when I blinked. I sank into my senses. I could taste the blood as the wolf coiled and stretched, limbering. The ape in me was smiling in anticipation. Myself liked each other.

The Meat was just where they said they'd be. I parked a block behind them. It was raining a little harder when I called Izelle.

"I'm here," she answered. "Her lights are on and she's moving around. I'm across the street. The rest of the neighborhood is still dark."

"Okay," I said. "Go time shortly. Maybe less than three minutes from now. You ready?"

"Yeah." She sounded almost bored. It was an act, I knew. "Is it okay if I stop and get some shoes on the way home? Even two blocks in these heels is going to kill me in this weather."

"We can go out later. You'll just have to endure a blister."

"Fine. I'll get the fire going."

We listened to each other's rain pattern.

"Be careful," she said finally.

"Call me as soon as you're done." I hung up. Then I took out my big bugged phone and called Christophe.

"Gelson." He answered immediately. I was on speaker phone. "Cold feet?"

"Yep. And a cold head. And a wet coat. This sucks, man. In order to pull this off I have to sit in the fucking rain for ten hours and then drag a rich pervert around through more rain and possibly snow. And I'm hungry already. I think I want more money."

Christophe breathed out through his nose. "I'm beginning to lose track of your constant extortions, Verber. We've already discussed how your compensation is more than adequate and that your position, as it were, does not give you any kind of negotiating—"

"I have a few minutes to kill. I'm coming in. We can talk in person. Have my scotch ready. And a snack. Ten minutes." I hung up. One minute and thirty-eight seconds later the pink phone rang. The Meat.

"We're supposed to follow you in."

"Good. I have to keep this line clear. See you in five." I hung up and the phone rang fifteen seconds later. Izelle.

"Done," she almost shouted. "One to the chest and one to the face! She exploded but all of her blew back inside. I'm on the move."

"Okay," I said. "Just drive. Take an evasive pattern. Don't go too fast. Crack the windows about a quarter of an inch and put the gun back in the bag at the first stoplight."

"She exploded," Izelle repeated.

"It happens," I said calmly.

"I'm gonna throw the gun in the river." Her voice was high and fast.

"Good," I said. "Then go get that muffin. Drink that scotch. Take a couple different cabs home and get the fire going."

"Muffin. Booze. Cabs. Fire."

She sniffed and spit. Then she hung up. I put the phone under my seat and lit a final cigarette. When it was done, I got out and squinted through the weather. Whatever happened was going to be over with very, very soon. I put my head down and walked, listening, scenting. The world was empty except for the two dead men waiting for me. I knocked on the passenger window and they stared out, faces white and slightly sweaty. They were both extra bulky. Body armor under the suits. It meant they would last an extra few seconds.

"Hi guys," I said brightly. "Ready to kill some bad people?"

They exchanged a look.

"There aren't any good guys here, are there?" Dentures asked. Together they studied my face for a reaction. I gave them a brief, thoughtful look.

"Not really. Just soon-to-be-rich ones. Safeties off, gentlemen."

While they did a weapons check and prep, I unloaded my pockets and began passing items in. I gave everything to Dentures except the torch and the wire, which I tossed to Roids.

"Gun and knife go in the back of the belt. Once we're past the scanners and in the elevator, I want them in front of me. The camera is right above the elevator doors, so they won't be able to see me take them. All fire goes at Christophe first. Wait for my move and then unload. I need the bitch alive to wipe some computer stuff and transfer a small fortune to Antigua, so leave her. If she's armed and opens up, shoot her in the feet and we can wire off the ankles. Got it?"

They both nodded.

"Let's roll. You guys follow me in close, like I've been misbehaving. Just follow my lead." I started walking slowly to the Salt Street building. Behind me I heard the car doors open and close. The Meat fell in behind me, one to either side, a professional five steps back. I could smell their fear and their freshly oiled guns and, unfortunately, the polymers in their body armor. Christophe would smell it, too, but it would still probably buy us a second or two.

There was a buzz at the two huge glass double doors as we approached. We were already on camera. I pulled the door open and headed for the elevator. There was a soft crackle as the intercom activated.

"Please pass through the scanner, Mr. Verber." Linda's voice echoed over the speakers in the empty tile room. "Tony, Redmond, if he has metal on him, shoot to kill."

Tony and Redmond. Their real names. I held my hands up.

"Okay," I said, irritated. "I don't have anything on me. It's all in my car. But let's not make the guys with the guns jumpy, dumbass. I wasn't planning on killing anyone until later."

Behind me the Meat's fear stink ratcheted up a notch. I passed through the scanners and put my hands down. They went through one at a time and set it off. Linda silenced it both times from a control terminal in Christophe's office. Her office. The elevator doors opened.

"Christophe doesn't have all morning," Linda said, scorn coming through. "Let's go. Boys, don't get too close to him. He bites and scratches."

"In," Roids said, playing his part. We stepped in.

The doors closed. Roids kept a gun trained on my head, as far back as he could get. Dentures leaned out and pressed the penthouse button, and when he did I smoothly slipped the gun and the knife out and pocketed them, then yawned and stretched, reaching for the ceiling. I crisscrossed my hands and left them on the top of my head.

"How much do they pay you guys to get up this early? I'm getting, like, fifty cents."

"Shut it," Roids said firmly. Dentures turned and pointed his gun at my stomach.

"No talking in the elevator," Dentures said firmly. Lame. His back was to the camera. He smirked. Also lame. Behind him the doors opened.

Christophe was seated at the desk, staring at the rain beading on the window like he usually did. Linda was at the bar, decked out in a black power suit and holding a meat cleaver. She was chopping up something big and raw for my snack time. The Korean was slouched in the far corner, gun drawn and pointed in our general direction. Christophe spun and sniffed. A smile flicked on and off and he sniffed again. Then he moved.

Flowed is a better description. Dentures got off a single shot before Christophe crossed the distance between the desk and the elevator, faster than anyone but me could see. There was another fraction of a second that will remain etched in my mind forever, almost just an afterimage, as Christophe paused like a conductor before he tore the big man's head off in a single, claw-filled torsioning spasm of red and blur. I managed to shoot him in the right kidney as I dove over him and rolled to my feet. He made a hard gasp and used the severed head in his hand like a hammer on Roids, who staggered back under the terrible blows and then shot him point blank in the stomach. Christophe took a step back a fraction of a second and the Korean's bullet blew the top of Roids's head off. I dropped as bullets ripped past me and put a round through the Korean's face, an inch to the right of his flat nose. He dropped and as I spun to face Linda the meat cleaver flashed past, clipping the tip of my ear. She'd thrown it.

More than half the room was dead, just like that. Christophe looked at the head in his hand and then down at his stomach, covered the wound with his free hand. There really wasn't much time to think. As Linda fumbled for her gun in slow motion, I raised the Luger and shot her, just above the belly button. Then I turned. Christophe was struggling to focus, so I crossed quickly and kicked him in the chest as hard as I could, sending him flying backward into the elevator. Then I reached in and hit the ground-floor button and backed away as the doors closed while he thrashed in the blood, trying to rise. Two more steps back and then I shot the elevator control panel. I turned to Linda, who was clutching her stomach with both hands. She looked up at me, her eyes wide with disbelief.

"Hi," I said, smiling. "I can't believe that actually worked." And then I laughed. A real, solid laugh of joy, filled with life. I crossed to the bar and poured myself a double. The glass was freckled with blood, but I didn't care. I sipped and savored the burn, then let my eyes play over the blood-splattered room before I looked down at Linda. The area in front of the elevator looked like someone had dropped a stick of dynamite in a fifty-gallon drum of cow guts. Smoke was wafting up from scattered holes that marked the passage of bullets I hadn't even registered. I looked at the Korean, who in death had the same worried expression he'd had in life. The bullet hole looked like a bumblebee that had landed on his face, no blood at all, and the pool under the back of his head was dark and sticky looking. I could smell the urine spreading through the fabric of his crotch, whiskey corn and surprise, and it made me thirsty for a river of moonshine. I gestured at everything in general with the tumbler. "I hope you have an extremely discreet janitorial service."

TWENTY-TWO

"IT ISN'T FATAL, you whiny baby," I said. Linda gave me a look of such pure hatred that it was almost scary. Almost. I was in too good a mood for an interrogation, but it had to be done. I forced myself to look grim. "But that can change."

"You're dead. Dead. Dead. Dead."

I sighed and finished my drink. When I was done I poured myself another and left it on the bar. Then I kicked her gun across the floor to the far side of the room in case she made a mad scramble across ten feet of bloody marble for it and pocketed the Luger. When I drew my gutting knife she snarled, but remained still when I patted her down with my free hand. Cell phone, nicotine gum, and keys. They all went into my coat. Then I picked up my drink and sipped, watching her. She was pale, but I knew from experience that she would live if she got medical attention within the hour. She did, too.

"So," I began. "I know you're the boss here. I know what you do. I know you're blackmailing Christophe, just like you're blackmailing me. I already have Thomasini. Got him last night. He's in a safe location, one of mine you don't know about. I turned half your staff. The Asian desk lady is dead. Let's see. What did I leave out." I tried to look thoughtful. Linda hissed. "Oh yeah. Okay. This is going to hurt, but after I search the desk, I'm going to put you in a chair and drag you over to the big computer. We have about twenty minutes before you go into shock, so we'll have to be quick about it. I need you to erase my file, Christophe's file, and anything related to Thomasini. Then I need you to transfer everything Salt is worth into this account I set up. I'll leave you enough to start over somewhere else."

"Fuck you," she spat. There was blood on her lips. I tutted.

"Fine. I guess I'll just burn the place when I leave. Call me from hell and let me know how painful it was."

I carried my drink over to the desk and sat down. The computer was on and active, so I used the mouse to open various files, casually browsing. Linda would probably pass out soon, and I still had an hour and fifteen minutes before the first part of the Salt Street Development day shift reported in and found the bloodbath in the elevator.

"You're running out of time, Linda," I said. She didn't reply. "You know what I've been calling you? I have this habit of giving people whatever name I want, myself included. Know what I've been calling you?"

Still no response.

"Miss Misery. Like that one song on the radio a few years back. Except I don't think the guy who wrote it drank scotch and watched the woman in question bleed out. At least I don't think he did."

"You'll never leave this building." Her voice was still strong. I had to laugh.

"Of course I will. The question is, will you? I mean on a stretcher or in one of those big black bags. I'd choose soon. As in the next few minutes."

"Even if I gave you everything you wanted, you'd never let me go. And if I wipe Christophe's file, he'll kill me instantly."

"Maybe not instantly," I corrected. "It depends on how long you've had him on a leash."

"Jesus." She sucked in a breath through her teeth as a wave of agony rolled over her. "Jesus."

"Come on, then," I said, rising. I pocketed the knife. I had her and I knew it. Her choices were simple. Bleed out or gamble that I might take my money and my freedom and leave her to Christophe, who was in pretty bad shape at the moment. I could feel the variables tumbling through in her head as she unwisely calculated the odds.

"Listen," I continued, walking over to her, pulling the wheeled desk chair along behind me. "You do what I ask, I split and cap whatever is left of Christophe on the way out, plant the gun in his hand, and make it look like suicide. You dial 911 and say he went crazy. You get a ride to the ER, Christophe takes the fall, and you have just enough time to come up with a convincing story."

I stopped in front of her. She glared at me and I smiled back.

"Linda," I continued, "I'm not even mad at you. Not really. Why the hell would I be? I'm a criminal just like you. It's just that I'm better. I've had a lot of practice, almost a century of it.

Look at it this way. Your plan didn't work. I got a ton of money.
I have to shoot Christophe a few more times on my way out
anyway. I can't risk him healing up and holding a grudge. Shit,
you even gave me a detailed file with my personal history. I can't
blame you for who you are, as low and aesthetically wretched
as it may be. Just do what I ask and I'll be on my way. But I will
kill you if I ever see you again. Deal?"

"Get me in the chair," she said tightly. "And get me a drink."

"Chair first. Drinking comes when you finish."

She hissed. When I lifted her into the chair she almost passed
out. I had to hold her in place as I wheeled her over to the computer. I hummed out of tune in what I though was a soothing
way, which woke her into a boiling fury instead.

"If you don't shut up," she growled, "I'll just allow myself
to die."

"Zipping it on the Muzak," I replied. "Let's do the money
first, shall we?"

I pushed her into position. She had to hold her stomach with
one hand. While she wiped the other one off on a relatively clean
part of her shirt, I went through the desk. It held mostly standard
office supplies. There was a .38 in the top right drawer, which I
pocketed, and an envelope with what had to be cold operations
cash, somewhere between three and five thousand, which I took
as well. I pulled a plastic bag containing rubber bands apart and
flattened it over the keyboard.

"Can't get your blood on the pad. Nosey cops might want
to know why the hell you were typing instead of lying on the
floor."

She gave me a withering look, but there was a greedy hint of
hope in her eyes. I was outwardly aiding her in her exit strategy.

Which meant she had a chance of exiting. She turned back to the computer and began typing. I held the account number out for her to see, my eyes locked on the screen.

Outfits like Salt never keep all of their financial assets in one place. It was almost certainly spread out over several banks in a dozen time zones, with chunks of it tied up in real estate, metals, stocks, et cetera. She predictably led me to what was probably one of the larger accounts, $8.6 million holed up in the Caymans, then glared up at me.

"I guess I'll take 7.6. You can keep the rest and invest it in a new colon. With that and even a fraction of all the other shit you're hiding from me you'll be all right. Enter my numbers and let's move on to eraser time."

Linda Misery shook her head and dutifully pecked in my sequence. Two minutes later she coughed.

"Done."

"One moment." I took my cell phone out and checked the account. From zero to 7.6 million in two minutes. Technology. I silently thanked Lemont for setting up the new account for me and then teaching me how to change everything so he would never know what he did. He deserved a fruit basket at the very least, and he had definitely made my Christmas card list. "Good. Next item is me."

She tapped away for a moment. I watched, but even one-handed she went through data faster than I could follow. It was beginning to dawn on me that the research wizard behind my file was probably actually her alone, and not some team of nerd kids with otherworldly computer skills operating under her command.

"There you are," she said in a thick voice, "in all your glory."

I didn't bother to look. "Wipe it. Don't fuck around, either."

She hit a few keys. I looked back at the screen. I was gone.

"Christophe."

She began typing. This time I did look. It opened with a photo of him, taken within the last few years. He was in a café of some kind. It looked vaguely European. She was just about to delete it when I brushed her hand aside.

"Hold on." I quickly scanned it, reading fast. My old teacher would have been proud. What I found was fascinating.

Christophe's real name was Oleg Groff. Born in 1691 in what was now Czechoslovakia. His mother was pure werewolf. Father died old of natural causes. There was some speculation as to whether she was still alive. Christophe had been on the leash for almost four years. Hundreds of jobs. I whistled. He was probably extremely upset with Miss Misery if he was still alive.

"Delete that."

She looked up at me.

"I told you I'd kill him on my way out if he isn't dead already," I said. "If anyone looks, I don't want them to find out about creatures like him."

She looked back at the computer and her hand skittered over the keyboard. Christophe vanished. But when he did, something caught my eye. I'd done my best to watch what she was doing as she worked, and I thought it was possible to access what I was looking at, so I backhanded her in the side of the head and knocked her out of the chair. Then I sat down and started typing.

There were eight other files in the section Christophe and I had been in. Of them, seven were marked as deceased. I read through them quickly. All of them had been half-breeds or less, and all of them had been blackmailed into Linda Misery's service and terminated after five years. The records went back more than a decade. A fresh one had just been discovered, but had not been contacted yet. Maria Estrella. Christophe's replacement after I'd found a way to kill him, as I was just about to do. How clever. Maria Estrella was living in Queens and hunting well. She had a little bar with live music. A potent half-breed like Christophe, but only fifty-three years old and still using her real name. She looked about twenty and was smiling in every photo, except for the ones taken around the full moon. She was slated to kill me shortly after she got pinched three or four years down the road. A snarl rose up inside of me and then I howled.

As the air filled my chest and my head went back, just before the sound and the electric shudder in my spine, I felt it, the lost time of separation, the flash of realization that I was two things flexing as one. And then the ape screamed, a trumpet of fury and vengeance, a wail of remorse for how the most purely wrong things of the world seemed subject to an impossible distillation, and how amazing it was that it had all come so far, to a moment like this, so unimaginable a century ago. Woven into the same voice was the long, harrowing call of a wolf, surrounded by invisible cages, pulled further from that first clean thought, the first bright dream of every mammal, of light and milk and warm breath, before the punishment began.

The sound shook my skeleton, and I knew if I had been outside, or anywhere close to it, anywhere but in an office full of carnage, that a blackout would have wholly consumed me. Instead, the howl circled the drain and as it wound down my eyes cleared.

When my breath was finally out I looked down at Linda, who stirred a little. She was still clutching her stomach.

"You bitch!" I roared. I howled again then. It came out of the deepest part of me and I couldn't stop it any more than I could stop what I did next. I dropped and bit into Linda's throat, all the way to the vertebrae in two savage, snarling motions. Then I wiped my face with her hair, took three steps back, and unloaded every bullet from the Luger into the computer. When I was done I stood there, panting. I was suddenly blank. It took a long minute for some kind of person to look out through my eyes.

I'd briefly lost it. It hadn't happened in years. I shuddered as it dawned on me what I was calling myself. Gelson Verber. I was Gelson Verber. I collected books. I cooked. I was moving to Detroit. With . . . with . . . what?

I went to the bar and drank something straight from the bottle, three long pulls. My life, my memory, wrapped around my head like a tight new skull. I gasped and my eyes focused on my reflection in the mirror behind the booze collection. My ear had already stopped bleeding, but there was blood on my face and my hands. Linda's blood. My blood. I washed in the bar sink and stuffed the towel in the same pocket as the knife. I needed to get home. I needed a shower and some pills. I needed to cook and eat and read by the fire. I even wanted Izelle to tell me some kind of story that had every chance of making me sleepy, something about the history of the feather boa. I smiled weakly at my reflection. It was my ape that was smiling.

The room looked pretty grim when I surveyed it one last time. Miss Misery was in a pool of her own blood by the desk, her head mostly off. I was standing in a pool of her blood, in fact, from where she had been sitting after I shot her. The elevator doors were splattered and Dentures was facedown in front of them. The Korean had made his own mess. Roids had never even made it into the room and was still in the elevator. The stairs were off to the right. I decided to take them.

At the door I took one look back and it occurred to me that I should loot the place. See what the Korean had on him. Check Linda's purse. Riffle the desk one more time. Take the best scotch. I shook my head. Then I took a deep breath and opened the door on the stairwell.

Christophe was waiting.

TWENTY-THREE

IS OPENING PUNCH was all it took. His fist slammed into my sternum and knocked me back more than ten feet. He was on top of me the instant my back hit the bloody marble, his splattery face a snarling animal mask. He raised his right arm, hand flattened into a rigid killing plane, and then he . . . stopped. Christophe sniffed, scenting. A different kind of light flickered in his glacier-blue eyes. His mouth opened and a high keening came from deep in his throat. I struggled to turn my head and follow his gaze. He was staring at Linda's crumpled body. He cocked his head, listening for the rattle of her heartbeat. Then he looked down at me and smiled. The hand curled into a fist.

"Well, now you've gone and done it." It came out far too calm.

"You didn't even like her," I said. "The cancer in her armpit. You didn't tell her."

"You caught that?"

"I did. Before I did . . . all this, I had her wipe your file. Mine too. I shot the computer because, well, shit." I paused for a breath. The air was whistling around in my chest and my ears were ringing, but nothing was broken. Yet. "Lemme get a drink and I'll tell you why."

Christophe arched an eyebrow. "Temper? Poor impulse control?"

"Exactly."

He got up and looked down at me. He had already stopped bleeding, but his clothes were a mess. Somehow his hair still looked perfect.

"You know where the bar is. Get me a scotch. Neat. Considering I just got shot a few minutes ago, maybe make it a double. And tell me why I shouldn't kill you while you pour."

I slowly climbed to my feet. The room tilted and then righted itself. Behind me Christophe walked over to Linda and looked down at her. He didn't touch her.

"I didn't like being blackmailed," I began. "So I decided to kill Linda pretty much right away. The two muscle heads were easy to turn. I nabbed Thomasini early and he paid in currency and information, which is how I learned that Linda was the head of this circus and not you. So it struck me as likely that you had been set up, too, that she had enough on you to make something stick."

"She has backups." Christophe sounded mildly irritated.

I poured two big ones. "I have Thomasini in a place with some serious computers. He can find them, or his people can. His secrets are stored in the same place. When he's done I'll let him go. He sort of owes me."

"Interesting. Why shoot the computer?"

I skirted the pools of blood on my way over to the desk and handed Christophe his drink. He took it and sipped, waiting for my answer. I considered.

"You ever see all of the files?" I watched for his reaction.

"I read mine about four years ago." He shrugged elegantly. "I read yours from cover to cover as well. Why?"

"There were several more. Linda kept things like us around for about five years. Then she euthanized them. You were due to be replaced in a year or so by me. My eventual replacement is someone named Maria Estrella. Nasty bitch probably would have made me run a sniper team on you after she'd gotten all she could out of you. Then a few years from now Estrella would take me down. Once she hit the slave-dog list."

Now I had his interest. He sat down in the chair at the desk and pushed himself clear of the growing pool of blood, then turned his back to me and looked out the window one last time.

"I wonder why five years," he murmured. He absently drained the rest of his glass.

"Probably a formula she worked out in the beginning. Maybe we start to destabilize after a certain point." I finished my own drink and waited.

"Formulas. I really do miss a time when they weren't applied to things like me."

"Me too." I plucked up the bottle and walked slowly over to the desk, stepping over Linda. I sat down on the edge and he turned slightly and held out his glass. I refilled both of ours.

"Her formula didn't work on you at all." Christophe glanced over at the dead Korean. "Why?" He seemed genuinely curious.

"You read my file. I'm one-eighth moon dog. My best guess is that the human part of me was just born . . . off or something. Of questionable character at the very least."

Christophe barked out a laugh, a single sharp noise. "So you're saying that if you had been born pure ape, you would have turned out to be . . ." He let it hang.

"Maybe a serial killer. Possibly a cop. Parking ticket person. DMV. I was thinking about it earlier, but I never considered the job angle."

"But something bad." He was definitely amused. He spun in the desk chair and looked me over. I gave him my best breezy expression back.

"Yeah. I think the whole nature vs. nurture argument is . . . well, they change their minds all the time. I dunno."

"Maybe it was the human in you after all." The notion made his smile widen further. It occurred to me that he may have been mocking me, but I smiled back anyway.

"It's a theory."

Christophe drained his glass and looked at his watch. "Time to go. You have a car out there?"

"Three blocks down. You okay to walk?"

He snorted. "The lead passed right through me. Bullets are nothing compared to swords. Now those things fucking hurt." He got up and pointed at the walled-off area I had noticed on my first visit, the partitioned section of the penthouse office. "Wanna see my kennel?"

I didn't know what to make of that.

"I need a new shirt and a coat. Probably need some other things, too, since I'm not coming back." He glanced at me and then set off. "You could use a new shirt."

I reluctantly followed him. To one side of the enclosure was a door with no doorknob, easy to miss. There was a recessed touchpad to the left of it. He punched in the code and the door swung inward. I could feel the tension bloom in the half-breed as he stepped over the threshold. I watched from the doorway.

The inside was spacious, the spare furniture postmodern and sterile. The bed, raised on a black stone dais, had white sheets. It made me wonder if there had been a physical element to his relationship with Linda.

Christophe went quickly to the closet and pulled out a dark suit, shirt, tie, and shoes. He talked while he wiped himself off and quickly changed. I drank straight from the bottle.

"I could come and go after a while, but they always knew where I was. A lot of times I got the impression that I was locked in here and they only freed up the system to accept my access code when I got close to the door. Mai Chen was in charge, at her station by the front door, watching me on some camera I could never find. She should be here soon."

"She's dead," I said shortly. Christophe froze, one sock half on. He shot me a curious look, part surprise and part kid at the playground.

"Really?"

"Oh yeah. She evidently exploded. At least that's what I heard."

"Good. What color shirt you want?"

"Black. And a blazer, too, if you have one. I prefer an Italian cut. No tie."

He pulled his other sock and his shoes on and then went back to the closet, withdrew a shirt and the top part of an Armani and walked over to where I stood. On the way he paused at the single white dresser and opened up the center jewelry drawer. He took out a battered gold pocket watch and what looked like a deck of cards, also very old, pocketed them both, and then brushed past me, handing the clothes off and plucking the bottle out of my hand as he did.

"Hurry up," he said. "We don't want to have to kill too many of the secretaries."

I shirked out of my luxurious fur coat and changed. Then I put the coat back on. There was blood on it, more than a little, but I'd already resolved to stand under one of the city's many rain gutters on the walk back to the car. I'd grown fond of Lemont's gift. Christophe said nothing.

"Where to?" I asked. Christophe knelt next to the Korean and removed his wallet and two guns. Together we walked to the elevator. I picked up Linda Misery's gun as we passed it.

"Bank opens in thirty-eight minutes," Christophe said. "Salt has several accounts and they gave me access to more than a few of them. I need to transfer some money around before I leave."

We got in the elevator and he pressed "L" for lobby. Neither of us looked down at the pile of muscle on the floor between us. I nervously cleared my throat.

"There was this one account, like maybe eight mil . . ."

Christophe ticked off the floors with his eyes. "You took it. Just leave the rest alone."

I shook my head. "She must have actually thought she was going to live, " I marveled.

Christophe gave me his bark of a laugh again. "That woman thought she had everything figured out. She probably planned on getting it all back with interest in a day or two."

There was a soft *ding* and the elevator doors opened on an empty lobby. Christophe strolled out and immediately shot the reception computer. We headed to the front doors. The light was just beginning to change outside, from streetlight and black to a dull slate gray filled with rain and the reflections of neon. Morning was just around the corner. It looked like I was going to see another day after all. There was a fifty-fifty chance, anyway.

The cold hit me just right, tightening the skin on my face, taking some of the throbbing out of my ear. I took a couple of deep breaths and turned to Christophe. He had his face up and his eyes closed. Drops were running off of his angular features. He slowly held his arms out, palms up, and I knew what he was feeling. It was freedom, for the first time in years. He shuddered and then shook the rain out of his hair. I tossed my thumb to the right. We walked slowly, Christophe with a spring in his step, me trailing the blood sluicing out of my coat. When we passed a really active rain gutter I stood under it until the water ran clean. I was wet and cold and the coat weighed about twenty pounds more than it should have, but the wet animal smell was good. We got in my car and I tossed the sodden thing on the backseat and cranked the heater. Christophe rolled his window down.

"Cigarettes?" he asked.

"Glove box. Fifth of bourbon under your seat, too." I punched the cigarette lighter in and flicked on the headlights while he got everything into his lap. We were two blocks south when he passed me a lit smoke and spun the lid off the bottle, drank and passed it.

"What bank?" I sipped and took a drag.

"Doesn't matter. Not for what I'm doing." He had an almost peaceful look on his face. He smoked and stared out the window as if he were seeing the world for the first time in a long while. I drove us farther and farther away, angling for the bridge and the entrance to the freeway.

"What the hell is going to happen when the day shift shows up at Salt?" It was the sole remaining consideration. Christophe shrugged.

"People get killed there all the time. Standard procedure is to cover everything up as fast as possible. The top brass is gone, thanks to you. The junior butt sniffers will go in and mop up, try to figure out what happened, then spend a week or two trying to poison each other and form temporary alliances that will end in epic backstabbing and pedantic terror. Modern corporate sociology, essentially. I'm not sticking around to watch, of course. One of those little shitheads may have a brain."

"I'm not staying for the show, either."

"There." Christophe pointed at a US Bank. I pulled to a stop in front. He turned to me, unsmiling. We stared at each other for half a minute while he decided my fate. I already knew what he was going to say.

"Thanks for the break," he said sincerely. "If our paths ever cross again, even by chance in a crowded place, I will kill you." He opened the door and then turned his glacier eyes on me one last time. "Linda Morgan was a monster as people go, but . . . She wasn't the CEO. There was always someone more terrible than her she was answering to."

"I know. And tell Maria Estrella I said hello, and to move. That she's been made."

Christophe paused for an instant, and then he was out into the suddenly fierce downpour. I watched him for a moment, and then headed home. He'd taken my cigarettes.

✳

IZELLE WAS WAITING in the front window when I pulled into the driveway. On the way home my chest had stiffened up a little and my stomach was growling. My wet clothes were sticking to me and I was running low on nicotine and tar. But I waved cheerfully anyway and dragged my soggy coat out of the back before I went up the stairs. I didn't bother to hurry through the rain, as I was about as wet as I could get already. Izelle threw open the front door as I reached the top of the stairs and crossed her arms.

"What happed to your coat, Gelson? Did you fall in the river?" But she was beaming.

"Stood under a rain gutter. It had blood all over it." I stood there smiling back. She tossed her head.

"C'mon then. Leave those shoes on the mat and put your coat over that fancy patio chair. I'll deal with it after you make us lunch."

Izelle was wearing a vaguely bimbo black tracksuit, white athletic shoes that had never been anywhere close to a tennis court and never would be. Her hair was in pigtails and her face was sparkling as if she'd just taken a long bath after a nap. No makeup. She smelled like bubble bath.

"Move it," I said gruffly. She made way. The fire was going strong, so I wobbled over to it and crashed down flat on the bearskin. Steam began to rise from my clothes. A minute or two of blessed silence passed before something whumped down on my aching chest. I opened my eyes. A tracksuit, identical to Izelle's, and a towel.

"I thought I told you not to go shopping," I said weakly.

"You do not tell me when to go shopping," she replied shortly. "Change. I'll fix us drinks."

Behind me came the clatter of glasses and the sounds of pouring. She went into the kitchen and half yelled at me from there while I changed into the awful athletic wear.

"That took you long enough," she called. "What the hell were you doing?"

"Killing people and stealing money. I got all wet. And I cut my fucking ear."

"What happened to the boys?"

"They got killed. I didn't do it."

"Like I believe that. You done?"

"Almost. Preheat the oven to three-fifty. It's the white knob that says 'Oven' under it."

I zipped the cotton-lined jacket up to the neck and tossed all my wet stuff over to the door, then sagged back. Izelle appeared a moment later with two glasses of brown. She handed me one and settled next to me.

"I told you I'd be taking care of you at some point," she chided. "I just didn't think it would be so soon. You need a girlfriend, Gelson. Someone to help me when you track stuff into the house like this. Are you hurt? Other than your ear."

"I kinda got beat up. By the guy who killed the Meat."

"Huh." She didn't sound very interested. "What did you do with him?"

"Gave him a ride to a bank. He stole my cigarettes, too."

"There's more on the kitchen counter. I'll see if there's a wheelchair in the basement so I can drive your sorry ass out onto the porch."

We drank for a while. She went back into the kitchen and after a moment the blender turned on and off. When she came back she had smoothies. I tasted mine. Beets, ginger, bananas, and carrot juice. Some kind of tranny cocktail to make my skin look better. I drank some more of it. Eventually I sat all the way up and looked into the fire.

"We have to move," I said. "Sooner than I thought. Like within a week."

She didn't respond. I went on.

"I left a decent trail of bodies this morning, but some junior-grade dummy from the staffers I left alive will eventually put two and two together once the smoke clears and Salt Street Development has a new CEO. I need to get this house packed and have everything headed for Detroit in a series of relays fast. I figure I'll switch everything between various trucking and rail services for a month or so to throw anyone off the trail, maybe fly to Denver and pick up a car there, drive the rest of the way. How's that work with your timetable?"

Izelle considered. "Fine. Just fine. I fly out to Bangkok tomorrow. Seventeen hours, first class. Last time I'll use Antonio's passport. A week to adjust and pick out some new outfits, then two weeks of rehabilitation. You may have to make up my room before you do the rest of the house."

"Not a problem. You have to follow the antique code, as we agreed, so I was planning on outfitting your room anyway. I promise I'll try not to make it gloomy and . . . well, you know."

"Old folksie? Nerdy?"

"Yeah. And fuck you, kid. I am old."

She snorted, but didn't come back with anything.

We drank for a little more. I put another log on the fire. The warmth of the booze and the flames were sinking into my bones and driving me from hungry to famished. I rubbed my chest. Izelle played with her hair and watched the fire. I caught a whiff of rain and bullets under the soap and flowers.

"You going miss this place?" She asked the question in a quiet, neutral voice. I rubbed my face with both hands.

"Yeah. Yeah, I am. I've been here for years. But it was getting to be time to go anyway. Any longer and the neighbors would start getting gray hair. They'd begin to wonder, and right about then is when you discover that everyone is superstitious, even the ice-cold Volvo science types. It wouldn't be a leisure move with an easy story behind it at that point. This way I can go quietly."

That gave her pause. "Sounds sort of depressing. What do you know about Detroit?"

I shrugged. "Lemont comes from there. So I assume it's dangerous."

"We'll fit right in." She patted my shoulder.

"Yep. After the house, we tackle the cabin. I stung the dead bitch who was blackmailing me for a pretty chunk of change before I . . . before what happened happened, so maybe it might just be a good idea to tear the old shitty cabin down and have a new one put up. Three fireplaces. Maybe a Japanese theme."

"Unless the old shitty one has character. Then I say we rebuild. Add on."

I nodded. "And I need to get some new guns, pronto. I went through most of my stock in the last week or so."

"Maybe you should get a new coat, too," Izelle said. "The one you have is dripping pink stuff."

I waved that away. "It'll come out. I'll rinse it off in the bathtub with some shampoo and conditioner. Drop it at the dry cleaner after it dries in front of the fire tonight. Good as new. I'm sort of attached to it. Fur has that effect on me."

Izelle was quiet for a few minutes, and so was I. When she finished her drink she got up and went into the dining room. I thought she was going to get a refill, but instead she came back with the file. My file. She sat down next to me, holding it in both hands.

"I read this while you were gone," she said. "It was more than interesting. This is what you were being blackmailed with, isn't it." It wasn't a question.

"Yeah. I never read it, though. I'm Gelson Verber, just like I said. For now, anyway."

Izelle thought. "So you don't know your real name? Your mother's name? Your father's? How you wound up at a place called Mama Heads? Who the wolf was that . . . got into your DNA?"

"Nah."

And then she tossed the file into the fire. We watched it burn until the ashes were white. And then even the ashes were gone. That was when she turned to me and stuck out her hand. Her eyes shone bright and soft and warm all at once.

"Izelle Dellafortuna," she said. "Pleased to finally meet you."

I took her hand and shook it. I don't know what was in my eyes, but they made her look back into the fire. Maybe she somehow caught a fraction of what I was thinking. Considering what I had planned, I doubted it. I relaxed and let it settle into my face, my jaws. Even my teeth.

*

New Year's Eve and we were on the top floor of the Empire State Building. 1979. The guy I'd just strangled was safely ensconced in a bathroom stall and John and I were enjoying the view, the party swirling behind us, a hundred-plus hearts rising in tempo with the approach of midnight.

"This is the life, pal," John said, gesturing at the view with his martini glass. "Lets take Nisco's tickets and go to Alaska next week. Do some bear hunting."

"You know how to rumble, Johnny Boy." I popped a quaalude and handed him the bottle. We were having a great year. Up two mil that we'd already burned through for the most part, I'd discovered The Ramones so I liked music again, and John was on a gambling spree that verged on sorcery. Plus, women were exceptionally lovely and promiscuous that year. Life was good. Easy.

"I do. You know, I always wanted to go there after I read Call of the Wild *all those years ago, but I never had a free ride off a fresh corpse with the right itinerary."*

Theo Nisco was a big game hunter by trade, but he trafficked in humans and rare animals for sex and breeding, respectively. Totally offensive and potentially dangerous to us in life, but in death he made a fantastic travel agent. Tickets for himself and four more, plus a week at a cabin.

"Should we go sniff around some of these dancers?" I looked back. There were dozens of true beauties, but I remember the chandelier the most in that snapshot of time. New York was in one of its complicated phases of glory, peaking in some ways,

luridly desperate in others. John didn't even bother to look. There was something else on his mind at the moment.

"So, pal. New Year's Eve. I want to ask you something. This guy who taught you how to read? He knew your name and don't tell me didn't. He called you all kinds of things, I know I know, you already told me, but right there at the end, at the moment of truth, God watching and the whole nine yards, what'd he call you?"

I leaned over and whispered it to him, and then we looked at each other. He smiled, amazed.

"Ten, nine, eight!" they counted, swirling and bright behind us.

"Well," John began, shaking his head, smile widening.

"Seven, six, five!"

John cackled a little, his mad cackle, searching for the right words.

"Four, three, two!"

"You're fucked, man!" He gleefully raised his glass to mine.

"One! Happy New Year!"

Gelson Verber, Brian Clark, Mike Brannigan, David Hill, Ryan Talbot, Martin Green, Calib Myers, Herbert Franklin, Adrian Moore, Kevin Hicks, Emmitt Fielding, all the way back to what they called me so long ago, in that hardship farm orphanage by the cornfields called Mama Heads. I could never be bribed with my name, my identity, not even then, though he'd tried, just as John predicted. Clarence, the master of my letters, had called me a thousand things. Bitin' Boy. Little Mister Secrets. Burnie the Burn Baby. But I kept that last name, his final earthly words in fact, spoken like a curse and a revelation. He had a mouthful of teeth at that moment, and it was in the instant before I opened his head with his trusty woodchopper, to let in some of that divine light he was always going on about. It was a strangling, choking sound, followed by 'Lu! Lu!'

Choking Lu Lu.

Unconventional, as names go. But that name, that crazy sound, had a ticking time bomb element to it. John Bridger had seen that. Gelson Verber, well. That guy had been a straight up killer.

EPILOGUE

WHILE IZELLE SLEPT that night, I killed everyone. Lemont was the hardest. He liked me in his way, as much as the little murderer could ever like anyone, and there was genuine sadness and betrayal in his eyes in the second before I snapped his neck. Once I'd hidden the body in the rafters I strangled his mute gatekeeper. He let out one garbled scream as he clawed at me, proving that he had a voice after all. Then I'd used Lemont's computer to send Thomasini a private message concerning Salt Street and how they'd set him up.

The fat man showed without his guards, and after I broke his arm and tied him in front of the computer, he'd whispered in Spanish while he worked, only switching to English at the very end. The face of the architect of his undoing, the man who had hounded him to the end, the inescapable, relentless genius who had driven him to this, his final moment, in a cold warehouse. With me.

"My God," he whispered. "How did you know? How did you find this?"

After I snapped his neck, I strolled around in the computer myself for a few minutes. Then I stole his wallet and lit the warehouse on fire.

It was raining on the post-midnight drive to Vince Percy's place. I parked across the street and two houses down and went over the floor plan in my head. I'd spent enough time inside in the dark to still be able to find my way around, so I went to the back and picked the lock with tools I'd stolen from Lemont's desk. My chipper little fence had set me up and was due to collect the bounty that had been put on me for killing Leon, and once I was in a trash bag all the property he'd signed over would revert back to him. I was of no use to him financially if I moved. Leon had been sent by a Detroit heroin syndicate Lemont had ties with. Leon hadn't been looking for Lemont. He was working another deal, and at the same time trying to find out if Lemont had anyone sniffing around his operation. By killing him, I'd implicated myself and a price had been put on my head, with a photo courtesy of the Verber ID. Lemont would neatly collect the bounty and his property titles in the same move; killing me. Very clever, except he was dead.

Vincent Percy's house was dark and quiet when I snuck in. I didn't need the lights and I never made a sound, but the Insect Lady was still sitting up in Vincent Percy's bed when I ghosted into the room. She looked up searchingly in the darkness for me before I broke her neck, and she never made a sound, either. I didn't feel surprised. I didn't feel much of anything that night.

✳

IZELLE LEFT EARLY on a Thursday morning. It was raining and cold, but she insisted on wearing a summer dress. She had one piece of luggage and a giant purse, and informed me in great detail how shopping was a top priority after she checked into her suite, got properly drunk, and had a long nap. It was weird watching her sashay into the airport, and it surprised me that I felt lonely as the doors closed behind her. I decided to park in short-term and walked back to watch the planes take off, inside out of the rain. I didn't want to let go. John Bridger would have smiled in that sad, knowing way he had.

The first in a string of movers were preparing to pack up my entire house in one tremendously long day. I'd be gone by the time they started. The estimated seventy-eight boxes of books and all the furniture would fill an entire semi. They would be taking it all to Phoenix and putting it into storage. Another company would pick it up the next day and drive it all to Houston, where everything would disappear into the most confusing web of madness I could engineer, and after a solid ten days of shifting through various shipping companies, it would all eventually depart from New Orleans courtesy of a trucking company so primitive they didn't even have a computer and took cash only. A final company would pick it up at the Michigan border and take it the rest of the way. It was enough, though it burned most of my fake IDs, with the exception of my Verber ID, safe once again with the death of Lemont, and an old one from Arizona. I was going to move the contents of my safe in an hour and then cement the empty into the foundation, then pluck all of my stashes. My new ride was a restored 1961 Lincoln Continental, black on black. I needed the trunk space.

My neighbor Barry was supervising the movers the day after tomorrow. Once the house sold, I'd set it up so that the money would be his, for the kid's college fund. It would have been too risky to try to move it, plus Barry had been so good over the years. He's never suspected me of anything. Never probed or prodded or sniffed around. He'd just been neighborly. And I had been the kid's English tutor, after all. Even if it was just a cover, the little guy deserved a chance at a worthless English degree if he wanted one.

A private jet had taxied into place on one of the runways. I recognized the numbers on it, so I took my phone out and called Izelle. She answered on the first ring.

"Gelson?" She sounded relaxed, tipsy, curious. Confident.

"Hey, kid," I said warmly. "I got you something. A present for your new life."

"You kook," she replied, giggling. "I'm on my plane already."

"Don't worry. It's in your giant purse. Little wooden box I snuck in at the bottom. A good-luck charm."

"Hang on . . . It's heavy!"

I heard rustling, and then the little snap of the lid on the wooden box. Three seconds. She had three seconds.

"You knew," she said.

The jet on the runway blew in two phases, one as the grenade went and then a fraction of a second later as the incandescent white phosphorus shrapnel ripped through everything and the tanks of jet fuel made lateral mushroom clouds of themselves. The safety glass on the bank of windows spider-webbed in the shockwave and the screaming started all around me. The Portland airport was a cathedral of glass and metal and plastic, designed for screaming, as it turns out. I pocketed my phone and calmly made my way to the exit, following the commands coming over the loudspeakers, pushing through the swarming panic all around me. And then I was outside. I lit a cigarette and sat down on one of the empty benches.

The wolf in me never would have guessed. It was the man, the unexpected, unanticipated man that had spoken, had made a list, had turned the pieces of the puzzle over a thousand and one times and then wanted blood, rivers more than any part of me that hunted simply because it was hungry. No, the monster, the true monster in Gelson Verber, was the ape with stars in its eyes.

Vincent Percy and his house. It had been too blank. Because it had, in fact, been a hotel, made for Salt Street and used by their staff. The night I'd killed Percy, it had been stacked to make it look like he'd lived there. The man Max who had called his cell phone, which had later disappeared, had been the black man I had scented, the man who had staged the play, and whose employee file and travel records Thomasini had uncovered. There had only been one caller, and only one other scent. It fit. Vince Percy was nothing more than a tool, a pawn, a plant. Max had lured him to town with the perfect job, the perfect cover, at the perfect time. It was all there.

Max had then called from a DC area code, and the call had been an error. From the head office there, Antonio Reyna, a shadowy powerhouse and one of Thomasini's many enemies, had waged war; political, economic, and with proper bullets, against any number of targets. Thomasini's final act had been the one that made him speak English in the moment just before his death. The one picture of Antonio Reyna, grainy and distorted and three years old, was Izelle Tatum. He'd never put it together and he never would have. Countless surgeries later, the only evidence was the eyes, and the long and undeniable chart of Reyna's actions, open to him for the first time. Thomasini had known in that final instant what had happened to him. Antonio's greed, his relentless pursuit, had rocketed them both into the stratospheric twilight dementia formerly reserved for kings and queens, emperors and dictators, transforming them into things as strange and foreign to most people as people are to me. Drive and ambition had turned them into machines, and broken them in the process.

The look in Linda's eyes when I'd stabbed her in the hand had not been for me. It was for the cameras, for Reyna. The perfect corporate servant indeed, which had been my observation at the time.

Izelle had thrown my precious file, containing my actual name, the names of my parents, the lineage that made me what I am, into the fire. Not to liberate me, or to have a hand in my freedom, but because she was the architect and author of it. The freedom of seeing it burn had only been an illusion for one cruel instant, briefly unbearable. My first job as the new Christophe was to destroy Salt Street, kill everyone, and make Thomasini disappear. And I did. But I kept going.

The villainy of it all was more than a little disgusting. Thomasini and Izelle had both been sociopaths in the end, and that I'd killed the warring creatures was marginally satisfying. Their battle with each other was over. The top of human society had always been thick with monsters of a variety I had—in the end—little in common with. When they held a book, they held something like an equation, to be dissected, parts of it used, parts of it masked, parts of it digested. Same with paintings. Music had been made for brainwashing and misdirection. Windows were to keep things out instead of to look through. I'd never understand their Other, but if I were to visualize it, the thing in Izelle and Thomasini would look like a baby with a hard black beak for a nose. Not screaming. Not hurt. Just sitting there, blankly staring, waiting, watching. Planning.

The Insect Lady from the Salt Street Development front desk who had been hiding out in Vincent Percy's house might have been able to elaborate, but I'd killed her without asking. There was also a chance she might have whispered something disgusting in that final wide-eyed, quiet strangulation, and I was better off not hearing it. The amped-up Japanese noose porn she'd had in dead Vinnie's bedroom TV in no way invited conversation.

The end of the show for Lemont's computer had been conducted by me over Thomasini's warm, twitchy body. Salt Street Development was a subsidiary of CVRS, which the late communications genius discovered an instant before the neck snap. I'd perused it until some obscure security countermeasure cut me off, which is why I torched the place.

CVRS had more than one subsidiary. They were all over the world, but most of them were clustered on the Eastern Seaboard. It all radiated from the pestilent swampy floodplain where the founding fathers had surrendered enough unusable land to build their capitol. All of the CVRS satellites had slaves of one kind or another. I'd managed to find that Max guy in the big office in DC. He was a handler of some kind, for special cases I was unable to learn more about. Another Linda, so he had to die just on general principles. But in the end even CVRS was only the beginning. As an entity, it was not alone.

The final bit of proof regarding Izelle, in case there was any question left at all, was of course the grenades themselves, which would have never made it through commercial security. But they would make it onto a private corporate jet departing for DC. And they did. But it was that first night at my house, on the back porch, when she had cupped her hand in the rain that had tipped me off. She was so familiar with the motion, in a way that could only have come from watching me night after night on a video feed, the same kind the Insect Lady had used to monitor internal activities at Salt Street, flicking from screen to screen.

So a week after I'd killed a man in an alley, one day after I'd stepped over Linda's body, a handful of hours after I'd gone on my last local killing spree, and only one minute after I'd blown up an airplane, I sat in front of the Portland airport, smoking. It was still raining, one week after the full moon. I was fashionably dressed in an Italian suit, the only one I hadn't packed, I was a few million dollars richer, and a fur coat was waiting for me at the dry cleaner. I'd pick it up on the way home, and then I planned to shop at my favorite grocery store one last time. And then make dinner in my house. Sleep in my bed for one more night, maybe with Katie, the woman from Jake's.

It was going to be cold everywhere I was going. I still planned on Detroit, because every trap has bait, and I meant to change the nature of the trap and become the bait myself. Plus, the dead industrial capital was a perfect place to begin the hunt for the emerging corporate monsters of this new era. They had been there, and killed, and left a trail. The last week had shown me something I was keen to explore. A wolf, or a man, was at the top of the food chain in nature, but something new was eating them both. A wolf ranges over hundreds of miles. It makes no sense to have them as a primary food source. It is unnatural.

Humans are the same. You cannot live on them alone. Until now, in this bright new time. The imagination, using the deformed playground of economics, had given birth to a new hyperpredator. The new top of the food chain was an idea. It was so big and so fast, with a thousand faces and yet no face at all. In many ways, the new corporate super-killer resembled the final, global evolution of Vincent Percy, who had started me down the road to its discovery in the first place.

I wanted this new thing's blood. I wanted to touch its glass and steel entrails, to foul the electricity in its mouth. Specifically, I wanted to hunt something bigger than myself. Something awful, with a glorious maze of sewers for guts, a pumping furnace of a heart fueled with mountains of tiny stolen hopes, with a hydra collection of heads to add to my collection. Just thinking about it made me feel good. My dream prey, because I wasn't perfectly natural, either. It had been a mistake for these gluttonous new things to give me knowledge of their existence. The destruction of Salt Street had been amazingly profitable, but it was more than that. Natural or not, anything that had the power to put me in a cage, however briefly, needed to die, and so did the rest of its kind.

On impulse I walked to the edge of the huge glass awning that covered the departures zone and stuck my hand out into the rain, let the big drops play over my hot skin one last time. One last time.

I was leaving. Moving. In a greater motion, for the first time. Waiting for dark and the rise of the waning Blackberry Moon. Alive in a new way. I'd probably never come back to this place. It's rain. The obscure byways I'd found where only the animals played. The little things I'd left hidden in their houses. None of it mattered now. My territory had never truly been just a grid of city blocks, a neighborhood with borders, or even a town. It was everything under the moonlight.